I SPY A BUTTERFLY

LAUREN LOGAN

COPYRIGHT

Front Cover Art: Sean.Ex.Savior
Instagram @seanexsavior

Interior Character Art: Liz Castro
Instagram @neothenine.art

Front Cover Design: Allen Wahlström
Instagram @Bafacoach.W
www.asenzathletic.myportfolio.com

Editor: Beth Sullivan
BSullivanEdPro@gmail.com

Writing Assistant: Kathy Hunter

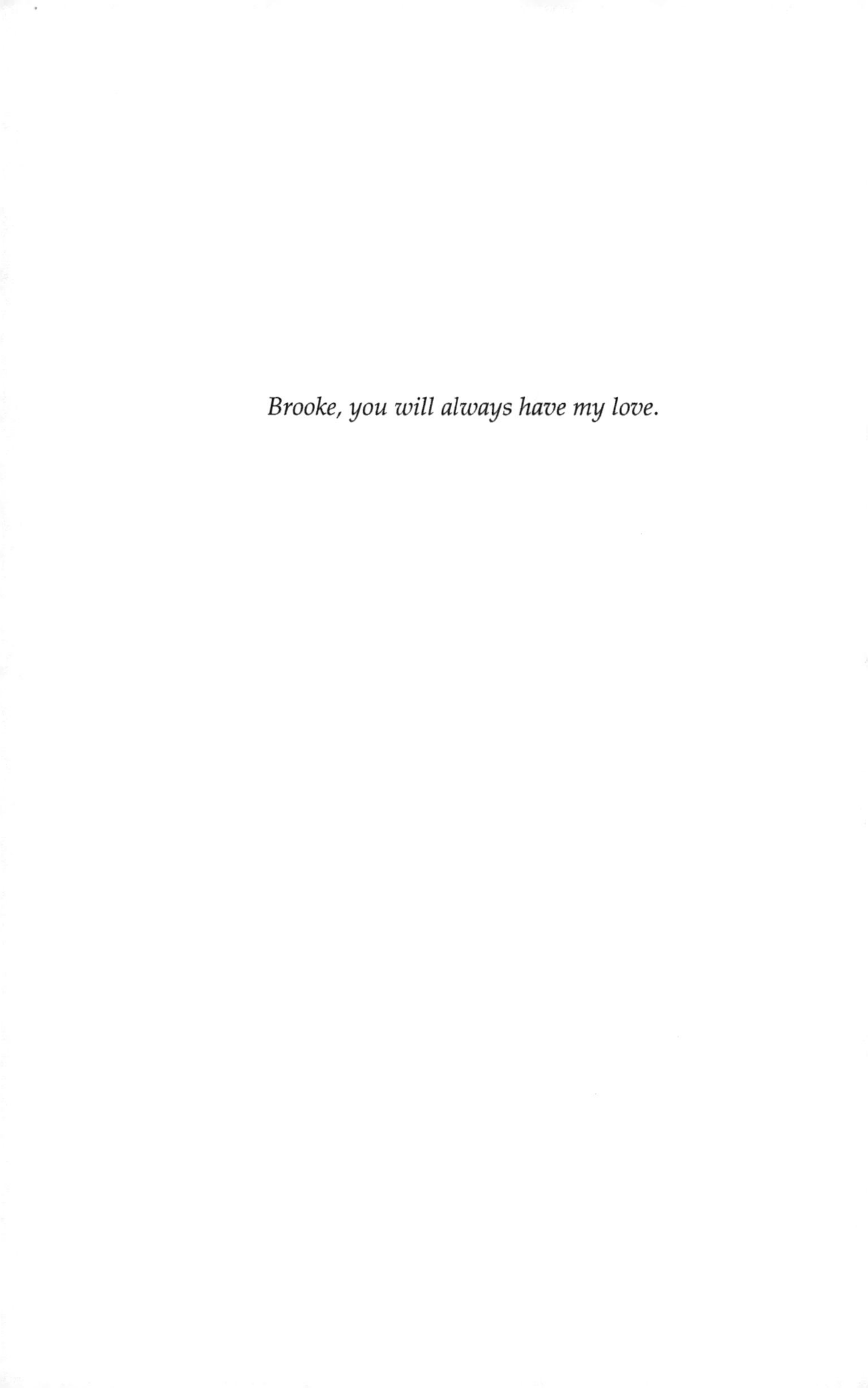

Brooke, you will always have my love.

CONTENT WARNING

Trigger and content warnings for I Spy a Butterfly are
listed on
www.authorlaurenlogan.com

I Spy a Butterfly is strictly from mature readers of 18+

Please protect your mental health.

ONE
INTRUSIVE THOUGHTS

I could tip my drill forward three inches and spin his brain into a whirlpool. The metal handle of the drill chilled Laye's skin as she clenched it in her fist. With Leem's head mere inches away from the gleaming tip of spiraling metal, her thoughts were on one thing. *I think I'm going to do it this time.* The gel in Leem's short brown hair shone under the bright lights as he worked on the circuits of the wormhole navigation system under the ships control panel. The back of his head seemed to taunt, *just do it. You know you want to.*

She was supposed to be drilling the stripped screw out of the panel above his head, yet she angled the pointed drill bit downward, closer. *I can do this. I can make it. All I need to do is turn Leem's brain into soup.*

Laye could feel a smile grow on her face as she swore she could taste the flavor of freedom on her tongue. It was intoxicatingly spicy and sweet. Leem lifted his head up and it aligned with the console ledge. *Now or never, honey butt!* Pressing the trigger, she grinned like she had been given a treat as she plunged the spinning drill bit into Leem's temple, pinning his head against the ledge. His body convulsed as she held her wrist steady and turned his brains into mush. His clear blood sprayed from the drill as she pulled it out, and he slumped to the ground. Laye dropped the drill, and it clattered across the floor as an alarm blared above her head.

Unraveling her antenna, she stared up at the alarm light. *Did Leem the Lousy sabotage our ship?* She poked her head under the control panel and found a bundle of severed wires leading to the navigation system. They sparked and arched against the side of the panel like teeny firecrackers. Laye slid to the floor and sighed, "Computer, shut off the warning sound."

Silence filled the bridge of the small, sleek ship as she stared at the hole in Leem's head. His grey and white brain matter mixed with his clear blood as it seeped out and slid down the grate. *It was always you standing over my bloody broken body, smiling at the damage you had caused. You deserved this end, or maybe you deserved more. I guess that's not for me to decide.*

Another warning sounded above, and she lifted her green eyes to see what the view screen would tell her. *What could possibly be more important than killing my life-long bonded, and the appointed heir of the Vo-Pess Dynasty?*

Oh, we're crashing. Laye ran for the captain's chair before remembering she had no navigation controls, and she closed her eyes, standing silent for a moment. *I knew that lump of droppings would maroon us again.*

Laye pushed all the thrusters to maximum before she grabbed the emergency pack she had prepared weeks ago from the under-bridge storage bin. She kicked Leem in the crotch as she climbed inside of the escape pod. She had given him far too much of her body over the many years he kept her trapped. *Never again.*

She peered out of the pod view screen at one lifeless, dry planet nearby. *Sugar tits!* "Computer, where are we?"

A kind, feminine voice spoke above her, "You are located in the Sarter Kingdom territory. The nearest system has a dry world which harbors life. You are compatible with fifty six percent survivability. The planet is named K'hurian, and the people are called the K'hornibus. The southern hemisphere is controlled by the Shardlow clan. The north continent is a warring faction."

"Send pod one to the south and make sure I land where I have the highest rate of survivability." Laye leaned back in the small pod and attached her harness.

She didn't know much about the K'hornibus other than they were ruthless warlords who lived on a desert world. K'hornibus evolved from a hearty desert lizard and with rough scales on their arms, legs, and backs. Horns grow along their skulls, ending in a point behind their head with the points angled away from their face. *Wait, don't they have prehensile tails? Giant, muscular, and terrifying, and a fun time tail, just like I like them. Actually, I am not really sure how I like them, or what I like. Who am I kidding with all this talk of a man, I am probably about to die.*

Laye was just thankful she was crashing in Sarter territory. What if she had landed on UTC soil? She patted her shoulder where her dual location tracker and self-destruct switch resided. *Nighty night, Honey butt, for good.*

The bright system star blinded her as she was ejected. Now below her, the hull of the ship ignited as it entered the atmosphere. She aimed in a southern direction while the ship, and Leem, had a collision course for just above the planet's equator. A secluded mountain range, she hoped.

She grasped her belly. Her insides were still sore from his last rutting. She was sure he had torn something inside of her. In that exact moment, when he had held her down and hurt her had been the moment, she decided he would die. He had forced himself on her for years, but that was perfectly legal on Vo-Pess for married couples. They had to repopulate their species. They had to adhere to every rule precisely or they would be harshly punished, so she withstood it, no matter how much she hated it.

She had tolerated eighteen years of Leem and his torture, but he hadn't even been the worst of it. It had been her training. Years of painful physical and psychological torture and for what? For the First Human's faction to fall when she was finally given the ultimate assignment? When Leem had made plans for home, her heart broke.

It had been the one goal she worked to accomplish. She studied and trained her entire life to track down and eliminate Fausta Ursus III of the House of Venus, not the Genil descendant who now reigned. All the work Laye had suffered through was *for nothing,* but that was over now, she would never go back.

Freedom from the shell of her former life was at her fingertips, but she had never dreamed this day would be possible. A thrill ran over her light blue skin, pebbling it, as she tightly coiled her antenna against her head. The computer signaled the landing gear was preparing to drop down from the pod, and she grasped her pack to her chest.

After a few rumbles, she dared a peek over the side of the pod at the vast desert. She desperately hoped she would survive. It would be hell escaping the planet if she couldn't make a life here. *I really hope they don't eat stranded people.* She snarled her lip at the idea of stealing a ship from a K'hornibus. That would be a terrible plan. They were territorial and possessive, she bet they would do anything to have it back.

She pressed her armor tab, and the familiar metallic material spread from the tab and crawled over her skin. Laye touched the side of her neck where her helmet tab folded up and it spread the protective nano material over her head.

The suit sent a jolt down her spine as it connected with her neural port at the base of her neck. *I hate that part.* Her antenna tingled as the suit connected with them. She knew reflective colors would keep her coolest, so she set the color of her suit to a light silver. Laye knew the Vo-Pess government would be vying to have her back as she tapped her shoulder. *I'm going to have to dig that damn thing out as soon as I land.* She was the only empath in generations. They had done selective breeding for over five hundred years, and she was currently the only one of her people who could read emotions without physical touch. With her armor amplifying her abilities, she pushed her senses out as the suit synced with her neurons. She couldn't detect anything with feelings for miles. Either she was alone, or she had some dangerous neighbors. Who knew with the K'hornibus? They might all be emotional voids.

Her pod landed with a crunch in the sand, and she popped the top, the heat searing her lungs as she sucked in a breath through her helmet's filters. Laye lifted over the edge of her pod to survey the area and found nothing but reddish sand. Her ship's computer must have made a mistake, she could never survive here. She climbed out and slung her simple, black sling pack on her back before hiking up the dune.

The sand slipped away with every step as she made her way to the top. On the other side were a few more dunes and some rocks protruding from the sand. When she made it to the rocks, she found a shallow cave where she lay her pack down. She had some work to do before she could go any farther.

Retracting her armor, her skin felt like it was melting in the heat. *Is it always this hot here? Why couldn't I have landed on the water covered world, Keru?* She retrieved her med kit from her pack and pulled her white, snug fitting under-shirt off. Prepping her shoulder, she scrubbed it clean before biting her lip and cutting her skin straight down to the edge of her tracking device.

Clear blood spurted from the wound, and she clenched her teeth while she dug around trying to find the tiny transmitter. Having enough of all the digging around, she began squeezing at the skin surrounding the wound. The end of the pea size device poked out, and she pinched it with her fingertips, and as she did, she could feel tension in the long wires running through her chest. Carefully pulling them, she shivered as she felt the wires slither away from her heart and slide from her shoulder.

She stared at the teeny machine before crushing it between her fingers. *They might track me to this planet, and even this rock, but after I step away from this spot, I am on my own. Free.*

Fere's beautiful face framed by her black curly hair appeared in her mind and her gut twisted like she had been stabbed with a knife. Knowing her escape meant she would never see her best friend again, Laye wiped away the tears sprouting in her eyes as she blinked away the memory. She would grieve her friend eventually, but today she needed to survive.

After slipping her shirt back on, Laye pressed her armor tabs, and it spread over her skin. She had sampled her own DNA and had her replicator make a spare hand. Pulling the jar from her pack, she shook it and the hand flopped around, it had remained in the stasis jar for months.

She pressed the crushed tracking device into the open flesh at the wrist before laying it on the ground. She took a few steps away and waited for the stunning little jeweled beetles and other insects to start chewing on the hand before she felt confident her deceased bio signature would be detectable in the area. Laye hoped if the Vo-Pess send a team to look for her, they would accept the planted DNA as her death. Orienting herself, she made her way east, she had seen another rocky outcrop during her descent, and she wanted to make it there by dusk. She had a good idea of what kind of creatures were on this planet and the last place she wanted to be was out on the sand dunes after dark.

TWO
DESCENT

I feel like I'm being roasted alive, why the fuck did loser Leem have us in this area? Laye stood on rocks jutting from the endless sand and spotted a deep cave to make her camp. Climbing down, she lost her footing and slid against the sloped rocks before hitting the dusty stones below. Fine grains of sand filled the air, and she waved it from her face. Before her was a small opening that she easily crawled through.

Laye stood in a small cavern with fairly flat ground, and she found a spring toward the back. Pulling her pack off, she retrieved her survival kit for a small lantern to see and she tested the water. It showed to be contaminated with salt, and she huffed at it, deciding this cave was too close to the crash site for comfort anyway. She and Leem weren't due to check in for another few weeks, so she knew the Vo-Pess wouldn't be looking for them just yet, and she had time to make it further before trying to stay in one place. Unless… Laye froze with fear, *what if they send Fere and our team after me? Old team now, I guess.* Laye missed Fere so badly the memory physically ached in her chest. She rubbed the place over her heart. *Oh, my friend, my sister, I am so sorry.*

A cramp began in her lower belly, and she slid her hand down and rubbed it. It was not in the same place as the pain from Leem. This was new. She wondered if it was just hunger so she pulled her syrup sticks out and drank a few before sitting back against the rock.

Oh, what I would give to access the ship computer, I need a map. Laye wasn't sure how long it would take to reach the next island of rocks in the sea of sand, and she didn't want to be caught out at night. She wiggled her toes. *I would give up a toe for a map right now.* She imagined her foot looking like a toothless grin and giggled to herself as she lay down on her back, hoping for sleep. Looking up, Laye noticed the ceiling of the cavern was covered in tiny dimples. *Are those baby stalagmites?!*

Sleep was not something she achieved easily; her memories liked to remind her of her past. Everything from her metamorphosis, to being claimed by a powerful abuser right as she emerged, to being cut and beaten during her training.

While Laye had no visible scars, her body had been used by everyone. Used for her unique biology, used for her wing type, and used for her female anatomy. She had never belonged to only herself before.

Sprawled out on the hard ground, Laye closed her eyes and tried to sleep no matter how much she hated it. Visions of her long, multi-legged child form dissolving over time and becoming a liquid before rebuilding into her adolescent form. It was agonizing, the nauseating feeling of everything becoming a liquid and to make it worse, her very aware nervous system was floating in the goo of her former body. Being awake during the lengthy process, trapped in a cocoon and just wanting to be free made her feel vulnerable and entrapped.

After emerging and being forcefully claimed by Leem on the spot, she lost all hope. The back of her head still tingled from where he grabbed her neck and dragged her from the spawning forest. Leem, with his warm brown hair and beautiful sapphire eyes. A part of her broke inside. *How could I have ever grown to love him?* He didn't ever love her back. He loved what she could give him, and her heart felt like it was trapped in a vise as she finally drifted off.

She awoke with a start with the beginnings of daylight reaching her eyelids. Dusting herself off, she picked up her pack before exiting the cave.

Dune after dune, the sand all looked the same and her mind didn't know what to focus on, giving her more memories of her former life which she shoved away. The armor she wore repelled some of the heat but not all. If she wasn't wearing it, her skin felt like it might burn up and the resulting ash blow away in the wind.

She paused, sensing something. Raising her antenna, her armor protected and amplified them as she felt out into the desert. There was nothing specific she could find, but something deep inside told her to run. *Run now!* She went on high alert as she took her next step.

Laye felt the ground moving under her feet as a sink hole formed in the sand and she slid into it just as two beet red pinchers emerged from the growing darkness beneath her. A massive creature hid under the sand and she was falling right into its grasp.

She only had two wrist spikes, and they would take months to re-grow, yet she knew there was a high possibility she would be wasting one on this creature. She had to do whatever it took to claw herself out of this sand hole. Laye kicked at the sand under her, trying to climb, as the beast's pinchers grabbed her legs and she ground her teeth at the pain. It sunk spikes from its pinchers into her flesh and she hissed, *now you're going to die sandman!* The creature pulled her toward its mouth, and she desperately searched for some kind of head so she could have a clean shot. *Does this fucking thing not have a head?!*

The creature finally pushed its head above the sand and opened its mouth full of razor-sharp teeth. Just as she thought it couldn't be any worse, from the sides of its head two sharp, long horns arched inward and closed in on her.

My computer lied! What a bitch! She did not have a fifty six percent survivability rate on this planet. She was probably going to die now, and it had been one day. Pulling her closer to its awaiting mouth, the creature stretched its jaws, and she called on the wind spirits to guide her as she aimed her wrist at the middle of its face.

A spike, made of her bone, tore through her skin, and lodged into the head of the beast causing it to still. The pinchers fell against the sand with a slap, and she patted her legs for damage. *Ha! No butterfly snack for you today. Asshole.*

Finding her skin bruised and torn a bit, but otherwise fine, she took a slow breath and shook her wrist. *Fuck, that stings.* It always stung to use her spike, the skin would heal over in a few hours, but it never felt the same there. It became more sensitive every time.

After several long minutes of digging, she made it out of the conical hole. *Does nothing on this planet have emotions?* She cringed thinking about how easily something could sneak up on her here. She had relied on her empathic skills too much. Laye had always fought her superiors, but they didn't listen. They had forced her to witness hundreds of hours of live torture before forcing her to participate.

Something is not right.

She stopped and moved her hand to her lower abdomen. Something was wrong with her. There was another sharp cramp, *I had been well just before I landed. Hadn't I?*

Terror, like nothing she had ever dreamed, enveloped her as she stood in the screaming starlight of the day. The world seemed to cease to exist around her as she pleaded to the wind spirits. *There is no way. Please, Relit, tell me this isn't happening!* Feeling around on her low abdomen, she dropped to her knees. Tears were not something Laye allowed, but in that moment, nothing could have stopped them from pouring from her eyes. *I am carrying eggs.*

Her heart broke in a thousand pieces. She had no way to feed them. She had no way to care for them. Her eggs would dry up in the arid environment and shrivel. *I will have to crush them.* Laye had to find somewhere to make a safe haven for herself and fast. She had two days or less before the eggs would be ready for her to pass. *I think I am going to be sick.*

There was nothing she could do; she had made her choice to run. She rubbed her shoulder where her transmitter had been as she climbed to her feet. *This was a mistake.* If she had known she was carrying eggs, she never would have killed Leem. She would have returned home and been a sire like her oath dictated. *My fucking oath?!* Nausea surged within her.

She had not dreamed of the possibility of this before this moment. The Vo-Pess at one time had two systems they populated, but one fell under an attack from the First

Humans and every Vo-Pess person on their home world died of a virus. Their second world thankfully had not been discovered. They all had made oaths to return to the spawning woods of their metamorphosis if they given the chance to sire. They were made to swear to return after finding their way out of the forest on Hyret, their adapted home world. They had to repopulate and regain their numbers, regain their power in their own little area of the galaxy. They must stay unseen, undetected. Everything was always to benefit the Vo-Pess, never the individual.

Another cramp in her lower belly made her nausea churn, and she needed to pick up her pace. She was moving too slow and needed to find shelter before night-fall. Her pack felt heavy on her back as she drudged on. Her legs were becoming sore the longer she had to trek through the loose sand.

The system star was setting, and it would be night soon, the sky was turning a brilliant tangerine. Laye was a whirlwind of emotions, but when her training kicked in, it would all be erased by human screams. Oh the delight she had found in their suffering of the FH commanders she helped torture. Delirious with her eggs now bearing down and her body prepping to lay them, she squeezed her dreary dry eyes shut for a few minutes before opening them just in time to find herself standing on the edge of a canyon. It stretched for over a mile in the center, and she slung her head back in frustration.

The last thing she wanted to do was unwrap her wings and use her waning energy to fly, but now she didn't have a choice. She moved her pack to her front and secured it around her waist before concentrating on peeling her wings from her skin. As blood pumped into them and the main veins stretched out behind her, they began rapidly unfolding from her skin and her nanotech armor moved out of the way before it reformed over the places where the wing peeled away from her body.

Her wings were solid black and jutted out to each side before sloping into a downward point, which was why they were called Angle Wings. They had a beautiful pattern of raised veins unique to her and she loved them like they were everything. Although they were massive compared to her small body, they had evolved for high speed and maneuverability.

When they were fully extended and ready for flight, she began flapping them back and forth. Lifting off the ground easily, she flew into the canyon and landed at the bottom where a small river ran through. The sounds of open moving water set her at ease as she retracted her helmet to see better and spotted a cave across the water. She flew across the river and landed on the opposite bank. The cave was directly ahead of her, and she noticed former signs of life. There was a fire pit, and the cave had a natural clay wall built up. *The wind spirits answered my calls. Please allow me peace while I have my eggs*, Laye truly wondered if they had guided her here. It may rain on this world once or twice a year and all ash and soot from the fire pit had long been washed away. Clearly abandoned, she would be able to have a discrete fire to warm herself, and she might even be able to stay there long term.

Laye fell to her knees with sharp, all-consuming belly pain followed by an ache beginning between her legs.

THREE
SEVEN EGGS

She knelt by the fire and gave her offering of a droplet of honey in the flames to the spirit mother, Relit. Any one of the Vo-Pess would skin her alive over a fire for such blasphemy, but she had found proof of their cover up. She had borrowed viral protective gear from the lab. *I don't know why I still can't admit to myself that I stole it. I stole it. There, that felt good. See? I'm growing as a person, even in this hellish wasteland.* With the viral protection, she had ventured to the Vo-Pess original home planet, now inhabited by primitive humans. Laye had found a cave spoken about in her history books which was suspected to hold some of their ancient texts, the contents of which she found to be highly controversial. Her find had stirred up the Van-Well Dynasty circle and was eventually rejected as false, forever shaming her in her family's eyes.

She didn't care, *I believe what I saw and that's all that matters.* Relit had guided her here, and she could at least give thanks for a moment of peace and comfort.

The fire was small but burned with smoldering intensity and she sat as close by it as she could while her time to pass her eggs drew near. The ache had become constant, and she braced her hands on the ground before tapping her armor tabs, causing it to retract.

She pulled her tight-fitted, long underpants down and kicked them away before moving back by the fire pit. Pain erupted in between her legs as she began passing her first egg. Laye knelt down with her knees spread and leaned forward until her forehead touched the ground. With her hands between her legs, she waited for it to emerge. She pushed and it landed smoothly into her hands, so she set it down carefully, curious at the odd color. *Why do my eggs look so strange?*

She had the second and third. It became easier as she had the next few, and when she finished, she counted a total of seven. Laye rinsed her aching flesh between her legs in the cool, rushing river before returning to dress in her undergarments. She pressed her armor tab, and it spread over her.

When she approached her eggs, she wondered if she was seeing things correctly. Dropping down on her knees, she inspected them, and the color was wrong. They were grey. The Vo-Pess only had pure black eggs, and if there was a color to them at all, the eggs would not hatch. She wondered then if her eggs would have ever survived to begin with. Her heart sank. She had not even come close to fulfilling her sire oath. The heated air in her chest became heavy. This was her punishment for running from her duty and her oaths. *I can't even develop viable eggs.*

Leem would have killed her. The moment he had seen the eggs, he would have slit her throat and found another to replace her. *Maybe this is all some odd type of mercy from*

Relit. She would have had to crush them anyway, there is no vegetation here.

Her entrance burned after being stretched beyond its capability, and she lay down next to her eggs with a groan. Her antenna extended, and she reached out to the eggs, wondering if there was a chance. She reached, and reached some more, but found nothing. Her eggs were empty. *What would I have done if I had discovered a life-sign? I couldn't have saved them.*

She took a handful of ruddy sand and let it shift between her fingers, watching it dust the ground.

What now? Should I bury them? Toss them in the river? She hated the idea of any of it. She rolled her antenna back down onto her head and tapped her helmet tab before she rose from the ground to find a place to sleep in the small open cave in the cliffside.

She stared at the dying fire for hours before her eyes became too heavy and shut, only to wake, what seemed to be moments later, when she heard a scratching sound outside of the cave. The canyon was well lit by large, bright white double moons, both covered in deep craters. Her eyes focused, and she remained still as a large rodent appeared from the left of the cave. The rodent's young gathered around it expectantly, hungry.

Laye watched as they took her eggs and scurried off. Her heart ached more than it had ever before, but she was unable to force her emotions to the surface. They always stayed deep, far away from her exterior. She had to maintain composure, no matter what. She buried her grief deep within in her graveyard of lost dreams, it was time to sleep. She knew it was. The moons were illuminating all the meager bushes while creating shadows against the ground, taunting her with images of her sweet baby cater-pillars foraging. *Sleep will not come easy tonight. I wish I could have figured out how everyone always just turned it all off. How did they push away their feelings so easily?* She moved in every position she could, but every way she tried to lie down, her bones would ache.

Lying flat and closing her eyes, she willed sleep to happen. It was the one thing she had epically failed at in her training. Everyone else had mastered forcing sleep except for her. When she did sleep, her dreams were filled with torment, and she dreaded it despite knowing she needed it. She squeezed her eyes shut and tried again. Hours passed, and she hadn't moved, but hadn't had a single dream. *What is wrong with me?*

She rotated on her side as she noticed the colossal moons hung low in the sky. The moon's impossibly deep craters made them looked as though they were some of the First Human's planetary victims, the skeletal aftermath of their planet destroying core mining the faction was well known for. It would be daylight soon, and she would need to go in search of food. She must find a sugar source before she ran out.

Placing her hand on her lower abdomen, her thoughts fell on her eggs. The children who would never be, her children, how lucky she would have been in another life to have sired seven. Laye imagined her offspring hatching and finding their way through the woods. She jolted upright with a memory of her time as a very young child, crawling through the woods, trying not to end up eaten by birds. There was terror, and she grasped her hands together.

Wait, that can't be right? My time in the woods was joyous and safe. Right? Where did that memory come from? She racked her brain, but all she could recite was, her time in the woods was joyous and safe. Something told her the time in those woods as a child, was not so safe after all, and maybe the joy and the safety were programmed like everything else in their lives.

FOUR
HAPPENSTANCE

Laye's eyes snapped open as she was hauled out of her peaceful sleep on the cavern floor and thrown onto the uneven, rocky ground of the canyon. She landed in the shadow of a giant K'hornibus man wearing black riding leathers with shoulder spikes, a mask resembling their skulls, and a black cloth concealing his neck from the elements. He seemed angry to find her in what she was just realizing was likely some rarely used hunting hole. Too bad today was the day these men chose to occupy it.

As a product of her training, she rolled to her feet and bolted by the giant man with horns protruding from the back of his head. She didn't look behind her as she wiggled her wings free from their resting place against her skin, and they began expanding. Within a few seconds they unfurled and were flapping, her pounding heart filled them quickly. Taking off while running was difficult, but she had done it many times before. She ran as quickly as she could and angled down as she flapped her wings. On her second down stroke, and she felt a hand wrap around her ankle. *Sugar balls! I should have tucked my legs!*

With an iron grasp on her ankle, the K'hornibus growled, "Get my rope!"

Laye strained her wings with all her might and kicked at his grip, desperate to not waste her last spike. *Fuck it, I'm living today.*

Twisting herself, she angled down and pointed her wrist at him before firing her spike. It burst through her skin aimed directly at the K'hornibus face. Her bone spike could penetrate most anything from the force the Vo-Pess shot them with.

She beat her wings furiously thinking the spike had landed, but his grip remained. Laye snuck a glance behind her to find her spike had simply passed over the mask and lodged in his thick skull. *It didn't penetrate?! Honey butt, you're fucked now!*

She gritted her teeth and bucked as she forced her wings against the wind and lifting them from the ground. "Yarle! It's lifting me up, grab my arm!" Yarle, another K'hornibus, grabbed his arm and yanked him down, pulling Laye to the ground in a great cloud of dust.

She slammed against the dirt, and her wings shriveled up, sliding back against her skin as her suit covered over them. A moment later, when she was back together, Laye leaned up to find four seven-foot tall K'hornibus in skull masks surrounding her. Their tails were all curiously swaying behind them. Yarle kicked her leg, "What is it, Mac?" She pulled her knees up to her chest and wrapped her arms around them, feigning meekness.

Mac, the K'hornibus who had a hold of her ankle answered, "It's a bug. It looks like dinner."

Fucking sugar tits. I am on the menu? She had crashed on the wrong planet and fallen asleep in the wrong cave.

She desperately stared at the dirt under her like it would tell her what to do, and she frowned as it slid away while he dragged her to her feet. Laye was only as tall as Mac's chest, barely, now standing next to him, she thought he was possibly even a few inches over seven feet. How many she wasn't sure, but he towered over her. She was tall for a Vo-Pess at five foot ten, but it didn't help much standing next to this giant. *I really hope they kill me before they eat me.*

Staying silent, she wondered if she retracted her armor that she might graduate from the dinner plate. Her body had never been her own anyway, how was now any different? Maybe if it was her choice it would be different. Laye couldn't take her eyes from Mac. He was so broad and thick. *So, very juicy. Whoa, did I really just say that?* She angled her shoulder up and retracted her helmet, causing her curly, black hair to fall free. Meeting the sour, lemon eyes of the powerful man before her, *why can I not read their emotions? How can they block me?* He had a damn mask on, and she couldn't see his expression. *Fucking sugar balls, this is so bad. I'm about to be roasted and toasted over an open fire.* This was hardly her ideal end, and her mind went straight to internally begging for the self-destruct option she had dug out of her shoulder and crushed. *Honey butt, you're an epic dumbass.*

She kept her antennae hidden in her hair as Laye pushed her gift out again, only finding the void. Mac reached up and peeled her helmet tab off her neck and put it in the pocket of his utility pants. His rough hand brushed the soft skin of her neck, and she held her gaze on him, studying him. He angled his head and stared at her, *what is he looking at?* She could see him blinking behind the mask. After a moment, he took her hands and bound them before forcing her to move forward.

There were long and sleek hand-crafted bikes parked at the end of the canyon. They were moving her somewhere else, which presented more opportunity for escape. Who was she kidding? *Do I have the will to run anymore?* She imagined her end, and something about it gave her great comfort. It would all finally be over, and she would be at peace. Her drive to live was slipping away with each step.

As Laye was marched to the bikes, she noticed the pile of her broken gray eggs. She guessed nothing mattered anymore; she would die soon. It was probably for the better, and she became accepting of the idea. A normal life for her was a fallacy anyway. Her own mind would have claimed her eventually. Her people experienced terrible mental health problems as seniors, and many of the Vo-Pess who had her job eventually developed psychological failures. She knew it was the training; it had to be. She felt her emotions crawling up her gut to climb her spine and finally reaching her brain just to eat her mind away, bit by bit. Burying emotions came at a high price.

Shaking her head, memories of screams rattled in her mind as she was hauled over the side of a bike. *Silence!* she cried out into her own mind. The assault of thoughts quieted, and she could finally think clearly for a moment as Mac started the electric engine. The sand blowing all around them reminded her she needed her helmet. She faced the hulking beast of a man and when he turned to meet her eyes, she tapped her neck where her helmet tab had been.

He leaned in close and studied her face before reluc-tantly reaching in his pocket and gently placed it back on her neck where it had been before. Mac's fingers brushed the skin of her neck, this time sending a flutter through her. She gave him a nod of thanks and pressed her neck to her shoulder to activate it. The metal particles slid over her face, and they formed a helmet.

She felt his hard body slide on the bike behind her before he picked her up by her waist and moved her forward so he could settle. He sat her down directly against his dense torso, and she smirked. *So, maybe I do have this Mac guy hooked after all. I wonder what a K'hornibus penis looks like. I wonder what it feels like. I'm sure he likes it rough.* She nearly fell off the bike and had to reposition herself. *Well, no wonder he put me in front of him.*

Laye was busy wondering if she truly had swayed him, and how their intimate moments would transpire when he twisted the throttle, and they took off. The force of the bike pushed her against him, and she had nothing to hold onto with her hands bound, so she gripped like hell with her legs and hope to not fall off. *If he had put me on the back, I would be flapping in the wind.*

It was like flying and she had to admit, she was having a bit of fun as they moved through the canyon. She had never been on a motorized vehicle like this. Her people flew everywhere, and their world was designed around it.

But this, she liked this, a lot. After a few hours of riding, she was in love. *With the machine under me, not the big scary lizard man.* Just to be clear. *What is a K'hornibus again?* Weren't they an evolved lizard? Or did they come from an early bird like animal? She couldn't remember, as their species didn't come up much. They didn't leave their home world often, and they were mostly private people. That's all she could recall.

They pulled to a stop, and she noticed a small cave

which looked identical to the one she had slept in. Distracted by the pain of laying her eggs, she had thought the cave was natural with ancient additions. It was obviously still being used. Maybe she had greatly underestimated these people. If she had her head on straight and wasn't preoccupied with her emotions, she would have been able to avoid this.

They climbed from the bikes while two of the K'hornibus started a fire and spread out sleeping mats. Mac stood by his bike and held onto Laye. Once the camp was erected, he pulled her off the bike and set her on a bed mat toward the back of the cave. Mac knelt in front of her, and waved his fingers toward himself, signaling to hand over her armor.

Laye stared at him as it occurred to her all she had worn under her armor was her tight fitted underclothing, which was quite sheer. She hoped he just wanted the helmet. Reaching up, she tapped the tab, and the helmet receded. She leaned her neck over for him to peel it off, which he did. This time his fingers lingered against her skin, and his eyes bore into her with more heat than the daylight star.

He tilted his head as he pulled his hand back and pointed to her chest, "I know there are more. Hand them over."

She pretended she didn't understand and ignored the vivid, intruding memory of cutting her translator out of the throat of a dying First Human Commander. He thrashed as she dug his vocal cords from his throat with her knife, and the experience was rather healing now that she reflected on it. He was dead before she retrieved the implant in his ear.

Bringing her green eyes up to Mac's, he was completely

unreadable with his mask on. He reached up and grabbed her ankle, yanking her down onto the bed mat. Mac crawled over her and grabbed her by the neck. He lifted her so her nose lined up with the nose of his mask. "Give me the armor."

Laye nodded and he let go of her throat slightly, allowing her to breathe. Laye didn't want to give it up, but she complied anyway.

With her hands still tied, she tapped her chest at her sternum for the armor to gather there in a tab. The armor receded, and Mac stared down at her sheer white underclothes, her dark blue nipples evident through the fabric. Nothing was spared to the imagination.

He paused for a few long, drawn out moments before reaching down and carefully tapping the tab, causing her armor to engulf her again. Crawling off the mat, he stood over her for several minutes, his eyes focused directly on her. When he was finished with his staring game, Mac sat in front of her bed mat and didn't move for a few hours.

Peering around him, Laye noticed a few of the K'hornibus from the group had been missing for a while. Mac remained a statue in front of her as the missing men re-appeared with a several hundred pound dead sand viper draped over their shoulders. One assembled a spit from their gear to roast it with while the other skinned and prepped it for cooking.

When it occurred to her, she wasn't being eaten *tonight*, she leaned back against the cave wall. She sighed, wishing she had some of her syrup from her pack, but that was long gone. Laye knew she could go months without eating but she didn't want to. She loved her curves and wanted to keep them.

They slid a section of the snake onto the spit as the fire

grew under it. The system star fell, and the double moons rose, lighting up the canyon. Visions of her former life crept to the surface. *Why so soon? Why are they coming back already?* Had her one moment of relief in life pulled the plug which held back the raging flood of her emotions?

The quiet became loud with insects, and Laye focused on their teeny symphony projected into the night. Anything to keep her mind from drudging up old memories and tormenting her.

FIVE

THE STREAM

After days of blistering hot, uneventful travel the river had become a stream, and the canyon walls tapered down. Wildlife was sparse, and she wondered when they would be crossing the large expanse of sand with their bikes. Laye observed the planet briefly on her way down, she knew what was at the end of this canyon, and it was nothing but endless desert dunes. A walled city was located in the center of the vast sands, but that was it.

The K'hornibus set up camp, and she sat next to Mac's bike with her hands bound with rope. She could easily untie it, but why, just to get caught and tied up further? No. She had cooperated, and Mac had even tried to offer her food. It was roasted snake meat, and that was an absolute no, but he offered and that meant something right?

Mac hovered over her and pointed to where two of his men were bathing in the stream. She turned back and stared at him as he bent down and tapped her neck, causing her helmet to recede. He peeled off the tab and pointed to the stream again. He wanted her to bathe. *Do I smell that bad?* Laye tipped her face down and sniffed herself. *Maybe he has a point.* She did have a pungent odor.

Complying, she rose to her feet, and as she did, two K'hornibus men passed by her with no clothes. Their sex organs were hidden behind a bulge with a nearly invisible slit down the middle, right at the apex of their thighs. They were all solid muscle and each around seven feet, with different patterns of spike like horns protruding from their heads. She wished she knew more about their anatomy. They didn't have their masks on, and she was infinitely curious if she would have the opportunity to see Mac without his on.

Mac had four horns, two large horn spikes jutting back along the arch of his temples and away from his head and a smaller one protruding from under them on either side. The other man she had come to understand was his closest brother, Yarle, had six horn spikes. Laye discovered the other two men were their younger brothers and border guards, Inex and Kote. They had four horn spikes each.

When she reached the stream, she noticed not one of them stood around ready for her stream show, except Mac. She stood in his shadow, and he had his hand out for her armor tab.

She pressed the suit at her sternum and her armor receded. Laye reached under her shirt and peeled it away to hand it over. He took it and slid it in his pocket. He untied her hands, and swiftly pointed in her face, "If you run, I will gut you, and we will have you for our meal tonight."

She didn't respond as he removed the rope. Laye knew he was not turning around and wondered if she should give seduction one last try. *Fuck it.* She might have sex with him and still end up dead afterward. She would have with Leem, *so what's new?!*

She stripped off her underclothes and boldly revealed all her light blue skin to Mac. Her wings were flush against her skin and ran along her backside from her shoulders to her calves, like swirls of night against the daylit sky. She stood several feet from the water and didn't rush as she approached it. Laye had only been with one person, but she wasn't stupid, she knew what they all liked.

She stepped into the chilly water and her skin tightened. Laye needed to make this quick. She scrubbed her underclothes under the water, knowing they would dry when she wrung them out. When they were free of her body odor, she handed them to Mac who she noticed watched her intently. Although she couldn't see his eyes behind his mask well, there was a small shadow visible, and she was positive he hadn't blinked once.

She noticed he had tossed soap on the bank. Laye stood up, and took the soap, lathering it in her hands before she ran her hands over her arms and cleaned under them. Keeping her eyes on Mac, she lathered again and slid her hands over her breasts, before rubbing the soap down her stomach. *I could really use a washcloth about now.* She lathered her hands one last time, and she swore he mumbled something under his mask. Laye wanted him to take it off, she needed to see the man underneath. Gliding her hand through the top of her thighs, she watched him take a small step to the side, ensuring no one else could see her behind him.

It was working. She wondered how far she could take this as she turned and carefully spread her lathered hands over her rear. Laye met his eyes before she put her hand between her butt cheeks and shifted as she bent over to begin lathering her legs. She was angled so he couldn't see her center, and she watched as he tipped his head trying to see without seeming too obvious.

Mac began to lean for a glimpse, so she dipped down into the water. Laye swore she heard a huff from under his mask. She rinsed herself and lightly shook her wet hair as she rose from the stream.

On the shore, she couldn't hold back as she made her body vibrate to remove the water. Droplets shot out from her in every direction as she shook, creating a small Rain shower all around her.

Mac stood perfectly still, holding her dripping wet clothing as he watched her every move. She approached him holding her gaze to his as she reached for her clothes. He handed them back and stared at her while she wrung out her underclothes. Laye dressed herself and put her hand out for her body armor.

He carefully reached in his pocket and pulled out the tab, handing it over. Laye noticed him roughly swallow. She put her hands together in front of him after her armor was on, and he rebound her. Mac led her over to their camp where he tied her to one of his packs.

Yarle sat next to her and watched her as Mac headed to the stream. Was she going to receive a show in return?

Mac dropped his jacket along with his shirt, revealing his patches of scaled skin and muscled body. He sat down to remove his boots but stood back up to slip off his pants, giving Laye a full view of his round ass, and she was not disappointed. Mac was incredible. He was thick with muscle, and he had a tattoo of a sand viper covering his back.

Take off the mask! She wanted to yell at him. He did take

it off but didn't turn around as he waded into the stream. *Is he really going to hide his face from me? Why?!*

She was more disappointed than she cared to admit. He finished washing and never turned around. All she had was a glimpse of the side of his face when he reached for his towel. Instead of it making anything better, it made her want to see it even worse. *I just know he's attractive. His brothers are, sure as sugar!*

When he came back, and Yarle took his turn, he sat in front of her and didn't turn around. She was thirsty. She reached up and tapped his shoulder, he jolted a bit and turned to her, seeming to be furious. Laye made a signal for water, and he growled, "Don't fucking touch me."

Her face fell, *that was fucking disappointing. What is wrong with me?* Had she lost her edge?

He seemed to lighten up as he handed her his jug. She struggled to lift it with her bound hands and spilled some on herself before she handed it back. He snatched it from her and turned away before he lifted his mask partially and guzzled some of the water. All she could see was his jaw and lips, and she was not disappointed.

After replacing his mask, he signaled his younger brothers to start the fire for their meal. They roasted a large rodent, like the one that had taken her eggs. She watched as it slowly spun on the spit for hours before they devoured it. Laye was slightly hungry, but she would make do with water for now. She knew she would eventually lose weight but that didn't matter if she didn't survive for much longer. Especially if she failed to seduce Mac.

Nothing really mattered anymore. Her mind had fallen quiet, and she believed she might be regaining her wits, but she wasn't going to put all her weight onto that assumption. After the meal was over, they each prepared to sleep, and Laye did the same. Mac seemed unhappy with where his bed mat was and he moved it behind hers, she didn't turn over as she heard him lie down.

It was a cool night, and she was too far from the fire to feel the warmth. She would have done about anything for a blanket. Her armor was not made for insulation. It was just made to keep her protected from whipping winds, nothing else. If she was cold, it was dipping to freezing temperatures. Not long after she began shivering, she saw her breath turn to frost. Laye studied the breathing of everyone she could see, and they were all fast asleep. She could hear Mac behind her, and his breathing told her he was far from asleep.

Mac slid his hand over her hip, and hauled her over to his mat, pressing her against him. He lay his arm over her, and she could feel his warmth seeping into her chilled body. Laye expected a roaming hand, but he didn't move, he draped his arm over her small frame and kept his hand flat on the bed mat.

With him close and his breathing becoming steady, she tried to wait until he fell asleep to slide off to sleep herself. She was glad she waited because the moment he began to doze off, he slid his hand against her belly and pressed her to him again. Mac's heavy arm held her close.

Maybe my little show worked.

SIX

THE END

They had been traveling all day along a road she couldn't see from the wind sand blasting them. Her legs were sore from gripping the bike, and she instinctively slumped to the side against Mac. He slid his arm down and around her to hold her up. When he did, he pressed her into his firm torso, and Laye angled her ample rear to grind into him.

She swore he muttered something, but with the wind, the sound blew away with the dirt cloud swirling behind them. They were rapidly approaching the walled city, and from what she could see, it was made primarily of metal. She guessed the right metal was the only thing that could withstand the desert heat and winds.

As they approached the great doors in the wall slid to the side with gears the size of her former ship. Laye watched men lean into giant chains draped over their backs to pull it open. The four bikes passed through without slowing and headed down a central road to a building at the far end. The city appeared derelict and rusted, apartment buildings seemed to lean onto one another for support and between them were tarp covered markets. The street was hardly bustling, and its people were all weary and shuffling along. Malnutrition among the unhoused squeezed at her heart, *no one should ever go hungry in a galaxy full of food.*

The building was constructed into the side of the wall at the back of the city. Another set of doors opened ahead of them, and they blew through the gate without reducing their speed. It wasn't until they were approaching a garage, did they slow down. All the bikes came to a halt in a line under the metal roof. Mac lifted Laye off the bike and set her on the ground before taking her arm and leading her down a path around to what she thought was the front door.

They entered a large reception room where an old K'hornibus man sat in a tall back chair at the end of a long table. Laye was marched to face him.

Yarle spoke first, "Father, we found this in the desert. It's a butterfly being. What should we do with it?" Mac stood silent as he gripped her arm.

The man leaned back in his metal chair, and it creaked with the motion, "Looks like she could feed a lot of people. Mac, take her to processing. We need to have a discussion later about your duties here. You're being relocated to the north canyon and leading up the watch there." Mac nodded and disappointment mixed with sorrow wrapped around her heart. Laye would be sliced up for meat after all.

Nothing could have prepared her for the room Mac led her into. She almost broke her silence when she saw metal butcher tables before her. The rest of the room wasn't much better with meat from desert creatures hanging on hooks behind the tables, as well as a skinned leg of a higher being. Mac forced her onto one of the tables and she turned to face him, doing her best to hide her devastation. She wasn't even sure she had earned a humane death at this point.

He tied her onto the table, arms over her head and feet tied together at the end before he tapped her below her sternum. He lifted her sheer shirt and peeled the tab away from her skin. Mac took a pair of scissors and cut away her underclothes, and the freezing metal under her bit into her skin. It was so cold it burned, and she trembled as she exhaled frost. *Is this the meat freezer?* She looked up and wished she hadn't. Meat was hanging all around above her.

She squeezed her eyes shut, but they flew back open when she heard the buzz of a saw start up. Her head popped up and she watched Mac casually approach her with the small bone saw. She absolutely did not earn a humane death and her mind spun trying to comprehend what horrific pain she would soon endure. She went to the place she always did when she needed to hide. Laye imagined herself flying free above her world, unbound to Leem and free of her military obligation as an angled wing. No oaths, no screams, just air and clouds and freedom.

Mac slid the handle of the single blade saw along the center of her chest as he peered down at her through his mask. His brilliant yellow eyes shined back at her as light from the polished table shone onto his mask, illuminating it. She tried to find a reason to beg for her life, but she decided she was ready to die, and she closed her eyes preparing for his worst.

He slowly drug the handle of the running bone saw against the skin of her thigh before lifting the saw away and sniffing between her legs. Mac trailed the handle of the saw along her skin and when he grazed her center, her eyes flew open. He turned the saw off and inhaled deeply at the apex of her thighs. Laye felt his hand slip down and feel her seeping wetness.

He brought his fingers to his mouth under his mask before bringing his face even with hers. His hollow eyes focused on her and she wasn't sure what he would do next as he stared at her.

Mac started the saw again and brought it down on the rope holding her to the table, below her feet. He cut the rope extending her arms and turned it off.

He kept checking the door as he slung her nude form over his shoulder, careful not to stab her with the shoulder spikes. The rough leather scraped against her skin. With the saw still in his hand, he checked both ways of the hall before sprinting down to a door at the end. It was another freezer with the same setup, but the door had a lock, and she noticed there was no meat in this one. It was clean.

Her heart sunk as he set her on the table and again tied her down. She had thought for sure he wasn't going to butcher her, but she wondered if he just wanted a clean, private place to do it. She internally sighed and tried to hide her face behind her arm when she heard the saw start up. Laye had been through horrific torture at the hands of her teachers as a student in training for her duties. This would be no different, only more permanent.

Laye again felt the handle of the saw run down her exposed flesh, but this time he lingered at her lower belly. Mac, slowly, brought the shaking handle of the saw between her thighs, and pressed it against the strip of nerves above her entrance. She was tied to tightly to move, but her hips demanded it. She had never felt something so intense.

Her head shot up from the table, and he met her wild gaze with a growl as he rubbed the tool up and down against her most sensitive place. Her hips clenched, and her lips parted as she tried to comprehend what was happening. She had never had anyone touch her there, and she had never so much as grazed that area. Her mind spun wildly. Something was growing, and she wasn't sure what was happening, but she was afraid she would lose her mind when it happened. It was intensifying and she couldn't help panting.

Laye tried to squirm away, and he pressed his hand on her lower belly as he moved the handle up and down her delicate strip. Her hips fought his iron grip, and she was at a loss at how her body was reacting. *Is this a form of torture?* Unending pleasure which caused involuntary movements and sounds of her ecstasy would surely be following if this became any more intense. *Is this how he plans to break me?*

She writhed as she felt the end of his tail slide against her taught nipples. Her body had never experienced such a thing, she had never been allowed. Laye felt something flowing within her and she yearned to whimper as he increased his speed.

At the point of unbearable, something delightful inside broke free and slammed into her. She trembled violently and arched herself back as the euphoric feeling flooded over her. Mac tilted his head and stroked his fingers against her lower belly as he pulled the saw away and turned it off. She couldn't help it as she tilted her head up to watch, Mac as he lifted his mask and brought his mouth down between her legs to lap up the results of her pleasure.

When his long tongue grazed her strip of nerves she nearly jolted so hard she felt her wrists pop against the rope, and he released a low growl of satisfaction. Mac slipped his hands under her ass and lifted her before he licked her clean and he purposely slid his tongue over her swollen, sensitive row eliciting another jerk from her hips before finally setting her back down.

She was out of breath, *was that a fucking orgasm?* She had never in her life dreamed it could be so overtaking and satiating. Her mind slowed, and she watched as he took what looked to be a big black duffel bag from a locker.

After untying her, Mac leaned over her, "I don't know if you can understand me, but I'm hiding you in this bag, and I'm taking you out of here. If you scream, or try and run, you will die."

Is this man serious? Move over big guy, I am diving into that bag. Mac placed her armor tab on her chest before tapping it. The armor spread over her as she climbed off the table.

There was no use feigning understanding, she couldn't hold herself back from jumping into the open bag. She would probably follow him off a cliff after what he just did to her. Before he closed the bag with her now inside, he leaned over it, "I knew you could understand me. Now be silent, and don't move."

Mac zipped up the bag and her world became dark. Her training had not prepared her for this type of interrogation at all, she had *never* given in so quickly.

SEVEN

A QUIET MIND

She was knocked around in the bag as Mac moved. She had no idea what he was doing until he unzipped the top of the bag and stuffed some black cloth over her before zipping it again. The bag was stuffy, and she felt him slide her on his back while she did her best to remain fluid.

Laye could hear the engine on his bike rev up as he took off. She was confused but glad to be alive as she felt him reach top speeds. She remained in the confides of the bag long enough she began to sweat long before she felt him begin to slow down.

Mac pulled to a stop and set the bag down on the ground before opening it up. Laye looked up to see Mac staring at her from his position straddling his bike, "Get dressed." He pointed to the clothes he had stuffed in the bag, and she sorted them out, it was a small, fitted tank and a pair of leather pants with a leather jacket. *Look at us, already wearing matching couple's outfits.* She dressed as quickly as she could, and he didn't warn her as he grabbed her waist and sat her in front of him on the seat. He slid a K'hornibus skull helmet over her head, clearly made for a child, and stuffed a black cloth over her black hair before tucking it into her jacket behind her head.

Mac wrapped his arm around her, and they took off into the night under the light of the moons. She could feel his hand search for her skin at her side, he lifted her jacket and stroking his thumb along her flesh. Before long, his hand was all the way inside of her shirt and his rough fingers gently rubbed circles on her belly. Laye was sure to shiver if he didn't stop, but she wanted more so badly her palms tingled, and resisted succumbing to the urge to grind against the seat.

The journey was long, flat, and uneventful. They approached a bridge which dipped into a canyon, and he slowed only to cross it before he sped up again. After hours of travel, he leaned over her, "We are crossing into disputed territory, we have a checkpoint ahead."

She nodded in understanding, and he continued until they saw a fire in the distance. It grew brighter as they neared, and he slowed to a stop but she was unable to see with the light shining in her eyes. "I have the border assignment now. Tell Shin to head home."

Laye couldn't see anyone, but assumed there was a guard station in front of them but heard the checkpoint guard asked playfully, "Who's that?"

Mac growled and she could feel the rumbles against her back, "None of your fucking business."

The guard laughed, and waved him on, "See you at the border."

Mac sped off pulling Laye against him. Following another shorter drive through the canyon, he stopped at a metal rolling door and climbed off his bike. He turned, pointing to her in warning, as if she had anywhere to run.

He opened a door to a large shop and remounted his bike to pull it in. Once he was parked, he climbed off and closed and locked the door, slipping the key in his pants pocket. Turning around, he found Laye leaning against his bike.

Mac approached her and pulled her helmet off before he pointed to the stairs in front of them. *You're not going to take your mask off big guy?* Laye climbed the stairs to find a small but nice apartment with windows facing the inside of the canyon. The floors were wood from Vidar, and the walls were reddish clay bricks, he had a full kitchen, dining, and living space. Mac grabbed her arm and pulled her to the back where he had a large metal frame bed and side table. There was a door to the left, leading to what she suspected was a restroom.

He reached inside a drawer in the side table and took out a metal ring before approaching her and pointing to his bed. She obeyed and crawled on the bed to sit. Mac took her ankle and attached the metal ring snugly before pressing a button which caused a red light to come on briefly before turning off.

Meeting her eyes, he asked, "Do you eat?" She was starving and nodded. Mac leaned into her face as he asked, "What do you eat?"

Laye wasn't going to say a word. She knew better. When you spoke, they only had more ways to manipulate you. He grabbed her by the throat and asked again, "What do you eat?" She stared back at him with no intention of answering.

Mac growled, "How the fuck am I supposed to feed you when you won't tell me what you eat?" He stormed into the next room and put his hands on either side of the window as he peered out at the moons.

He tipped his head to the side and turned to glare at her in his room before he went into his kitchen and began opening and noisily shutting cabinet doors. He stopped and silence filled the kitchen before he appeared around the corner with a jar in his hand. Mac thrust the jar at her, "You're a butterfly, you eat sugar."

Laye was genuinely surprised, Mac had figured that out quickly. She reluctantly took the jar and slowly spun the lid, finding golden honey in the bottom. She could hardly contain herself as she dipped her long, hollow tongue into the thick sugary substance and slurped it up greedily.

Mac stood stoic in front of her as she cleaned out the jar, she hadn't ever been that hungry before, not even when they had starved her for two weeks for slapping her bunk mate during one of her long-term training sessions.

She handed him the now empty jar, and he grumbled, "Sugar. No wonder your pussy tastes sweet."

Oh?! Is that why he was licking me? Laye was starting to understand why he spared her and dragged her along. She had tasty lady bits.

Mac handed her a glass of water while he drank one down himself before setting his mostly empty cup on his bedside table, "Why don't you talk?"

Laye didn't move and had no intention of speaking as he loomed over her. He growled again as he wrapped his hand around her throat. "I can see your translator scar. What will it take to make you speak?"

She kept her lips sealed, and he lifted and tossed her on the bed. Mac halfway stomped into the next room before returning without his jacket on. He walked by the bed and went into his bathroom, *I knew it was a bathroom* before poking his head out again, "I'll detonate the bomb on your ankle if you leave the apartment while I'm showering."

With that, Mac slammed the bathroom door, and she could hear the shower start. She lay back on the bed a moment before she grew warm and needed to take her jacket off. Laye had just taken it off and put it on a wall hook when she heard the door open behind her.

Mac was nude, and he had taken his mask off. She did her best to hide it, but she was overwhelmed, *Mac is beautiful*. His jaw was strong, and his eyes were perfect, solid yellow almonds with a slit down the middle.

Her lips parted and he smirked as he approached her, "Get on your knees." She complied without thought and he grabbed her hair, pulling her head back, "Suck the left and stroke the right."

Laye didn't understand until his length emerged from his slit, it had a clear line that ran down the middle and she was beyond intrigued. She was wondering what she had truly gotten herself into when he slid his length into her awaiting mouth.

Mac tipped his head back and groaned, "Good girl, you can take it."

She felt him begin to pulse in her mouth before he pulled out and his length split into two parts. Each side formed a ball like structure at the end and could move independently. Laye did as she was instructed and put her mouth around the left side as she brought her still bound hand to the right side and began stroking him. He was impossibly hard, and she was drooling down her chin trying to take one side fully. He braced his hand on the wall and grunted before grasping her hair in his hand guiding her mouth up and down. Mac's length began to pulsate, and he curled over as he erupted onto her face.

Mac reached down with his hand and rubbed the cum from her cheek, "Let's get you washed up."

That was positively the sexiest thing that had ever happened to her. She rose from the floor and slowly made her way to the bathroom where he wet a cloth and cleaned her face.

As he finished wiping her clean, he leaned in closely and whispered, "What will it take to make you to speak? I have a few ideas. I want to hear that voice of yours scream for me." Laye was unsure whether she would ever speak again if her silence would result in more attention. She was starting to think her situation might not have ended up so bad after all.

Mac led her to the bed and pointed to her clothes, she complied and began taking them off. Once she was nude, he handed her one of his under shirts which fit her like a dress. When she finished pulling it over her head, he grabbed her and threw her on the mattress.

He took a rope from behind the bed and tied her wrist before he unlocked the ring on her ankle and put it away. She wiggled her blue legs under the covers as he climbed into the other side.

He hauled her against his hard, muscled body. *Well, that was unexpected.* Affection felt curious and foreign, and it took some time and energy to calm herself. A comforting touch was something she had never experienced. Leem had only put his hands on her when he wanted to steal a piece of her flesh. Mac wrapped his arm around her, and she had never simultaneously so felt safe and in danger. Either way, she would take this moment and appreciate it. She wasn't dead, yet.

EIGHT
SCREAM

Laye stood at the windows of the apartment, studying the sparse shrubbery inside the canyon. There were tiny rodents frolicking around under the bushes and they had been thoroughly entertaining her while Mac was gone. The little tails were whirlwinds as they performed aerobatics in play.

She had awoken to him threatening her with his knife pressed against her belly as he told her again, she was not to leave. *Where would I go anyway? Venture into the desert to die of thirst? After he gave me the first orgasm I ever had? No fucking thank you, my honey butt is staying here.*

He reluctantly untied her wrist and allowed her to roam his apartment, she had taken a shower and put his shirt back on. Her hair still dripped down her back because she had not shaken off in his bathroom. It would have shot water everywhere and she didn't want to clean it, so she toweled off instead.

The sound of his bike purring in the distance thrilled her, he had not told her when he would return or what he left for, but he had a new pack on his back when he returned. Before then, she had never felt anything but apprehension knowing someone was soon to join her. Well, except for Fere. *I miss her so much.*

She felt flustered as she heard Mac climbing the stairs. Laye was unsure what to do, and she ran into the kitchen and stood behind the counter. Mac opened the door and came in, taking his mask off and setting it down. He signaled for her to follow him into his room.

He set the new leather pack on the bed and opened it to reveal clothing, and she could hear jars clanking beneath the cloth. Mac pulled out the clothes and pointed to a drawer in his dresser, she took the clothes that seemed to be in her size and put them away.

Laye turned back to find him holding a box full of jars of honey and she followed him as he took the box and put it in the kitchen pantry. Mac tapped the box, "This is yours."

He cautiously studied her before he tipped his head to the side and sniffed the air. He narrowed his eyes at her and pointed to his room. She complied and he followed, pulling his shirt off her as she reached the end of his bed. Laye stood nude and waited for his instructions.

His hand ran down her back, his fingers running along the edge of where her wings rested against her skin, whispering, "What secrets are you holding? What are you? Why are you here?" He waited for her to answer, but she wouldn't dare.

"You will answer me little butterfly." Mac demanded. She didn't move as he went around her and tipped her chin up to face him, "That pretty mouth of yours will make a sound today. Do you understand me?"

Her heart jolted as he reached down to grab her and

threw her onto his bed before he tied her hands to the metal headboard with rope. Mac pulled something from his bedside table, and he hovered over her face. He scooped a bit of cream substance from a jar and rubbed it into the ends of his fingers before leaning over and applying it to the tips of her breasts. She watched as he removed his clothes, and when she began feeling the skin of her breasts tingle, she squirmed.

What in fucking sandy hell did he put on me?! It was increasing by the second and felt like tiny hands were all over her nipples, the delicious sensation made her rub her legs together, but Mac laid a hand on her thigh, stopping the motion. *Fuck, he might win before it starts!* Already desperate, she met his piercing gaze.

He knew exactly what he was doing as he held her legs down and watched her wiggle. "The oil of the desert sage, it produces an intense sensation on the skin. It multiplies your nerve reception." Laye was wildly spinning inside as she noticed him counting, *what is he counting to?* She felt his tail slip between her legs as he leaned over her, "What is your name?"

The tingling of her nipples intensified all at once and she was nearly in tears, desperate for him to touch her where she needed it the most. Mac gently ran his finger down the center of her chest, and it was as if he was stroking her very soul. Her breaths became quick, and she arched off the bed.

"What is your name, little butterfly?" He purred as he slid his tail just short of her entrance.

She had been through horrific torture, this was something else entirely, and she was cracking. Her name was pressed against her own lips, begging to be set free as he slowly flitted his tail at her opening. Still hovering, Mac leaned over and ran his fingertips along the sides of her breasts, but not touching her straining peaked nipples. Laye would surely scream if he didn't touch her most sensitive place, *right now*. Laye felt herself give in as she breathed, "Oh, Laye, my name is Laye."

Mac growled in triumph as he rubbed his knuckles over her screaming nipples, giving her a wild thrill of intense pleasure. She whimpered and writhed as she felt him ease his tail inside of her. "I'll give you what you want, you just have to answer some questions." Mac hooked his tail upward inside of her, giving her a hint of what was to come.

She furiously thrashed, breaking through all her years of training was also cracking her heart open. Emotion threatened to erupt, and she begged her mind to hold back the gates. Mac smirked and held his hands above her nipples. "Laye, why are you here?"

Laye couldn't hold back any longer, "I defected." The truth hit her like something raw detonated inside of her mind, but she didn't have time to think about it as Mac reached down and gently rubbed the tip of his finger against her line of nerves. Laye leaned her head back and cried out, "Oh, please! I am begging you!"

"Where did you defect from?" Now thoroughly intrigued, the way Mac narrowed eyes above her told her they were nowhere near finished. She bucked against the bonds as she answered, "The Vo-Pess, my people are the Vo-Pess!"

"I've never heard of the Vo-Pess, and I've never seen your kind before. Why did you defect?" Mac asked as he gently blew against her dark blue nipples.

The warm breath passing over her breasts nearly took her over the edge, Laye's hips shook as she felt his tail stop moving inside of her. "My assignment ended. I couldn't return, not to that life. I was desperate." Laye fought her welling feelings and prayed to the wind spirits she could make it through his questions without truly cracking.

Mac furrowed his brow as he stroked her, almost giving her what she yearned for, "You're still hiding something."

Fuck! How does he know?! Laye squeezed her eyes shut as she breathed, "I killed him, I killed Leem. I couldn't let him control me anymore, I had to kill him."

Something shifted in Mac as he leaned in close to her neck and inhaled deep as he resumed running his finger up and down her needy line of nerves. Laye arched up, unable to contain herself.

"Why did you kill him?" Mac whispered against her neck as he gently bit down on her shoulder. *Should I mark her as mine? I need her like I need air.* He couldn't help it as his teeth broke through her flesh, just enough to leave his mark on her skin.

With the pinch at her shoulder, Laye had a good idea what he had just done was a marking of some kind. He had just bit her during sex, and it certainly meant something. The impenetrable wall around her heart was chipped away further, and she broke down whispering, "He took what he wanted and left nothing, I was left nothing."

Mac growled as he slid his tail further inside of her, filling her up. Although he seemed to be angry at her answer, his movements were invigorated. He twirled the end of his tail inside of her as his fingers kept a rhythm over her line of swollen and sensitive nerves.

Laye began feeling what she had before, something warm building. Heat blossomed and sweat formed on her brow as Mac twirled his finger around her nipple, giving her more pleasure than she could have ever imagined. It hit her like a storm, the intense delight swirling in her crested, and she leaned her head back, ready to scream.

Mac gently laid his hand over her mouth as she crashed over the edge, and it muffled the scream she released into the palm of his hand. Her pleasure was indescribable as she slumped against the mattress.

Shivering from overstimulation, Mac rubbed his knuckle along her jaw. "Good girl. Now we will clean you up and then you will tell me about Leem and the Vo-Pess. Do you understand?"

She nodded the best she could as the remnants of her orgasm waved through her. He reached up to free her hands, before moving to her feet and doing the same.

He lifted her from the bed and carried her to his bathroom before setting her on the shower bench. Reaching up, he turned on the water and it was steaming in seconds. Mac peeled his clothes off and lifted her up before setting her down on her shaking legs. The hot water ran over her, removing the desert sage oil. Relief filled her as Mac held her in the stream, but she didn't dare meet his eyes. She had rolled over and told him almost *everything*. *How could I have caved so easily? What is this power this man has over me?*

His deep voice rumbled above her, "Who the fuck was Leem?"

She spoke softly as she felt his hand against her back, his thumb slowly moving against her skin. "He was my bonded partner. He claimed me at my emergence, and I didn't have a choice."

Mac continued, "And he hurt you?"

She felt his thumb stop moving as she nodded against his chest, *why does he care? More importantly, why can't I read him?* He grumbled, "You killed him? How?"

Laye leaned up from his strong chest and whispered, "I drilled through the side of his skull."

She could feel Mac shift on his feet as he frowned, "You used a drill?"

With a small smile she leaned her face up to him and confirmed, "A drill."

"Vicious. I like it." Mac growled as he took a bottle of soap from his shelf.

Laye felt the soap run down her back and he began cleansing her, gently running his fingers over her black wings.

"We are going to finish bathing and then you're telling me about the Vo-Pess." Mac demanded as he rubbed the soap around her shoulders.

She swallowed roughly and he leaned back to look at her, giving her a knowing glare. Almost saying, if she didn't explain herself, she might have hell to pay. *What kind of hell was it exactly though?* It left her wondering when there would be more.

He handed her the soap as he cleaned himself for her to wash before they rinsed. He handed her a towel before he went in the bedroom and slipped on some soft fabric pants. Laye followed and opened her drawer where she found a fitted, thin fabric tank and leggings. After she dressed, she joined him in his living area and sat down next to him on his couch. Mac gave her a glass of water, "You were a spy for the Vo-Pess?"

She took the water and stared down into the glass, "Yes. Long ago, every person on my home planet was destroyed by the First Humans. They dropped a virus in our atmosphere. My people had previously made a second home in a nearby system, and the planet had been shrouded by nebulas, so it was hidden from the First

Humans. The remaining Vo-Pess became secretive, and our society became authoritarian and militaristic. We've been in a secret war with the UTC for thousands of years. I was sent to find and eliminate Fausta Ursus III."

When she met Mac's bright eyes, he was intently staring at her as understanding fell over him.

NINE
CONFESSIONS

Laye knew the time to hold back was over, she had been captured, so there was no point.

Mac's eye's seared her as he looked at her expectantly, "You're still not telling me everything." Laye had no idea how he knew. The memory of her gray eggs was still fresh in her mind as she peered back at him.

"Leem fertilized my eggs, and I lost them," Laye admitted after a long pause, her voice barely above a whisper.

Mac's brow moved low over his eyes, "What are you saying? Leem impregnated you but your eggs weren't viable?"

Laye hated discussing this, Mac reached over and lifted her chin to bring her eyes to his before continuing, "I need you to answer me."

She pressed her lips together and nodded before complying, "He took what he wanted from me, when he wanted it, and he had no regard for the consequences. I laid them the day before you found me, they were gray and dead. I wouldn't have been able to feed them anyway."

Mac's face fell as he understood, "Will they be coming for you?"

She cringed as she drank some of the water, "I'm sure, especially if they find out about Leem."

He seemed uneasy as he shifted to lean toward her, "What are you still not telling me?"

Laye knew it was pointless to continue concealing herself as she closed her eyes, lifting her antennae from their curled-up position against her head. "I'm a long-range empath, the first in five hundred years."

There it is, exactly as I thought. She is precious to them, and they will want her back. Mac stared at her possessively before he took a step forward and loomed over her, "You belong to me now. They won't be taking you anywhere."

Not knowing what else to say, Laye asked, "Who are you?"

"My name is Voakes Mac'Kie. I am the first hatched son of the Shardlow clan." Mac reached his hand out and she took it. He lifted her from her place before pulling a communication device from his pocket. "I'm busy. What do you want?" She could hear grumbling cheddar on the other end.

"Deal with it. The Shrout clan is weak. Don't call me again today." Mac slipped his comms in his pocket. He swallowed roughly in his frustration, and aimed to change the subject. "You need food."

Laye did not, but accepted anyway, following him to his kitchen. He handed her a jar of honey after opening it, and she sucked it up with her hollow tongue.

As she slurped up the sweet liquid, Mac pulled his comms from his pocket, "What?!" He grimaced and clinched his fist, "Fuck. Don't allow them to cross into our territory. Use the cannons if you must." The person arguing on the other end of the communication device was causing Mac to boil. He snarled at their words, "You're fucking useless. I'm coming."

Mac pressed her into the counter as he slid his comms into his pocket. He reached up and gently wrapped his hand around her neck, forcing her face even with his. "You will not leave, and you will make no sound. If you are found here, you will be gutted and eaten by the K'hornibus who find you." Laye lowered her eyes in agreement, and he leaned in close, "I will return."

Her skin chilled from the absence of his warmth, she doubted he would believe her, but she wasn't going anywhere. She may not be free, but her situation was light years better than it had started. She was hiding from her people, and he was hiding her from his people. She wondered how long this would last before they were discovered, if not by his people, then by hers. She rubbed the scar on her shoulder where her tracking device had been. *I hope that gross hand I had stored in that stasis jar worked, I would hate to think I had my own hand hiding in my cabinet for nothing.*

Mac stalked to his room and dressed, so she made herself comfortable on his sofa. He came out wearing armor plates over his leathers, his rail gun holstered on his hip and a long-range rail gun strapped to his back. He looked as though he was heading off to war. Mac went to the door and slid his mask over his face before he turned back to meet her gaze.

Mac slammed the door behind him when he left, rattling the wall.

Why did Shrout decide to attack our borders today of all days? The system star shone hot against his skin as he guided his bike from his shop. Mac wondered if Laye would cooperate as he peered up into his windows. From the outside, nothing in his apartment was visible. He started his bike and the engine hummed as he passed through the canyon, and he could still taste her on his tongue as her scent lingered. *How long can I keep her hidden away before I am re-assigned again?* He was growing tired of being shuffled around. He knew this was all a risk, keeping her in his private home in the canyon. Mac had cameras in all his houses, he would check in on her.

He couldn't think about that now as he headed off to the edge of Shardlow territory, he had to focus on assisting Yarle at the crossing. The Shrout clan had been at war with them over the planet's dwindling underground water source for hundreds of years. They had not given an inch of their borders since the Shardlow clan came to power thousands of years ago, that wasn't changing today.

He crouched low on his bike as he raced down the canyon road and up a bridge toward the crossing. The sand dunes stretched into the north on his left as he made his way down the road to the border on the other side of the valley. He passed rolling, golden fields of ripening grain as he began to make out the top of the wall over the hill. Mac could already hear shouts as he neared the outpost, someone had been hit. The doors slid open, and he drove in, parking by the outer wall.

Screams came from inside the main building, and he ran for the door, finding carnage inside. Seven of his younger brothers were laid out on makeshift medical beds, all with fatal railgun wounds. They each peered up at Mac as the nurse appeared at his side as if she herself was a ghost. She was unable to speak from grief when he approached, she only parted her mouth and willed her words to happen. One of his brothers had been close with her, he looked at her sorrowfully as he moved passed her find Yarle.

"What the fuck happened?" Mac asked quietly, pulling his mask off as Yarle came inside from the trench.

"It was an ambush. Several other places were hit at once, and we expect more. The Shardlow home has had an attack since you've been on the road." Yarle removed his mask as he explained.

Mac stopped pacing and faced Yarle, "Call in Inex and Kote. We need to strike back."

Yarle made the call, but it was an hour before the two arrived. They came in and removed their masks as they met Mac on the other side of the room from their dying brothers. He had previously lost twenty border guards, and three had been his brothers. Mac had begun with twenty-six brothers from his father's two wives and the Shrout clan was responsible for all his brother's deaths. This day would make ten.

As they began to review their plan, their nurse approached. "Ponet is gone. Gunet is close. The rest will pass in the next day."

In a fury, Mac moved outside for air. He paced by his bike as his surviving brothers made their way outside after him. Dust clouds formed around his steps.

"Inex, you make a team and hit their west border crossing with the cannons. Kote, you are heading home. We need to secure the house and guard father. They will pay for ending Shardlow brothers, blood for blood. Son for son." Mac paused, looking over Inex shoulder as he replaced his mask on his face.

A bit of light blue fabric was flapping in the wind against a nearby rock from someone's ripped clothing. Shrout were attacking their homes and borders, Mac's heart nearly stopped in his chest. *They know where I live, and Laye is alone at my apartment.* No matter how skilled Laye was, she would be no match for a Shrout ambush. "What's wrong Mac?" Yarle asked, noting how focused Mac seemed. Mac shoved his brothers out of the way as he mounted his bike. "You know what to do."

He signaled for the doors to be opened and sprayed dust into the outpost as he maxed out his bike on the road to his apartment. Mac had extreme, unsafe driving speeds ahead of him, and he swore to the dusk star he would slaughter the heads of the Shrout clan with his bare hands if she were harmed.

He pulled his communication device from his pocket and didn't slow as he flipped it open. He pressed the key to pull up his home camera and felt the world slow to a grinding halt as he watched the feed. Laye, his little butterfly, was hiding behind the doorframe in his room from three of the Shrout brothers standing in his living area.

Mac slid his comms into his pocket as he willed his bike to move faster, every second bringing him closer to madness. Ushaw had left him after giving him his ten children and now that his kids were grown, he had been visiting the local jet house for a piece of flesh. It was never enough.

Soft blue skin flashed through his mind as he slammed on his brakes to make the curve of the bridge. He was still so far, too fucking far.

He shook his head, he had to focus. If he hit a jumping julep, he could roll his bike and break his neck.

Mac's insides screamed as he flew down the canyon road toward his vulnerable little butterfly. *How could I have left her completely defenseless?*

TEN

THREE SHROUT AND THE SPY

Laye, being typical Laye, had searched Mac's apartment the moment he left. She had picked the lock on his weapons cabinet, finding only a single, long, serrated knife. She heard the unfamiliar rumbles of bikes growing near, and the knife remained in her hand as she approached and peered out of the windows to see if she would be having unwelcome visitors. They briefly stopped, to kill the man her and Mac passed on the way in at the checkpoint, she presumed.

Laye figured the K'hornibus outside were Shrout long before they had parked their bikes. The sounds were a stark difference from the Shardlow's as their motorcycle engines cut off. They knocked the bay door off its hinges as they broke into the shop.

She went into Mac's room and shut off the light, standing behind the wall on the other side of his door. She was glad she had pressed her ass up against Mac, she knew exactly how tough their skin would be to pierce.

The door crashed open, and she remained silent, waiting. "I told you, he's not here. I didn't see his bike." She could hear one of the men sniff the air, "I smell something alive in this apartment."

Laye crouched behind the door frame as the shadows grew against the wall by the bedroom door. The first man's defined shadow showed he wore no armor, just riding leather. *Thank you, Mac, for spotlight lighting in the living room.* She gripped the knife in her right hand and grasped the door frame with her left as she used leverage to slam the knife through the large, thick leg which protruded into the open doorway. Bright red blood spurted onto Laye's face as she withdrew the knife, cutting through his leg.

A snarling growl sounded as the man crashed backward into the other two men. Laye shifted forward into the doorway and leapt. Bloody Leg was lying on the ground, gripping his flayed open calf. His blood spilled on the floor and poured from his open flesh. As the two men behind Bloody Leg scrambled to their feet, she lifted up before she dove down and thrust the knife into his gut. Bloody Leg stopped moving and died as he gurgled from his lips.

Laye had thorough defenses against these men, she was a lethal monster when she utilized her combat skills. As for today? Today was that day. *May Relit guide me.*

One of the men hopped over Bloody Leg, she would call him Scar Face. He reached out for her, and she dove next to Mac's couch, turned at the last moment, and grabbed the side of it. She hoped it was heavy as she angled the knife up while she held onto the edge. Laye jabbed the knife into Scar Face's thigh and dragged it down as she slung herself through his legs, using the couch to propel her. She continued to slice around his leg as he fell against the floor.

Scar Face cried out as the third man, Jump Scare,

slammed into her. He managed to stomp on the knife as he wrapped his hand around her throat. His eyes were murderous behind his mask as he lifted her from the blood slicked floor.

Jump Scare growled as he squeezed her throat, and she knew she had only moments left before she would lose consciousness. He slammed her against the wall and the apartment shook with the impact. Jump Scare looked over at Scar Face as he bled out and died, and Laye was helpless as his rage overtook him. He slammed her down onto the floor, and her fine bones lit up with pain.

"You're going to pay!" He landed over her and reached for her throat again.

She tried to move back but only managed an inch. Jump Scare gripped the front of her neck and his unfiled, sharp claws began ripping through the skin at her throat, tearing away her flesh. Laye forced her hips up around his waist and squeezed with all her might as she pulled herself toward him. His hand was still digging into her throat shredding her further as she brought her face to his and hissed.

While he was focused on her hiss, she reached her arms around his head to his two lowest horns and pulled down on them. His head shot back and Laye pulled outward on the horns as she used the anchor of her legs around his waist. He finally released her throat, and she knew she only had a second to act.

Jump Scare reached for her arms, but he was too late as Laye heard the crack of his horns. She yanked down and pulled the broken horns away from his head, noticing his pink flesh in the center hanging from the broken off ends. He threw his arms out and backward to grab his remaining horn stumps as he screamed in pain. Laye pulled her arms from under him, and reared back with a horn in each hand, her legs still firm around his waist. She could feel her own clear blood trickling down, it was hot, wet, and dripping from her neck as she aimed for her kill.

Laye locked her feet behind his back before ramming his own horns into either side of his neck. Blood squirted out onto her as he stumbled back. Laye jumped away and grabbed her own neck, feeling the oozing, open wound slippery under her fingers. She watched him fall backward as she took her shirt off and bound the hanging flap of skin on her neck. She needed sutures and she would not be able to perform the procedure herself, the wound was too high on her neck.

Jump Scare twitched for the last time as Laye heard the familiar purr of Mac's engine, except this time he was moving at tremendous speeds. She moved her eyes around the apartment until she spotted it, the little camera he had mounted over his door. *Mac knew, he was coming for me.*

His bike screeched to a halt in a cloud of dust outside causing the view from his windows to darken as she heard him storm all the way up the stairs. When he reached the top and rushed inside his apartment, he slid his mask off as he carefully surveyed the carnage.

He was stunned as he studied her kills, admiring the brutality of them. When his eyes fell on Laye, he paused before asking, "Are you hurt?"

Laye could not speak from holding pressure on her throat, so she rose to her feet and tapped her fingers against her neck to tell him.

"Your throat?" His voice sounded concerned. *Is Mac worried about me?* She could have fanned herself. *Listen, honey butt, it is not the time to get all hot for Mr. Horny. We have a hole in our neck which needs mending first. Dick can wait.* He was by her in three steps. "Show me."

She closed her eyes as she peeled away her soaked shirt, revealing the torn skin down her neck. Mac's breath caught in his throat, "Is it fatal? Do you need sutures or do you need a surgeon?"

She moved her hand mimicking sewing, and he nodded, the bright yellow of his eyes revealed solid black irises as he ran into his kitchen. After digging in a drawer she swore she looked through, he pulled out a small box and waved for her to come into his bathroom.

He helped her lie on the floor before he poured one bowl of water and one of alcohol. He knelt on the floor with the two bowls, and he prepped the needle and thread. Laye knew what was coming, the wound had to be sterilized. There was dried blood and dirt caked around it, she could feel it scratching her broken skin.

"After the carnage you left, I shouldn't have to tell you what comes next," Mac warned her as he reached for the water.

Laye did her best to speak as she rasped, "Too well."

Mac nodded before he reached for her shirt around her neck. She lay her hands on her chest as he peeled bloody fabric away and set it next to her. His breath was heavy as he reached down and took one of her wrists and then the other, holding them folded across her chest.

He took the bowl of water and gently poured it over her wound to debride it before he reached for the second bowl. "Are you ready?" He increased his grip on her wrists.

Absolutely not, hurry the fuck up. She blinked at him, trying not to move as he tipped the bowl over onto the torn skin. Laye tensed against the floor, and her vision blurred from pain as Mac sterilized the area. The sting was mind scrambling and she fought the urge to scream. She could hear as he picked something up from of the bottom of the bowl, it seemed to be a tool, and she felt him moving the skin with it.

When he finished, his brow furrowed as he stared at her. She knew that look, and she hated it, sorrow.

He took the needle and leaned over her, his eyes soft as he whispered, "I just poured sterilizing alcohol over your torn throat, and you didn't flinch. I've seen warriors thrash from sterilizing much more insignificant wounds. You seem to have more you're hiding. What have you been through?"

Mac knew she couldn't answer, and she held his gaze as she searched herself. She had been though everything but had experienced next to nothing. She had always endured but never benefitted. Laye had always suffered with no reprieve.

Mac pierced her skin with the needle and began sewing the jagged skin back together. She remained motionless as he repaired her. Laye kept her eyes focused on the ceiling to keep herself grounded, this was a process she experienced too often. The dusty red of the rock ceiling above seemed to call to her, she loved the color.

When he was finished stitching her up, he went to the kitchen and came back with a bandage to cover her wound. Mac leaned down and meticulously covered the area before starting the shower behind him. He pulled her pants off and tossed them away before undressing himself. Scooping her into his arms, he rinsed her off before setting her on the bench. He dried her before picking her up and laying her in his bed. Next to her, he had placed a fresh set of clothes.

"My brother will be here soon. I didn't explain why I took off, and Yarle will be curious. You will need to hide. There is a small office I don't use in my shop downstairs. We need to move you down there and lock you in or he will find you. He will help me clean up the bodies and you can try for some rest. I'll come for you when he's gone." Mac laid his hand on her leg, and she blinked at him.

He pulled his comms out and called Yarle, walking into the next room. He didn't answer and Mac came back as she was carefully dressing. "He's on his way. We need to move you downstairs." Mac scooped her up with his bed covers and took great steps over the pools of blood.

He kicked open the door of the old office. It was clean and organized with only a desk and a toolbox in the corner. He sat her down gently on the floor and she leaned against his desk.

He lay out the bedding and gave her a look he had not given her before as he helped her lie down. It was kind, and she was unsure of how to react. Mac closed the door just as she could hear the sounds of his brother's bike rumble in the distance. *I think seduction may have worked after all, good job honey butt.*

ELEVEN
LIAR

Yarle stepped in Mac's apartment and stared at him as he cleaned his knife at the sink in the midst of the three dead Shrout brothers. "You did this? Why didn't you use your gun?" Yarle grimaced at the extensive gore.

Mac didn't answer right away as he moved around the counter. *How the fuck am I going to explain this?* "I was angry," Mac lied. He could never tell Yarle he had taken the little butterfly home with him.

The wounds on the men were low, except for one. He leaned over the dead body with Yarle and marveled at how Laye had broken his horns off and killed the Shrout man with them. *What a vicious little thing.* They were still protruding from his neck, and his blood spread out under him. Yarle was bewildered, "Mac, I don't understand why you did all of this. You broke his horns off, and he wasn't even tied down?"

Mac just grumbled as he grabbed the dead man's feet and pulled the body toward the stairs. Behind him he could hear Yarle, "Were you trying to cut their legs off? Mac, this is some sick shit. Why didn't you just shoot them? Are we torturing everyone before we kill them now?"

Mac ignored him as he dragged the body down his stairs, the head of the dead Shrout man banging on every step and echoing throughout his shop. His people had become accustomed to burying all the dead in the sand, but not today. Mac was offering these bodies to the creatures of the land, like they used to do with their enemies.

Yarle was behind him with the next body. "Are you planning to tell me what happened, or just act like this is normal for you?"

Mac turned to him, and leaned in as he growled, "I am through with the Shrout, I'll slaughter them all like pigs." Yarle dropped the feet of the dead man he was still holding up and changed the subject, "Are your cleaning supplies in your office or closet?"

Mac spun around, a little too quickly, "I'll get the supplies, they're in the shop closet. You drag out the last body."

Yarle stared at him for a moment before he nodded and climbed the stairs. Mac watched and waited before he opened the closet right beside his office door. Mac wasn't stupid, Yarle didn't believe a word he was saying.

They spent time scrubbing the blood from the apartment and afterward Mac brought out some dried meats for them to eat. Mac noticed Yarle was covered in blood, "Do you want a shower before you go?"

"I'm staying tonight and heading home tomorrow," Yarle corrected. Mac had never sent him on his way and Yarle was staring at him with his eyes full of suspicion.

Mac needed to cover his tracks better but all he could

think about was Laye tucked away downstairs in his office. Yarle stood and headed for Mac's room. As soon as Mac heard the shower start, he went to retrieve honey for Laye, and he skipped steps as he ran down the stairs as light footed as he could. He still sounded like a galloping beast, but at least he tried.

Opening his office door, he found Laye lying on her back with her hands folded over her stomach and her eyes closed. She opened them but didn't say a word as he knelt down and handed her the jar. Mac reached over and lifted her carefully, slipping his hand behind her neck to guide her. When she was upright, she opened the jar and whispered, "Thank you," before she slid in her long tongue and slurped up the thick honey.

He lay his hand on her thigh and rubbed her reassuringly. "Yarle is staying. I won't be back for you until tomorrow."

Laye understood, "I heal quickly, I have manipulated genes. I will try to sleep." She paused and added, "I find myself more occupied with the fact that you're taking credit for my kills." He smiled at her for the first time. "Is that all you take issue with here?" She tried not to laugh. "Something like that."

If he didn't know better, he would have thought this little butterfly had K'hornibus in her. She was just like the women of his people, vicious and ornery. Mac reached in his pocket and handed her back her armor tabs.

Laye grasped them in her hand, "This armor was made for me. It's linked with my nervous system, and I can project my empathic gifts further with it. I want to help you, but I can't read your kind. I can't sense anything on this world."

He knowingly smirked, "We have thick skulls."

Mac frowned, recalling the disturbing scene in his apartment. "How did you break off the Shrout's horns?"

Laye responded, "Leverage. I anchored myself around his waist."

Mac paused and admired her, "I haven't watched the recording yet. I'll save it to watch together if you want?"

Laye had never been so thrilled about anything as he shut the door behind him. *Is he making plans with me?* She prayed to the mother of the wind, Relit, as soon as he shut the door. She wanted this big, double-dicked lizard man so badly it hurt her heart to consider a future without him. Laye knew how this would go, and she would never be able to be with him, not really. He would just continue to hide her, possibly forever. It was so much better than all the alternatives she didn't care in the slightest. *Even if he only uses me for what he wants? I could care less. He is fucking gorgeous, gives me honey and orgasms, and I would probably do anything he asked at this point.*

Love was rare on her world, you were lucky if your bonded partner cared at all. Sex for fun? Not according to their practices. The same practices she was still having to sort through. The Vo-Pess say the father Caer had to kill the mother Relit because the mother betrayed him and tried to imprison him. She later had to let him free when she faced too great a foe. That's why Vo-Pess women were to be claimed and broken from an early age.

Laye had found the ancient records, and she discovered what really happened. Relit was intended to be the leader, to be a matriarch, but the father forced her into submission. In the ancient text, the mother hatches eggs and kills the father knowing her job is finished and wanting her children to live free. It had all been covered up with the story that the father kills the mother so the males of her species could claim whatever females they wanted. They tag the eggs they want to track, follow the caterpillar's pre-metamorphosis, and claim them on emergence. *We have no choice.* Angle wing sires were highly regarded, and their egg location was only known to a few of the top Vo-Pess families.

Her thoughts of home stopped as she heard Yarle and Mac upstairs arguing. They opened the apartment door intensify the sound of their argument as they came barreling down the stairs.

"Grab the drill. We need to fix the shop door." Mac picked up the door and moved it into position to lift and align back on the track.

Yarle opened Mac's toolbox to find his drill and also found some rock taping screws. He saw some cement glue and grabbed that too. The Shrout brothers had torn his rolling door out of the rock, so they needed to remount it. When Yarle handed Mac the drill, he began their argument again, "I just don't understand why you would break his horns off when you had a damn rail-gun on your hip."

Mac snapped, "I've already explained this. You're not listening. I got too fucking angry when I saw our brothers were dying. This is ten total."

"The wounds were low. Why the fuck were you on the ground?" Yarle exploded. It really did not make any sense and Mac knew that.

Not caring in the slightest, Mac had enough, "We are not discussing this further. You're leaving tomorrow, and we're not talking about it again. You're not blabbing to father about it either, if you do, I'll cut your fucking tongue out." Yarle dropped the side of the rolling door and took off down the canyon. Mac watched until he was far into the distance before he opened the door to check on Laye.

She was smiling at him when he opened it. "You know I'll have to choose between you and my brother if he finds you?"

Laye responded with a widened grin and wagged her tongue at him. Frowning at her unserious attitude, he slammed the door and moved a shelf in front of the doorway.

He went back to fixing the rolling shop door, even more fuming mad than he had been before.

Laye had crawled right under his skin. All he wanted to do was bury his face between her legs, but fucking Yarle had to follow him. His brothers were too far into his personal business and always had been.

When Yarle finally returned, Mac started asking the questions. "What makes you think you can pry into my life anyway? I am the first hatched Shardlow. I inherit the region, not you. I do what the fuck I want. Do you understand?"

Yarle reluctantly ignored him and continued assisting again with the repairs as if nothing happened. When they were finished, they stored their bikes in the shop and headed upstairs to sleep.

Mac went to his room and slammed the door before pulling out his comms to watch his living area. He would stay up and make sure his little brother didn't wake in the night and search his shop. If discovered, Laye would likely kill his brother. He was just beginning to realize how truly dangerous his beautiful little butterfly really was.

He climbed on his bare bed and furiously sat up all night watching his brother sleep.

TWELVE
UNKNOWN TERRITORY

Yarle woke at first light. Mac watched him move and tried to not seem too obvious as he rushed out to his kitchen. He handed his brother a glass of water and kept his eye on him as he left. When echoes of Yarle bike were far in the distance, Mac locked up his shop door before moving the shelf away from his office.

He opened it, filling the room with bright work lights from the shop, and Laye was resting with her eyes closed. Her eyelids fluttered open, and she reached for him to help her up from the floor. He knelt and helped ease her upright by sliding his hand under the back of her neck. Mac carefully lifted her to her feet, before collecting the bed covers. He loaded them in his washing machine before he gathered Laye into his arms and carried her upstairs. He set her on his couch before filling her a glass of water in the kitchen, "You're explaining why you took your repair better than a K'hornibus warlord." He handed her the glass expectantly.

She sipped the water and kept her eyes on the glass as

she sat it down on the couch table. *I guess it's story time.* "My training included interrogation tactics and torture, giving, and receiving. My people have advanced medical and battle technology which we implement without regard to wealth. Our society is based on two things, the great fight and Vo-Pess repopulation. All Vo-Pess attend the military academies. In addition to intense training, powerful male Vo-Pess follow and claim their bonded as they emerge from metamorphosis. We are nothing as individuals and the Vo-Pess are everything. Complaining was frowned upon." Mac was sure of one thing in that moment, he and Laye were both children of unforgiving worlds.

Seeming to agree with her, a crease formed on Mac's brow. "Our male leaders have always ensured the regions will be run by their male children. They developed technology to spot the female eggs early on. They crush them all so every leader only has sons."

I think this big sexy man is sad about the sisters he never had. Why can't I detect his feelings? Laye tried to lift her antennae under her hair and reach for him but still didn't feel even a wiggle of emotions. *I might as well tell him more about Leem the Loser.* "Leem was twenty years older than me. He had already had one bonded partner before me, but she died without giving him eggs. I think he tired of her and killed her. He wanted someone he could torment who wouldn't break."

After he murdered Leem in his mind, imagery of a giant worm with long black curls filled his head, Mac scoffed in disbelief, "Stop. Metamorphosis? Were you a worm as a child?" She tried not to laugh, "Something like that, I had a lot of legs. I think the word is caterpillar."

Mac's mouth dropped open, "You're not joking."

Laye gave him a knowing grin, "It's no joke. I made a cocoon, and inside it everything except for my brain and nervous system became a liquid. I was conscious, it was terrifying, and the process took weeks. I was blue and black striped as a caterpillar, and unfortunately, I was already an empath. During metamorphosis, several other of my people had built cocoons around me and I could feel their experiences during the process as well. It was disturbing to say the least. I emerged with a new form, and Leem claimed me on the spot. My body was never mine." Laye eyed Mac, who was scowling at her, "It's still not mine, is it Mac?"

Softening his glare, Mac licked his lips, "No, little butterfly it's not. Your body belongs to me now, and so does that mind of yours. But something tells me you wouldn't have it any other way." *Maybe I landed in the right desert after all,* Laye watched herself diving into an endless pit labeled 'Mac's penis.' She felt his hands move to her hips and she could have cried with anticipation. Mac carefully slid her down so she was lying on the couch cushion before he moved to the floor. He sat down in front of her and pulled her pants off before moving her leg over his head. She could feel his hot breath against the inside of her foot before he dragged his tongue from her ankle to between her thighs.

He nipped at the skin just before her pleasure center, and she closed her eyes in anticipation as he set her thighs on his shoulders and lifted her hips off the cushion. He moved his hand up her shirt and toyed with her nipple as he slid his tongue inside of her. She tried to be still as he found her line of nerves and ran his rough tongue along it. Her hips instinctively thrust forward, and he flattened his hand over her lower belly, pressing her down.

She was desperate to writhe against him as he flicked her over and over, giving her everything she could ever want. The friction was enough to make her go wild, and she felt the climax nearing. *How have I lived without this my entire life?!*

"Say it," Mac demanded as he slowed for her to answer.

Laye panted, "Oh, fuck me, please don't stop. You own me, you fucking own all of me." He began again and she released a soft sound as she felt herself tip over. The rush of pleasure was smooth this time, calm and full. Her inner walls clenched with her release and Mac was happily squeezed between two incredibly strong thighs, his new favorite place. He ran his hands down her legs as he lapped up her release and she shivered as he passed over her spent nerves. Mac pried her leg from his head, and she moved back up the couch enough to elevate her head. Laye fluttered her eyelids as he went to fetch a wet towel to clean her. He replaced her pants and helped her sit up.

"Do you want to watch the visual recording of you killing those three men who were four times your weight?" Mac asked, and Laye noticed a bit of a thrill in his tone.

She bashfully smiled, she was elated he seemed proud of what she had done, "I would love that."

He pulled out his communication device and unfolded it. It opened to be a small but detailed screen. Laye watched as he selected the video from his media file, and she noticed his photo of his children, *he has daughters.* Her heart soared. She desperately wished she could sense his emotions. Laye was dying to know how he felt about her. He leaned over toward her so she could see better, and he pressed play on the video.

Laye leaned over on his shoulder, and Mac intently

watched as she sliced into the calf of the first man before stabbing him in the gut. She noticed his head slightly moving as he kept his eyes focused on her image. Laye knew what was coming and leaned in closer. The next kill was brutal, and as she flayed into the man's thigh, Mac's brow furrowed, and he leaned back a bit as he saw the moment she was caught by the third man. Mac snarled slightly as the man tore at her throat whispering, "You killed him with that neck wound?" He wasn't asking her; he was asking himself. He flinched as she broke off the man's horns and reared back before stabbing and killing him. He kept the feed going, sitting in complete silence until he saw himself walk in the door on screen.

"The Shrout had a planned coordinated attack on several of our border outposts and family homes. When I found out they had been attacking our homes, I rushed back here as fast as I could. On my camera feed, I saw when they came into the apartment, but nothing after that, I was moving too fast to check."

Laye had been so thankful to see him when he finally arrived. "Thank you coming back for me and sewing my neck back together. I can feel the tingle of it healing."

He cringed as he admitted, "We usually call the nurse out, but I have seen her work before. I knew what to do."

Laye reached out and put her hand on his forearm. Mac seemed to shiver, and he turned his head to glare at her, "What the fuck was that?" She had no idea what he was talking about, Laye hadn't done anything except touch him. She shrugged and touched him again, this time reaching up and running her hand down his shoulder. He shivered again and flinched before he reared away from her, "Are you doing something to me?"

She smiled, trying not to laugh, "No, I swear I'm not doing anything but touching you."

He was not buying it, "Snake shit, if you weren't healing, I would be interrogating you again."

"I mean, we can still do that." She blurted out.

Mac gave her a deep, knowing laugh, "You might be worse than a K'hornibus woman."

Mac's comms made a ding, and he frowned as he lifted it to his ear. "What?!" The washing machine downstairs buzzed, and he went to change the mode to dry as he talked. She could hear Yarle right before Mac went downstairs. "Mac, you need to come home for a few days." Mac knew what that meant, his father was on a tirade and was bound to make things much worse. If this meant Yarle was off Mac's ass, he would accept it. He put the setting on dry and headed back upstairs. He stood in front of Laye, and she peered at him with her hands folded in her lap.

Mac slid his phone in his pocket, "I'll be back in a few days. I'm setting up a comm device for you before I leave. If you have any trouble, contact me, and I'll come back."

"I understand." Mac huffed, "I hate my father. He's a selfish viper. I think he hates me too. If he hadn't made me heir when I was a youngling, I think he would have chosen Inex instead."

Laye looked up at him, *should I mention I saw his daughters in his family picture?* She knew he had not broken his daughters' eggs.

Mac admitted, "He named me after him, and I refuse to use it."

He rose up and prepared for his journey. When he gathered his things, he set his pack by the door and approached her.

She stood up and he brushed her hair off her shoulder, "Do you need anything?"

Laye peered up at him and answered softly, "Just come back." *I mean that.*

He bit his lip and rubbed his knuckles along her jaw before he took his pack and closed the door behind him. Mac's absence chilled her, and she curled up on his couch as she listened to the sounds of his bike fading in the distance.

THIRTEEN

TOO GOOD TO BE TRUE

Perched on Mac's countertop, squatting in front of the mirror, Laye was using sterilized nail trimmers to remove her stitches. Her head was angled up as she clipped at the last thread and pulled bits of it out of her flesh. Her scar was minimal aside from a tiny lump of what she presumed was scar tissue on the inside of her neck.

She heard a crack of thunder and hopped from the counter to look and peered outside to see the sky had turned black with storm clouds.

She squinted to see down the river, which was a long way from his shop door. Laye wondered how much the river would rise as the first drops of water fell. *Do I need to call Mac over some rain, or should I just see what happens?* She pulled the communicator from the kitchen counter and opened it. Staring at the screen she felt silly; she was a capable woman. She didn't need to call Mac to come save her, although it was very tempting because something told her he would drop anything for her.

When the river began to grow up to its banks, she waited patiently for the downpour. The sky cracked open and as the rain drowned the dry land, she kept her eyes on the canyon as the river rose over its banks in minutes. *I miss the rains of Hyret. I miss Mac more.* How had she let another possessive man ensnare her so deeply? Her thighs clenched with the memory of his tongue. *How do I tell my pussy to cool it? She really needs to calm down, she's tangled me in a whole mess now.*

The river swelled until it was almost touching the now visible concrete of the road. Mac had only been away two days, and she wondered when he would return. She hoped he didn't find himself caught in the storm. The calming sounds of the trickling water made her yawn, and when she did, her antenna instinctively stretched out before they curled back up against her head. She sprawled out on his couch and watched the rain slide down the windows until she was lulled away into a deep sleep.

A hand lifted her shirt, and she felt warm lips kissing up her stomach, Mac's smokey scent wrapped around her as he ran his tongue over her breasts. She reached up and stroked his horns, and he rolled his head into her touch.

He can feel his horns?! Intrigued, she stroked her finger down the sides of the two biggest horns on the top. He was motionless and his face was a picture of pure pleasure. He shivered at her touch and yanked her down further on the couch before propping her head up on a pillow. He moved over her and she was tempted to lick his abs, "Open your mouth." Mac was already nude, and she complied as he straddled her face. His length emerged, and she opened her mouth. This time she was determined to take both sides.

She opened as wide as she could and was able to fit

him with little room to spare. He roughly exhaled as he tipped his head down to look at her. "Fucking pit of sand vipers, you fit it all in." Mac grunted as he thrust his hips. Laye's eyes watered as she placed both of her hands on either side, waiting for the fun part.

When he split, she stroked the sides as the ends pulsed and moved in her mouth. She took him in as far as she could, and he groaned as his hips pressed down. She knew he was close and stroked her tongue down the middle. He angled his head back and panted as he exploded into her awaiting mouth, it was salty, and she gulped it down with him watching from above. "Fuck, you did so good." Mac admitted as he crawled off, and he caught his breath as he looked down on her. Her breasts still revealed with her shirt at her neck was a sight he never wanted to forget. "I brought something for you. Take your clothes off and lie on my bed," he demanded.

She licked her lips, and a thrill drove down her spine as she all but jumped from the couch. Doing her best not to run, she went to his room and had her clothes off before he crossed the threshold.

Laye stretched out on his bed, and he took her arms and tied them down before tying her feet to the ends of his bed, spreading her wide for him. She watched him retrieve something from his pack, it was the handle of the electric bone saw. Her eyes went wide as he set it between her legs.

Mac smirked at her, "Oh, I'm not finished." He pulled a small jar from his pack and opened it before he scooped some out. Leaning over her he licked each of her nipples before he brought his face to hers, "Let's see just how much you can withstand, my little butterfly."

When the scent passed by her nose, she realized what he had on his hand, desert sage oil. She tensed as he hovered his oil slathered fingers over her left nipple. Laye's thoughts had escaped her entirely, she stared at him speechless. Mac looked up at her before he brought his finger down against her flesh, "Now be a good girl and don't cum too fast. You'll ruin all my fun."

When his fingers circled her nipple and then the other, and she felt the oil start to take hold. It still had not fully occurred to her what he was doing until she saw the handle base of the saw had been scrubbed clean and the blade itself had been removed.

Oh fuck, Laye was about to be edged to death. He *knew* she couldn't cum without her row of nerves being stimulated. She was already rolling her hips when he started the electric saw handle and angled it to slide inside of her.

Laye whimpered as he pressed the vibrating tool inside of her, filling her up. He slowly pushed it in, and she felt enough pleasure to drive her mad, but just under what she needed to tip over. This truly was torture, Laye felt his hand on her lower belly as he pressed her down and held the tool inside of her. Laye was nearly singing. The oil began tormenting her nipples all while Mac was intently watching her figure flail around. Laye gasped for air, but he didn't seem to be moving any time soon.

Desperate, Laye begged, "Please Mac, please!" He shook his head no and she came unglued, using her strength and fought the bonds. The metal of his bed creaked as she pulled, bending the post.

Mac pressed her arms back down and shook his head, "Not happening. I've been waiting days for this." The vibrations inside of her mixed with the oil on her nipples were overwhelming her senses. She leaned her head back and screamed.

Mac smiled so wide he showed all his teeth, "That's what I wanted to hear, scream my little butterfly."

Laye's mind felt like it would implode as he finally moved the saw handle to her line of nerves. She froze and clenched her muscles. The moment he placed it against her center, her waves began, and she was falling over the edge. No, she was soaring over it. Laye released a high-pitched groan as her orgasm slammed into her. She lifted off the bed and he pressed her back down as he held the saw handle to her.

When her waves subsided, she fell against the bed but kept rolling her hips from the sensation on her nipples. He took a damp cloth and rubbed the oil from her chest, making her eyes go wide as the tingling sensation shot through her nerves. The wet, rough towel over her spent flesh was almost enough to fall over the edge again, eliciting a yelp from her.

Mac untied her and brought her a glass of water. She drank it down, her throat was so dry she couldn't speak.

"I would hate to be cut up with that oil all over me." Laye gulped down the rest of the water.

Recalling the many times, he used it for torturing information from a Shrout, Mac grumbled, "They don't last long."

They dressed and went to the kitchen, Laye peered outside to the beautiful bright day after the rain. She missed flying, it was the only thing she truly wished she could have again.

Mac came up behind her and braced his hands on the top of the window frame, "What's wrong?"

Did this big man just notice I was stewing? She leaned back against him, "I miss flying."

He sunk his head, there was nowhere she would be

able to fly without being spotted. Unless he took her to the other side of the mountains to the salt layer, it had been an ocean long ago, but it was now dried up. It was an entire day of driving.

How could he get away for that long? *Why am I so nervous?* He had never felt this way before.

What could I say to father to make this happen? There was a rumor of an old base the Shrout used to build weapons, and his father spoke about it recently. He wanted to know what they had been trying to build or do. If he took Laye, she could help him find it.

"I have an idea. There is a place with a dried ocean, it's nothing but salt. No one can live there, and you would be able to fly. There is one condition though. I need help finding a secret outpost my father has wanted information on for many years. I think I can convince him to send me." Mac explained as he reached for his comms device to send a message.

Within moments he had a call back, and it was his father, "I think it's time I find out what the Shrout are doing in the salt."

"Find out. Don't return until you find something worthwhile." His father truly did hate him, he would send him off a cliff if he knew Mac would comply. His father hung up, and Mac put his comms away.

Sometimes he dreamed of putting a bullet in his father, but didn't only because at one time, he had loved him. Long ago when Mac was a small boy, he had thought his father cared, but it was clear now his father loved nothing but himself and power.

He looked down at Laye and he could see her face reflecting in the window. She was so happy she looked like she would burst. "Let's get some rest tonight and we can be on the road at first light." Mac caressed his hand along her shoulder and ran it down her back, over her wings.

She leaned into his touch and melted into him. He could see her antennae curl up and uncurl slightly, just to curl tightly again.

If there was one thing Laye loved, it was to have her wings touched. Mac moved his hand along her back, tracing the edges of her flattened wings, and she closed her eyes. She was close to shaking like she did when she was drying off, she felt it coming and tried to suppress it. He moved down, along her rear, still tracing her wings. Mac's touch was everything, she was so close to losing her grip she could taste it. When the shiver hit, she leaned back to avoid smacking into his chin as she shook so violently her feet left the ground.

Mac jumped back with a loud, "What the fuck was that?!"

Laye slid a hand over her mouth to hide her smile, "I guess I shiver like that when my wings are touched."

Mac could read between the lines, and he heard exactly what she said. *No one has ever touched her that way before.* Sorrow filled him over what she had experienced in her life. He wanted to murder that monstrous Leem all over again. He deserved to have a hole drilled in his head.

Something struck Mac, "How old are you?" Laye shied away and quietly answered, "According to UTC time scales I am thirty-one."

Mac wanted to skin Leem alive. The drill wasn't enough as he did the math. She had been fucking thirteen years old when Leem claimed her.

Mac had to say something. "If any of my three daughters had been claimed by anyone at thirteen? That man would have roasted over a spit until his skin bubbled away. My daughters are all in study off world along with their brothers. I paid a small fortune for all my children to receive the best education the Sarter Kingdom offers. It's a boarding school on Keru, the Plana world. They are all in the middle of an ocean on Keru's floating City having the time of their lives. I sent them far away from this planet and its wars. It was one of the many reasons my father, my children's mother, and my own mother hated me. I am finished with this war when I gain the seat."

Laye was awestruck as she processed what he explained. He was changing things for his children. She wished for so much more. More of him, more for them.

I want to be on this man's arm in the light, not hidden away like his dirty little secret.

FOURTEEN
SALT

As the first light of the day shined, they mounted his bike after Mac, wearing his skull mask, rolled it from his shop. He wrapped his hard body around her and started the bike. The engine roared to life, and Laye slid the horned skull mask bike helmet over her face. She was wearing riding leather, so if anyone saw them pass, on first look, they seemed like a typical K'hornibus couple.

She leaned into him as he pulled on the road and headed into the desert. His bike rumbled under them as they passed nothing but sand for hours. By mid-day, in the distance she could start to make out the mountains. Laye was so excited she didn't realize she was grinding her ass against him, Mac reached down and held her still, or so she thought.

He moved his arm to wrap around her and popped the buckle at her hip. *What the fuck is he doing?* They were moving at high speeds on two wheels. Laye felt him slide his hand into her pants, but she complied and angled her hips forward so he could reach what he wanted. He found her row of nerves and she reached back to hang onto him as his fingers started moving against her flesh.

The wind, the high speed, and the heat, Laye was already so close she could feel herself tipping over the edge. She gasped as the pleasure knocked into her, she had never dreamed it could happen so quickly. Her heart raced as his hand receded from her pants and lifted his mask to suck his fingers. It left her wanting so much more.

Mac pressed her into him with his hand just under her chest. It felt like he was squeezing her between his legs as he ramped up the speed.

By that afternoon, they arrived at the mountains and the road sloped up. They rounded curve after curve as the road twisted between the tall mountains. It took until dusk, but they had finally made it to the salt, it was so arid, Laye found herself trying to blink away the dry eye.

Mac stopped and parked his bike, he hid it behind a rock which jutted out from a hill, before opening the back hatch and pulling out a pack and a bedroll for her. He slid her pack on for her as Laye removed her helmet and stored it where the pack had been.

"How far of a hike is it from here?" Laye asked as she looked out on the evening system starlight shining onto the salt. The land glittered, and she was mesmerized by the sparkling mix of shadows and light.

Mac pointed in the direction they would take, "It's a few miles away. We should check out the base and see if it's abandoned or not before we make camp."

She agreed, "If it's not, I'll help you take it."

Mac nearly missed a step at the suggestion they could conduct this mission *together* sunk into his mind. It was as if he had dreamed of it all his life, the idea of running a job with his woman? He was so hard he thought his length would burst from its hiding place.

My woman? Had he really admitted that to himself? He watched her ahead of him, her pert round ass bouncing with every step. Mac could almost taste her on his lips as he thought about lapping at her pussy. This little butterfly had wiggled herself under his skin, and he didn't want it any other way.

Mac found himself afraid of what he would be willing to do and give up for her. If he had to choose, he knew what the answer would be. She was irresistible. It had been her big, beautiful emerald eyes, her perfect figure, and that sweet scent which hooked him, but her viciousness and cunning made him want to keep her, *forever*.

She seemed like an innocent flower, but she was a ruthless monster when she wanted to be. He found that fact so sexy his dual length was beginning to emerge. Mac willed it away and told himself just a few miles before they stopped.

Ahead of him, Laye had her head in the sky, dreaming of flying. The wind against her face beckoned her to join it and soar. Her wings begged to be released, they were lifting up at the edges and rippling down the back of her legs.

When they reached the area of the supposed base, and Laye spotted it first, "I see it, over the hill and beyond the rocks. I can see a door. We need to turn here and move around the back. Follow me."

Laye couldn't help it, her training was too strong, and it demanded she take control. Mac didn't say a word as he followed her. *Did I just boss around the big guy, and he let me? What is happening? Whatever it is, I love it.*

They found a place to stow their things and made their

way around the back of the building, which had been carved directly into the rock. Laye tip-toed around to a window and reached one of her antennae out to press against the edge of the glass. If she felt tiny vibrations, they had company. After a few moments, she could feel a pressure change and the window briefly moved. She confirmed movement inside, and they needed to fall back. Laye signaled to Mac to fall back, and he led them away. When they retrieved their packs, they back tracked and ventured further into the hills for some privacy. On the mostly barren salt, it wasn't easy to hide.

The only reason his planet had any oxygen was because their last ocean had an algae which had adapted to the growing salt levels in the water. Most of their ocean life had died off long ago but low pockets of algae still existed and survived on the little rain and endless salt the planet provided. More algae died every year, and there was nothing to be done.

This world was slowly dying, and Mac knew it, he didn't need scientists to tell him as he peered out over the miles of salt that had once been an ocean on the planet. On top of their bad industrial and pollution choices as a people, their system star was moving into a red giant phase, and their world was slowly being cooked. Without intervention, it would die over a million years prematurely because of his ignorant people.

While many of the K'hornibus ignored it, some, like him cared for the continued existence of their species and sent their children off world for better lives. Mac though, he was trapped here.

His eyes focused on the stunning woman in front of him, and he wondered what he did to deserve this spark of goodness in his life. Mac knew there was no way this could continue without them being discovered, and he was doing everything he could to keep himself from digging in too deep. Part of him was screaming, he was already in over his head. The more time he spent around her the harder it was to leave each time.

Mac had never felt so conflicted in all his life. He had accepted his duty long ago and had submitted to the life. *Now?*

Laye turned back and surveyed the area, "We should be fine here." He followed her line of vision and realized she had put them in the perfect surveillance point. They would easily be able to see the building from their location, but the people in the building would not be able to spot them unless they walked over the hill they were camped behind.

She was damn good, he had been lost in thought as she led them and now, he was standing in front of her wondering who was really in charge here.

Laye was, *obviously*. He watched as she drew out the layout of the building and began collecting rocks so they could construct a plan. She moved the rocks around and stopped to think, then she moved them again. Each time, she moved behind the rocks to find her angles. At one point she began counting on her fingers as she moved the rock little by little down a path she had made.

Mac hovered over her, "You could have killed me, and my men at any point. Why didn't you?" After he asked, he wished he hadn't. The way she looked up at him was enough to fill him with fury. The way she had been treated before he found her made something in him burn so hot he was afraid of what he would do.

Laye did her best to answer without breaking down, "I had, um, given up."

She stared at his feet for a bit before she returned to work on her plans. The way she just returned to work and kept going, not stopping to process anything worried him. She was a ticking time bomb, Laye had admitted she was an empath, and the only one born in many years. Her world was all military.

Mac was simultaneously in awe and concerned, he felt a strong urge to protect her but find her help. He had to find a way. He knew her type, they suppressed everything until one day it overflows.

His mind went to two of his uncles, both had lost their battles with depression. They had been used as spies and assassins by his cruel father, but their hearts had been kind. They were better men than him, they fought with their trauma and lost. There were repercussions for deep suffering, and he feared for Laye. She was so focused, so sharp. She was incredibly determined, but her heart and emotions had not been made for any of this. "What about now?" *I need to know.*

Laye didn't understand as she put a rock down and then moved it, "What do you mean?"

Mac knelt down to her eye level, "Is this the real you?"

She stopped when his question settled, "Right now, I am more of my genuine self than I have ever been in my life."

"You've never met this Laye before?" he asked as he held his eyes on her, she shook her head as she smiled, "No. This Laye is all new. I feel like I've just completed another metamorphosis, but this one wasn't filled with trauma like the last one. This one was an awakening."

Mac was glad he asked. He had seen her eyes, and she had given up on the butcher table. Not for one second did he have any intention of harming her, but did he plan to do exactly what he did to her? No. He had to wait long enough for his father to think he had cut her up. He had seen her nude figure laid out for him, and when she had accepted that he intended to kill her, he couldn't help it. When she had given him the little show in the stream, the way she had pressed against him on his bike? He had planned to keep her either way, but the plans became much more involved after that. Making her cum in the moment she thought she would die had been worth the way her eyes gleamed with confusion and hope afterward.

"You thought I intended to kill you?" he asked, he wanted to hear her say it.

Laye stopped, "What is this about?"

Mac finally took his mask off and narrowed his eyes at her, "You are a machine on the outside, but inside you're so soft. It's conflicting."

"Yes, I thought you were going to kill me. Are you happy?" Laye gave him a side eye.

Mac stopped her and took her hand, "When I realized you were a *woman*? I admit, I'm not a good man, but I'm not my father. I don't eat the off-worlders we find in the desert like he does, and I'm certainly not eating a woman."

She laughed with delight, "You think an average man could handle this?" Laye pointed to herself.

Mac bit his lip, imagining his little butterfly, pouring acid over a male body crumpled in a tub. "You would be dissolving his bones in a week."

Laye pinched the bridge of her nose, she felt a little *too* understood. "You're probably right. Good thing I found a big scary war lord to make me his sex toy."

She thought she was his sex toy? Mac laughed to himself, *she has no idea.* "You make a good point, take your fucking clothes off." Laye's eyes flared at him, and she began undressing on top of her dirt plans.

The sun was setting behind them as he laid out the bedroll. He undressed and hooked his finger at her to come to him. She closed the gap as he sat on the bedding. She stepped over his thick, muscled legs, and his face was level with the apex of her thighs. Mac grabbed her hips to steady her as he slid his tongue where she wanted it the most. He devoured her, and she leaned her head back, trying to catch her breath. Laye reached down and rubbed his horns, his tongue moving faster and harder as a result. Mac's rough tongue was perfect for her, she decided as she felt herself reaching the plateau. Laye was overwhelmed as he buried his face between her legs.

She began to tip over and she knew she couldn't be loud. It was hard not to cry out as she felt the orgasm send blasts of pleasure through her. Laye panted as she caught her breath. "I didn't know sex could be fun until you." Laye admitted, her eyes glossed over and satisfied.

Mac licked her clean before guiding her to straddle him, "I'm going to fuck you now. Do you understand me?" She nodded, she had been desperate to have his dual length inside of her since she first saw it, "Yes, please."

Mac tipped his head to the side to kiss her neck and his length sprang free, the tip already beginning to separate. Laye couldn't wait, she angled herself onto his length and sat down.

He had not expected that from her, and sucked in a breath as her heat surrounded him. She ground onto him, and he laid back with his hands on her hips.

Laye wanted it all. She felt his length separate, and as each side began to curl and pulse, she came undone. The way he felt inside of her, how he filling her was sending her mind to the stars. Was she breathing? She wasn't sure. He was made for her, her insides were wheeled with delight. *Is that another climax coming?!* Her wide eyes met his as she breathed, "I'm going to cum again."

Mac smirked up at her, "Of course you are, my little butterfly. You'll always cum on my hemi." She wanted to scream as she felt herself tip over again. Panting and shaking, Laye watched Mac curl forward as he emptied himself inside of her.

Laye burned the moment in her mind. This all felt like a ticking time bomb, waiting to blow up in her face. She had never been happy before. She felt safe here, and she absently rubbed the scar on her shoulder.

Why did she feel like this was all going to come to an end, that she was meant to suffer and never be happy. *I feel something coming.*

FIFTEEN
STAY

Shining in the early morning moonlight, Laye had her nano-tech armor set to black and she hovered above the main door of the building. They heard people outside, and she suggested they make their move. He had given her a silenced rail gun, and showed her how his worked, to which she had promptly shot a rock off the top of a boulder many yards away and Mac just stared at her. *She is a better shot than me too?* He didn't know how he felt about that. He watched as she made her way across the roof, and she crouched down.

Laye heard the men using the restroom, and there had been three so far, she knew there had to be more. *These K'hornibus seemed to like larger groups.*

She was right, two men came out in lab coats and she sighed internally. She knew what that meant.

Laye waited until they came back from using the restroom down the hill to listen for the door, the moment they opened it she rolled off the roof and landed behind them. She grabbed one by the horn and yanked his head back as she shot the other in the back of the head point blank. Shooting the man she had by the horns under his chin, she stuck her leg out and caught the open door all in the span of seconds.

Mac came around the corner and shook his head at how efficient she was. He dragged the two bodies around the building as she held the door. Inside, they found a stark white room with a single interior door. Laye approached the white door and shook her head, "It's a soundproof door. I have no idea what is behind it."

Mac thought about the geology in this area. "There are no caves here. They would have had to dig this out before building on top and hiding it. It can't be that big."

Laye nodded and pursed her lips, "I like your logic."

Leem had always sat in the ship and waited on her to complete her missions, it was repulsive. He never really did anything. Mac on the other hand? He would have made a great partner. *Maybe we can do this again.*

Laye signaled Mac to move to the other side of the door as she reached for the handle. She turned it slowly enough that it made no sound, and she opened it a crack to peer inside, she held four fingers up and swung the door open.

She shot each man, one after the other. Laye had not given them enough time to think or react. Each one received a perfect head wound between the eyes before they slumped to the floor.

Mac whistled, "I don't think I've ever seen anyone make a kill like you."

Laye turned to him, and holstered her gun, "Let's drag them out and find out how long they've been here. We need to know if we will have any company. Search for any trackers or comms."

Mac shook his head. "We won't have company, this is

still Shardlow territory." Mac checked all their pockets with Laye, and they found nothing. Not one electronic device. This had been an untraceable operation.

Mac pointed to the crate of emergency rations, and she nodded, her shoulders set back a bit as she surveyed the room. A lit-up glass case with sand in the bottom and a skeleton of a K'hornibus inside caught both of their attention, and they approached it tentatively.

Laye spotted something interesting, "Boxes from Aduro. Those are imported from the former Claudius Kingdom. The king was overthrown by his daughter Livia who won the recently opened up UTC Empress seat. After taking the seat, she banned all forms of slavery, established widespread food banks throughout the center, and even legalized adoption. Livia Claudius is determined to flip the galactic center upside down in the best kind of way."

Mac had no idea Fausta had been beat, "I don't keep up with UTC galactic politics."

Laye narrowed her eyes at him, "Lucky you."

The sand moved in the glass case, and Laye turned and lifted the lid of the wooded shipping box finding something that resembled a dead worm in the bottom. It was silver and half buried in the sand.

Laye dumped the box over, and the dead creature fell out. She saw the sand move again in the glass case before she knelt down to inspect the worm, keeping a cautious distance.

She spotted the tool they opened the box with and used it to lift the head of the worm like animal. Its mouth became visible, and she frowned, there were lines of sharp teeth. Mac shifted on his feet and pointed to the skeleton in the glass box, "Do you think that silver creature did this?"

Laye nodded, "That's exactly what I think. We need to

kill them before they find their way out of here and into your world."

Mac licked his dry lips. "Shardlow territory is mostly on the sand while Shrout has only rock. He is trying to kill us all. I might win some favor with my father over this discovery."

Mac knew he needed to prove it, so he broke into the lab supplies and pulled out a pack of dried meat. He lifted the glass on the case and dumped it in before pulling his comm device from his pocket and recording. Silver creatures swarmed the meat like piranhas and the dried flesh was devoured in seconds. He started to send the message to his father, but he stopped himself.

"What if we stayed out here for a little while." Mac suggested, as Laye pulled some liquid fuel from the supply closet.

Laye gave him a bashful grin, "I would like that." He watched as she lifted the glass just an inch to insert the fuel spout before she dumped the fuel into the tank. "Can you bring in a heavy rock from outside, please?" she asked as she searched for a lighter. Mac went and retrieved a large rock and held it up as she lit the end of some paper. She slid the flaming paper into the glass coffin. Mac set the rock on the thick glass, and they watched the silver worms thrash in the flames. When they were certain the flames were out and the worms were dead, they began collecting supplies.

When they had a bag filled with food, Laye slung it over her shoulder and Mac grabbed two jugs of water before they headed back to their campsite. Dawn light was pouring over the land, and Laye tapped her neck to remove her helmet, she wanted to see it with her unaided eyes. They stood on a hilltop together and watched for a moment, Laye leaned into him and soaked it all up.

The warmth of the morning star on her face was soothing. Mac leaned over and set the jugs down before he took the pack from her back. "Go fly."

She twirled around with her eyes wide, "Thank you. You have no idea what this means to me." Tapping her neck for her helmet to cover her head, Laye ran down the hill as her wings unfolded and began flapping. They were fully extended by the next hilltop, and she sprung into the air. She was like a rocket, her wings fluttered so fast he could hardly see them as she shot over him. Laye flew back and forth over the small hills before she landed in front of Mac.

Panting, she tapped her neck, and her helmet receded, "I needed that, and I think I spotted something."

Mac studied her inquisitively, "What do you mean by something?'

"If I'm not mistaken, it's my ship's crash site." Laye admitted. Mac seemed intrigued, "Let's go then."

They sorted their supplies and headed off on foot. Laye led again and Mac truly began to wonder what the hell had happened to him. Aside from his father, he had always been the one vying for control. Now he was just freely handing it over to Laye, someone he should never trust. *A spy? The way she can kill? Why should I trust her at all?* She was nearly skipping in front of him, and he bit his lip. He already wanted to bury himself in her again, the power she had over him was almost more than he could bear.

Ahead of him, Laye was busy plotting out the best route to reach the ship. Within a few hours they were approaching a charred vessel. Laye stopped and stared at it as Mac leaned over her, "You don't have to go in."

"I want to." She answered as she headed inside. It wasn't much more than a two-story transport designed with a cloak so she could remain invisible. The cloak was inoperable and charred to a crisp, so she wasn't concerned about tech being stolen and released, but she couldn't find Leem. She searched everywhere and became frantic when Mac stopped her, "I'm sure bugs ate what was left of him."

Laye hadn't thought of that. *That must be it, right?* The Vo-Pess had not come to find her yet, had they?

"But what if they found the crash site? What if the Vo-Pess general has already sent operatives to find me?" Laye met Mac's gaze. The memories of the general watching her training was etched in her mind forever. His obsession with her had made her feel like she was an animal being kept on a chain.

She had been through training with the people who would be tracking her down, they were too good. Laye knew they would find her eventually. Mac didn't seem concerned, "I won't let that happen."

"They trained alongside me. My planet has hundreds of operatives who have my training, but I'm the only empath. If I was one of the average Vo-Pess, it might be different." Laye explained her voice becoming softer with each word.

Mac was silently boiling, he would not be preventing anything from happening if that was the case. She could best him ten times over, and he was not too prideful to admit that. His insides spun as his nature fought his logic, he knew this little woman was too good to be true and he knew there was a real possibility she could be taken from him. How could he have let himself dig this deep? He should have known better. One woman had left him already, and he could feel Laye being torn away from him as the fear of her absence set in.

She ran outside of the wreckage and dropped to the ground. Mac followed and sat down next to her, putting his arm around her. "If they dare to take you from me, I'll come find you. I don't care how far, or what I have to do, I will always come for you. You're mine, and I don't let what's mine go without a fight." Mac promised her, and he meant every word.

Laye leaned into him, "If they catch me, I'll be put to death for defecting alone. If they know about Leem? They will torture me until I die, then they will probably revive me, and keep going."

Mac wanted to kill everyone she ever knew.

SIXTEEN
BURNISHED

Sitting on the ground in the early morning and eating some honey with her long thin tongue unraveled and dipped in the jar, Laye had the urge to explore. Mac was tearing into a piece of dried meat as he intently watched her eat. Laye pulled her tongue out of the jar and wound it back up so she could speak, "Can we hike the mountain today?"

Mac swallowed roughly, "We can do whatever you want." He was doing everything he could to hide his fear, but he had hardly slept, and every sound had him searching the area for the Vo-Pess. The sensation that he would burn the world down to have her back was not far from his mind. She was his and his alone.

She finished her honey and handed the empty jar back to Mac. He pulled her to him, and she knew why. Laye put her hand on Mac's arm, "There's nothing that can be done when they come for me. We need to make the most of the time we have."

"I can't accept that. K'hornibus fight for what belongs

to them," Mac admitted, holding her to him. Laye knew there was not a thing he could do if they came, or when. They would wait until the right moment and steal her away. He would never see any of them, and she would disappear without a trace. The memory of dragging an attempted defector home rang through her, she had forgotten all about that job.

"I found a defector once. I took them back. Defectors have their wings and antennae cut off before being drowned in the north lake. I watched it all happen, and believed I was doing something good. I had helped make the Vo-Pess stronger. The way he begged me to let him go? He just wanted peace. Whatever end I have at the hands of the Vo-Pess, I will deserve it. The fact that I was allowed a little slice of happiness is beyond my under-standing." Laye spoke from her heart and meant every word.

She was a horrible being, Laye had committed atroci-ties in her life. The depravity of her past threatened to eat her alive as she curled into Mac. Mac wasn't having it, "You were doing your job, you're not a lowly murderer driven by selfishness. You were trained and forced to do the things you did and like I said before, your insides don't match the outside. Who you were before is not who you are now."

"Mac, I killed several people last night. They were dead before any of them could blink," Laye reminded, as she ran her fingers over the scales on the back of his arm.

He laughed but sincerely hoped she listened to him, "Again, you were working a job. Those men were trying to destroy the dunes, and you stopped their plan. You also killed three Shrout brothers. If we're going by Shardlow clan law, I owe you nine life debts and one planet debt."

She sighed and her big green eyes shone, "Fine. You win this one."

Mac rose to his feet and set her down, "Let's ride on your hike."

Laye pushed away her raging fears of being dragged back to Hyret, and they took off up the hill. The mountains were bare until high altitudes where the only trees on the planet existed. She was determined to make the most of every moment of the time she had left, and she wanted to see those trees up close.

After an hour, they stopped for a rest, and she drank some water when something occurred to Laye. Mac seemed to be giving her a lot of water, wasn't it rare on this planet?

"Why is it you seem to have so much water when your planet is so dry?" She asked as she took another sip. He shifted his weight, "Water is one of our rarest resources and drinking water is one of the K'hornibus' highest expenses. I have recycling systems on all my homes, as do most people."

Laye had been part of plenty interrogating, but she didn't need that to know he was hiding something, and she wasn't asking. This moment in time seemed so fragile, and she was far too afraid of spoiling it. She was fearful if she accidentally said or did the wrong thing, it would all be over.

A few more miles up the mountain and they were passing the first meager tree, it has succulent like leaves and seemed to be a cross between a pine tree and a cactus. The trees became thicker and taller as they ascended. Mac heard a crunch nearby and jumped in front of Laye who put her hands on her hips as she tried to sneak a look around him.

When Mac heard a second crunch he reached for his railgun and held it up, waiting. He hadn't noticed Laye was already triangulating off to his left with the gun he gave her, his eyes went wide as he watched her approach the source of the sound. He was beginning to feel like he had found himself a bodyguard with the way she acted, and he didn't know if he liked it or not. He was supposed to be the protector. *Not* her.

A soft growl told Mac exactly what they were dealing with, and he whispered, "It's a Burnished cat, don't kill it!"

She nodded and holstered her gun but continued to approach, Mac was going to lose his grip with her. Laye would end up getting herself killed.

The copper and black patchwork cat finally made itself known as it came from behind a tree and made a clicking growl at Mac. Laye was off to the left, and she was approaching silently as the massive cat zeroed in on him, the cat licked its teeth jutting from its mouth before it crouched down. Mac knew what was coming, but couldn't do a damn thing as the cat, which was easily his size, came crashing into him.

It bit down on his shoulder, and he growled as he tried to pry its powerful jaw apart. Before he could do anything else, Laye leapt onto the female cat's back and moved up, so she was straddling the beast's neck. She locked her legs and squeezed its neck as she carefully pressed her fingers into the cat's eyelids, only trying to deter it, but not cause any ocular harm.

Mac grunted as he gripped the animals lower jaw and held it down to the ground so it couldn't reach up and scratch him, "What are you doing?!"

"What the fuck does it look like, Mac? You think I'm trying to go for a fun little ride or what?!" Laye gritted her teeth as she squeezed her thighs, and she could feel the Burnished cat slowing. Laye used her arms and pressed them into the sides of her thighs to keep the pressure on its neck, *this thing had to have veins in its neck, right?*

After several more seconds of squeezing, the cat slumped over. Laye helped Mac pry the cat's teeth from his shoulder, and it lost consciousness before floping onto the ground. "We need to go, it's just knocked out." Laye leaned back as she helped Mac up and they took off down the mountain.

Laye waited until they were far enough away from the trees that they felt safe before she asked, "Why didn't we just shoot it before it bit you?"

"It's extinct, or was. No one has seen one in the last few hundred years," Mac was holding his shoulder, and the wound was oozing.

"We need to patch your shoulder," Laye reached in her pack and pulled out the med kit they had taken from the Shrout supplies. Mac sat on a rock and peeled off his jacket and shirt as Laye prepped some bandages.

He studied the wound, "It's not that bad. Laye narrowed her eyes at him, "I'm putting a bandage on it."

He rolled his eyes as she rounded him, her small hands near his neck sent a bolt of lightning down his spine and he jolted up. "You are doing something to me for that to happen." Mac twisted his upper body around to glare at her.

She couldn't help the grin. "I'm not doing anything, I swear to you. I just laid my hand on your shoulder." He did not believe her at all, Mac slowly turned back around but kept his eyes on her. She tried not to laugh as she attempted again to apply the bandage to his shoulder.

She worked quickly but when her hand brushed his

neck again, his head shot back, and he jumped to his feet from his seat on the rock. "You're a fucking liar! What are you doing to me?! I almost snapped my own fucking neck!" He rubbed his throat, and his eyes filled with fury.

Laye slapped a hand over her mouth and pointed to his crotch, his length strained against his pants. He put a hand over down over the bulge, and his brow went low over his eyes. "You're a little witch!"

His eyes flared in fury, and he was positive she would die of holding in laughter with how violet her face was. When she finally let loose, Laye collapsed onto the rock as she laughed, Mac was eyeing her like she had cast a dangerous love spell onto him.

She bit her lip and pointed to his bulge, "You're full of lies if you say you don't like it." His eyes flared again, this time he straighten as he sincerely asked, "Are you a witch?"

She grinned as she shook her head, "I am not a witch, but I guess I don't have to be to make you jump for me."

Mac didn't want to admit he liked it, but his length split in his pants, giving away his true feelings. Laye came up to him and unbuckled his pants, taking one side of his dual length in each of her hands. He exhaled roughly as she stroked him, his length pulsing and rolling as she gave him what he wanted. His hips tensed, and he felt the rush of his climax nearing.

Mac leaned back and a guttural sound came from his throat, Laye jumped to the side just in time. Mac's cum shot out and flew by her as he folded forward. "Fuck, your hands are much softer than K'hornibus hands," Mac admitted as his length receded inside of him.

Laye smirked, she loved his rough hands though.

SEVENTEEN

SOMETHING LIKE NORMAL LIFE

Their return was uneventful, and Mac waited until he was inside his home in the canyon before he sent his father the video. Voakes was calling within moments, "What the fuck is that?"

Mac smirked, "I found the Shrout lab behind the mountains on the edge of the salt. They were planning to infest our sands with creatures from Aduro who devour flesh to the bone."

"They broke a Sarter environmental law. They brought an invasive species onto our world. We may not agree completely, but you did well this time. The Shrout will be tied up with the Sarter Queen's guard for this, and our borders will be quiet for a time. We need to strike again after the dust settles," His father commanded, his breath heavy over the comms. "Mac, as long as nothing comes up, you can take a few days," he offered, a rare gesture.

"Thanks." Mac ended the call, and Laye nodded she heard everything.

He dropped his bag on his couch, and unloaded his

gear as Laye did the same. Once they had unpacked, they showered and made their way into the kitchen. Standing in towels and eating in the kitchen, Mac soaked up every second. *This is what it would be like*, he thought as fear crept back in. The way it stung to think of normalcy made him feel nauseous. He could hardly swallow. He had to take his mind somewhere else.

Laye leaned up against the counter slurping down her honey, and he had to know, "How long is your tongue?" She grinned and rolled it out, and like a butterfly's mouth, it was long and thin, reaching halfway down her torso. When she rolled it back in, she smirked, "I keep it rolled up."

He gave her a wide smile and she melted, "Our first overnight freeze is tonight, I'm starting a fire when we undress. Spread out the bed mat, and bring the bedcovers in so we can rest by the fire, from the report the cold front will bring clouds. We may have a second rain this season."

They undressed and put on nightclothes, and she prepared them a place to rest while he built the fire, she found it quaint and felt like this was a date. She had heard of dates, but she had never been on one. Her heart danced as he lay down next to her on his side. She could hear the tip of his tail slapping the ground, *is this big scary warlord nervous?* Mac tugged her to him, and he slid his hands in her shirt as he curled around her. He didn't move for some time as he held her, Laye wasn't sure what to expect but it hadn't been this.

The fire crackled and outside clouds began to roll in, so Mac opened his comm device which had been sitting on the edge of the couch to check the weather.

Over her head Mac tossed the comms back onto the couch, and slipped his hand back in her shirt, "We have rain coming." Laye kept anticipating more, "What's happening right now?"

Mac's brow creased and he scrunched his nose, "What?"

"I don't understand what we're doing," Laye admitted, she felt painfully awkward. She knew nothing about how normal people acted or what they did. Mac nuzzled his face in her neck, "This is called enjoying your life."

"Oh." *Well, now I feel stupid.*

Rubbing his hand down her side he leaned up to her ear, "It's alright to live for now, and not for the future. We could die at any time and then what? I live my life one moment to the next, and right now? You are who I want to spend my time with. Even if it's just sitting here by the fire, waiting for the storm."

He felt her sink into him, and he kept rubbing her side when he accidentally grazed the edge of her wing. She made a small sound, just enough that he barely heard it. Mac leaned over and whispered in her hair, "Take your clothes off and lie on your stomach."

She pulled her shirt off, and her breasts fell free but he seemed more interested in her, than her body, something had changed in Mac. *Is he starting to genuinely care about me?*

Laye slid her pants off and turned over. Mac moved next to her and traced his finger down her right wing started at the top. He made his way over her ass and all way down the end of her wing on her calf, she suppressed her shiver like her life depended on it. When he moved to her left wing, she couldn't hold it back anymore and trembled violently for a few seconds before resting back on the floor.

Mac laughed, "I will never get bored of that."

Laye laughed into the covers, "If it makes you touch my wings more, I'll stop holding it back."

"You move so fast you seem to disappear, I've never experienced anything like it." Mac couldn't hold back a grin when he started on her left wing again.

She moaned into the covers and let out a whoop before she shivered again, this time Mac fell back onto the bedding laughing and pulled her onto him. She snuggled her face onto his chest and thunder cracked outside. Laye felt his heartbeat faster when the sound of rain began to fall outside, and the droplets started sliding down his windows. *Mac must love his planet.*

Laye moved to dress, but he held her to him, grumbling something she couldn't hear. *Is he asleep?* She looked and saw his eyes were closed, and his mouth still moving. She pried out of his grip, and leaned in close to see if she could hear what he was saying.

Mac mumbled, "Laye," and she distinctly heard it. *Is he dreaming about me?* It occurred to her that he may have much deeper emotions than she was aware of. She knew it was intrusive and wrong, but she had to know. Laye moved up his still body and reached her antennae out. Nothing. She watched his face and peered down at his horns. She wondered if she wrapped her antenna around his horn, maybe she could sense something.

She leaned forward and pressed her forehead against his as she reached down with her antennae and wrapped them around his top horns. The explosive emotions that poured into her caught her completely off guard and she gasped. She felt more love than she could have ever dreamed coming from this man, he whispered her name again and there was another rush of love flowing into her. Laye pulled her antenna away and her heart sang with joy.

She sat up next to him and studied his face, he seemed so peaceful. It was all too perfect. Laye decided not to dress, and she lie next to him while he slept, the sounds of his breathing comforted her.

Mac woke from his slumber, and she felt his lips on her shoulder. His hand came around her and cupped her breast as he kissed her along her neck to right under her ear.

He flipped her over on her back and lay her down so he could hover over her. He brought his lips to hers and kissed her, slipping his tongue in her mouth and sliding it along hers. Mac stroked her nipple with his thumb as he deepened his kiss. He was so gentle with her she was overcome with emotions, how was she so lucky to experience this?

He moved along her throat and to her chest, tasting and kissing her everywhere before moving further down. He crawled between her legs and lay himself out on the floor before his mouth descended on her most sensitive place.

This time he was slow and careful, taking his time to taste every inch of her. His fingers moved along her hips where he held her, the attention he showed her was heartbreakingly sweet and she was beside herself. The sensations of his rough tongue against her line of nerves was sublime, she felt like she was floating on a cloud. Mac spread her out and slipped a finger inside of her as she licked her.

He had given her some epic orgasms, but this one was different. It was so much more, she could feel it building up and she could have whined at how slowly it came on. She could feel herself slip over the edge, but it was smooth and heavy, the sensitive nerves were pulsing slowly, and she took deep breaths of air into her lungs. The way it was still there as he kept licking, extending it. She didn't move as it finally crested, and she leaned her head back to unabashedly moan.

He growled as she came, and he licked her clean. Crawling back up, he kissed the scar on her shoulder before she felt him line up with her entrance. Mac towered over her little body as he entered her, and Laye gasped as he filled her. She angled her hips up and he slid his hand under her, lifting her. He thrust a few times before his length split in two and began rolling inside of her. She arched back and ground her hips against him as he groaned.

Laye felt herself building toward another orgasm, "I'm going to cum again." She let out a soft cry as she felt the orgasm rush her senses. Above her, Mac smiled as he continued to grind into her as she flailed. Her hips shook as he felt her inner muscles grip him and pulse.

He squeezed his eyes shut as he felt himself start to fall over the edge, the sensation great enough it was causing him to curl up. He shook as he emptied himself into her, his insides felt like they were being squeezed in the best way possible.

Mac peered down at his spent little butterfly and willed the universe to allow him to keep her. He wanted nothing else more than this woman.

His comms rang and he sunk his head, *so much for a break*. Laye reached up and ran her hands down his muscled abdomen as he answered. "What?" Mac's tone was sharp.

Sensing he was interrupting something, Yarle spoke quickly, "We caught the second born Shrout brother. We need you to come interrogate him."

Mac rubbed his eyes, "Fine. But I'm not coming until morning."

He didn't want to leave her, not for anything, but he couldn't get out of this. Mac threw his comms at his couch, and Laye stopped moving her hands.

He leaned back and put his hands over hers. She smiled at him, "I heard. It's all right." It was not all right, and something ate at Mac to find an excuse not to leave her.

EIGHTEEN

CONSUMING SILENCE

Taking Laye into his arms, he leaned her back and reluctantly kissing her goodbye, Mac mounted his bike and drove away. She couldn't feel his anguish, but she knew he would have done anything to stay. Laye sat down on the brick-red dirt and watched him drive toward the checkpoint a few miles away. Little white and pink flowers were blooming in the canyon, and she remained seated for some time admiring and soaking up the floral scents.

It was a beautiful day, and she warmed her face in the bright morning system starlight. She finally rose from her spot and headed inside, she needed to stay in Mac's home and out of sight.

She climbed the stairs and went back to his bathroom for a quick shower before she dressed. Her hand moved to turn the handle of the door to Mac's bedroom when her gut twisted, *something is wrong.* Laye burst into the next room and discovered her worst nightmare was already surrounding her. Three Vo-Pess operatives were leaning on various surfaces of Mac's home, Laye met the eyes of each one.

Therow, Gerne, and Fere had been sent to collect her, three people she knew better than anyone else in the galaxy. They were the other members of the Angle Wings, and all of them were on her skill level.

Therow spoke first as he ran his yellow finger down the wall, and acted like it was too dusty. "Did you really think this would work?"

Laye had no intention of answering him.

Fere approached Laye and she used a soft tone, "If you cooperate, we won't kill the K'hornibus and his brothers." Fere had been her best friend. Even now, her maroon face was kind and sorrowful. Laye put her hands out but said nothing as Fere attached a tab to the back of her wrist and tapped it. The restraint slid around her wrists and tightened down as Fere reached for her arm.

Lowering her eyes, she saw Mac's security camera in his living area had been disabled, and it was in a pile on the floor. He would have no idea what happened to her. *It was better this way.* He would be killed if he came looking for her.

As they led her out, Fere leaned toward her, "What were you thinking? Why did you defect? The reclamation team found Leem!"

Gerne slapped Fere on the shoulder. "Stop telling her information. She's no longer an Angle Wing. She's the enemy now." Fere silently led Laye out to their cloaked ship, which was next to the river, the delicate flowers she had been admiring earlier were crushed under the ship's landing gear.

The ship's loading bay dropped open, and Laye was taken inside, she looked longingly back behind her at the open shop, and at one of Mac's old bikes. Her heart broke into a million pieces, for she knew she would never see him again. *It is over, it's all over. My little slice of life has ended. Have I even experienced a month with him?*

Fere had known all along Leem abused Laye, and so did the rest of the Angle Wings. They had all witnessed how he targeted her and treated her after he claimed her. Fere had been claimed in a similar way, and she had been claimed by someone who had used her like Leem had used Laye. Most of their ruling class men were so focused on repopulating that they claimed their women by force was a necessary sacrifice for the Vo-Pess.

The inside of their ship was identical to her former vessel, and she found a seat where they usually put prisoners. She waited for the force field to buzz around her. Within a few seconds, the sound of the shield was already irritating her. It was designed to block her empathic reach, but all it really did was piss her off.

The bright lights of the ship shone in her eyes, she had forgotten how uncomfortable their ships were. Sleek and white with holo-screens on every surface.

She guessed she better grow accustomed being uncomfortable, when they returned her to Hyret, she would wish she were dead. She had killed the heir of the Van-Well Dynasty after all. Laye wondered how much torture she would endure to make her regret all of this. *It would take a lifetime of torture, and she would still never regret her time with Mac.*

That would be their aim when they find out she hadn't given away any real information about her people or their planet. Gerne approached her with her official arrest decree, "Laye-Ce Olin-Trew, you are being charged with defection, treason, and the murder of the Van-Well Dynasty heir, Leem-Der. How do you plead?"

Fere spun around and held her eyes on Laye as she answered solemnly, "Guilty."

Gerne furrowed his lavender brow and shook his head at her, "You're so fucking stupid. They'll sentence you to be connected to the neural cycle until you die. Do you understand what that means?"

Fere walked up behind him, and scolded, "Just leave her alone Gerne. You know what Leem used to do."

"Sit down Fere, I'm lead on this mission for that exact reason. Therow, take us home. I want this piece of shit off my ship," Gerne spat back. Everyone found their seats and as the ship broke the atmosphere, a wormhole opened, and Therow brought them in. Within moments they were in orbit around Hyret, the white glow of the nebula surrounding them.

"Hyret City space control, AW-3 you have clearance to land on pad A-17."

Therow brought the ship down, and they landed without incident, the ship bay door opened behind them and the bright lights of their triple stars poured inside. The beauty of Hyret was overwhelming and Laye found herself hating it now that she was back. She had never dreamed she could look upon her high-tech, and vibrant, lush world with such disdain and loathing.

Knowing what came next, Laye shoved everything she had experienced with Mac into a little box in her mind, locking it up and tossing away the key. They could have her body and her mind, but they could never have Mac. He was hers, and she would never allow them to take his memories and twist them. She knew what she would endure, and her gut was in a knot, the Vo-Pess loved psychological torment.

Fere held her arm as they brought her inside the Vo-Pess prisoner processing building which was located beside the court she would be in within the next few days. The court which would seal her fate.

When she was brought inside, Fere handed her off to the guard and he took Laye's arm in a bruising hold. Taking her down the hall, they passed the typical processing door and Laye internally sighed. She guessed since she was a defector she didn't have the benefit of a pre-court hold.

The guard brought her into the interrogation room, and she cringed as her eyes fell on the indention in the wall that was person shaped with a neural link cord hanging from the base of the neck area. Laye was lined up to the wall, and Fere reached around to connect the neural link to her spine at the base of her neck. Fere didn't speak but her eyes said enough. She still cared about Laye. The guard left the room as Fere secured her to the wall with straps over her legs, waist, and arms. The bonds tightened and she was cinched to the wall. Her broken heart couldn't even beat in fear as she watched Gerne approach the controls.

The sensation of bugs crawling down her spine was just the beginning, it was followed by a rush of mind split-ting anxiety. She did her best to breathe deep but the strap around her middle was too tight, restricting her air. A signal inducing terror was pushed through the link as she stared blankly at Fere.

Fere exhaled roughly, knowing what horrors her friend was experiencing, "What did you reveal to the K'hornibus?" Laye remained silent and held Fere's gaze, Fere lowered her eyes before she gave the signal. The sensation of her nervous system being ripped from her spine flowed through her, Laye's breath caught as it cycled through and finally ebbed. The pain was otherworldly, and she gasped for air.

"What did you reveal to the K'hornibus?" Fere asked again, her eyes brimming with grief.

Laye had no intention of answering until she was forced, and she wasn't sure they would be able to pry a word from her. As she stared back at Fere, Laye began to realize that her shattered heart might end up a superpower here. Nothing could truly hurt her now. *I am invincible.*

Fere gave the signal, and the agony moved through Laye's nerves again. Her eyes blurred and she tensed trying to take a breath, but she was still unable.

Gerne from the controls lowered his brow, "Fere, we're already at the top."

A creased formed between Fere's eyes, "Laye, please. What did you reveal to the K'hornibus?"

Laye glared at Fere, they were already at the top of the neural link's input. They would have to do a lot worse to make her crack, but she knew it was coming. This was only the beginning. Fere closed her eyes as she signaled to Gerne once again.

This time it was longer and Laye fought for breath as her world darkened. Her head shot back up when the second round slammed into her nerves, but Laye remained silent. She wouldn't reward them with as much as a whimper.

NINETEEN
GRAIN OF RICE

Mac smeared the desert sage oil on the chest of the Shrout brother strapped to a wooden chair, while Yarle behind him was preparing his tools. The chair creaked as the man shifted away from Mac's hand. Through his mask, Mac could clearly see he was already nervous.

"You're not extracting shit from me," The Shrout sneered at Mac. Crouching down, Mac brought his face even with the Shrout's. "The fact that you're already speaking, tells me you will be easy to break. We just need to know if your father was aware of the project to introduce the invasive silver worms into our world and what his role was. Did one of your brothers lead the project? Simple questions and simple answers."

The Shrout brother hissed at Mac, showing him his sharpened canines. Mac chuckled and flicked the man's tooth causing the Shrout man to rear back.

If one thing was certain, Mac had a love for tormenting the Shrout. They were stuck in the old ways, and their territory had become destitute while their father became more jealous by the day. It was their brand of destruction and thoughtlessness that would lead to the end of their home world, K'hurian.

Yarle handed Mac a serrated knife, and he leaned forward, dragging it across the Shrout's chest. He screamed and thrashed, not understanding how the pain was so intense. "It was my father's project! Fuck make it stop!" the Shrout cried out as Mac stared at the small cut on his chest.

Having enough, Mac raised his fist and knocked the man out before facing Yarle. "Have Inex deposit him across the border with a squealer's mark."

Yarle approached him and grabbed his face before he ran a knife across his forehead, marking that he had given up information to an enemy. The Shrout started to wake and hissed as Yarle cut across his forehead.

All Mac wanted was to drive back to Laye, "If we're done here, I'm going home."

"Does father still have you at the mid check?" Yarle asked as he leaned back to knock out the Shrout again.

Mac didn't turn around as he headed to the door, "Yes," was all he muttered before the door shut behind him. When he had made it outside and was mounting his bike, no one was around, and he pulled his comms out to check on Laye.

The camera wasn't on. He selected the history files, and the camera had been disabled by force. Right before the cameras were disabled, Laye came inside and went to his bedroom. *Something is wrong.* He called the comms he had left her and there was no answer.

No, she can't be gone. Mac revved his bike and pelted the metal wall behind him with the stones from under his tires. Taking turns too sharply at top speeds, Mac raced to his main home in K'rin city. He leapt from his bike and allowed it to skid to a stop in his courtyard, the dust stirred a cloud into the air.

He barreled through his front door and barked at his guard, "Get out!" Parn, his guard, fell over himself, and Mac shoved him out of his way. As Parn shut the door and moved to the front gate, Mac released a roar into his home.

Where the fuck is my tracking box? Closet? He rummaged through a storage closet and nearly put his fist through the metal wall before his eyes fell on the black case.

He flipped it open and found a plug to connect it to power. In seconds, the galactic tracking device formed a map on the screen, the various items he hid tracker's on were pinging. He waited and waited; Mac sat for an hour staring at the screen. He had put a tiny tracking device inside of Laye's neck when he sewed her up, one the size of a single grain of rice. Mac had tagged all his children before they went off planet, and now he was thanking the sands he had been overly paranoid about their safety on Keru and already had the system before he ever met Laye.

He rubbed his eyes when he saw it, in the corner of the screen. One small little dot. His heart hopped into his throat, *could it be her?* Mac zoomed into the ping spot, and it took him several seconds of dragging his fingers across the screen to reach it. When he did, he sat back and took a rough breath trying to figure out what he would do.

The ping was in the Singer's Nebula, which was a star nursery. It was an undocumented planet, and the ping didn't give anything but an approximate location. He would need his father's entire fleet. He recorded the coordinates and plotted near it to avoid opening a wormhole on the planet surface. Mac checked his rail gun, and it had a full ammo tank.

He rose from the floor, and opened his comms to contact his father, "What, Mac?"

"We need to talk. Meet me up front." Mac opened his front door and headed toward his bike. He pulled his now scratched bike off the ground in a fury, "Pern, back inside!"

Pern fell over his feet, and he ran toward the house as Mac blew through his gate, causing it to swing back and slam against his metal fence. The dust flew around him as he traveled to his father's house, passing Yarle who threw his hands up at Mac like he had lost it.

He dropped his bike outside of his father's front door and ran into his home, blowing passed the front security guards. "I have urgent business off world, I need the ship fleet and teams." Mac never made demands, which had his father eyeing him suspiciously. Voakes moved to stand directly front of Mac before he quietly responded a simple, "No," in his face.

Without second thought, Mac pulled the trigger on his rail gun and the round went up through Voakes heart. He dropped to the ground at Mac's feet and the guards rushed in, pulling their weapons on Mac before looking around at one another. Mac peered down at his dead father, "I'm the Shardlow first son, put your fucking weapons down. The seat is mine. Call in my brothers and send double replacements to the border, and I need the treasury report before you drag Voakes away."

The guards slowly lowered their weapons, and nodded to one another, they knew Shardlow law. Mac was the boss now.

Mac pulled his comms out and found a number he never dreamed he would be calling for help. He needed fire power and there was one place he knew he could find what he wanted, plus some assistance installing the software.

One of the guards presented Mac with a folder and he opened it, the treasury report was inside. He read to the bottom and had to lift the paper to see correctly. That couldn't be right, could it? He took his mask off and read the bottom of the form.

Voakes had discovered an element called neodymium in mass concentrations around the south cap of K'hurian. Their territory was worth enough he could afford the terraforming equipment to save his planet. Mac wanted to rip his father's head off when he read the date the mine opened.

It had opened the same year Mac was born. His father had been one of the richest men in the galactic center, yet most of his people were on the edge of not making it to their next meal. The lack of homes had grown substantially, and Mac felt the urge to kick his dead father in the face as the guards dragged him off.

"Toss his body in the sand," Mac barked at the guards before the door shut behind them. His thoughts drifted to Laye, and he willed her to stay strong. He knew if anyone could survive, it would be her. Mac formed a plan as he heard Yarle walking up to the house. Yarle opened the door, and Mac was standing on the other side, "I've taken the seat. We need to talk."

Yarle ripped his mask off, "You what?! Did father die, or did you kill him?"

"I killed the stupid fuck, what do you think! He was starving our people and allowing our planet to waste away." Mac shoved the file at Yarle, and he followed Mac into the conference room by the entry way. Mac shut the door and rubbed his face, "I need to admit something to you."

Yarle's expression melted, and he fell backward into a chair, "Well big fucking surprise Mac! You've been acting like you've got parasites in your damn head!"

Mac groaned, his brother was not going to take this well, "The blue woman we found?"

Rolling his eyes, Yarle scoffed at his brother's audacity, "You didn't kill our father over a blue butterfly woman you found in the desert, did you?"

Mac frowned, "No. Alright, yes, but listen. The Shardlow's owe her a life debt, and a planet debt."

"A, what? A planet debt? How is there such a thing? You fucking made that up Mac!" Yarle grabbed his own horns, and seemed as though his eyes would fall out of his head at any moment. Mac pulled his comm device out and pulled up the video of the silver worms, Yarle grasped the sides of his chair until the end of the video.

"Mac, what the fuck is that?" Yarle asked, unable to tear his eyes away. Mac closed his comms, and his brother peered up at him, finally ready to listen, "The Shrout were planning to release them into our sand, and Laye killed all six of the researchers before she helped me destroy the worms. The Shrout ordered them from Aduro. Before that, Laye killed the three Shrout brothers you helped me drag out to the sand. They had come for me, and *she* was the one who killed them."

Yarle's mouth hung open, and he angled his head to the side as if in deep thought, "Her name is Laye, and she slaughtered *nine* Shrout in the last few weeks? No wonder you want her back. Did she swear loyalty?" Mac snarled at Yarle before he roared, "No, you stupid fuck! She's my woman!"

Yarle blinked rapidly, "Alright. Let's retrieve your woman. Do you have a plan?" Noticing the setting system star, Mac smirked, "Not a good one. We buy weapons and we show up. That's all I've got. I've just transferred Shardlow first son heirship to Berem, he has signed, and it's been transferred to the guard. You and our brothers need to establish house heir's before we leave. Prepare the ship fleet. We leave in the morning for Sinex Station." Yarle deadpanned, "Pirates? Is this a suicide mission?"

"Something like that." Mac admitted with a wink.

TWENTY
LAYE-CE OLIN-TREW

A heartbroken Fere pushed Laye's wheelchair into the court room. She loved her friend, Laye had been the only good part of her life. Laye's slumped figure was a puddle compared to her condition a day prior. She was her best friend, and all Fere wanted to do was reach down and hold her hand.

When Gerne had grown tired, he had them retire for the night, but he instructed the guard to keep going with Laye. Fere had not slept, and her head pounded from trying to hold in her grief. If her bonded partner Pley had heard her, he would have ridiculed her endlessly for being too soft. Rumors were already stirring about Laye and Leem, and Fere could feel the stares burning through her as she continued through the courtroom.

Laye sat up with the slamming of the great doors behind them, signaling the court was in session. The row of elders stood before them, and Fere's heart twisted with the thick disdain and disgust in the room as everyone pointed at her friend.

Silence fell, and Fere braced herself, she knew death was a mercy but the idea of Laye no longer existing sent her mind in a tailspin. *Could I sway the court to spare her?* Why would she want her friend to suffer more? She deserved peace. But the way Laye had stared at her, Fere wasn't sure any amount of torture would ever break her friend. Not truly. Laye was stronger than anyone she knew. Something inside Fere screamed at her to demand the neural cycle. *But why was something telling her to ask them to spare Laye?* Having Laye's feet tied to a stone and her dropped in the Grete Lake would be infinitely better.

The elderly, lavender skinned Dynast Van-Well stood, and announced, "Laye-Ce Olin-Trew, you are being charged with defection, treason, and the murder of the Van-Well Dynasty heir, Leem-Der. Upon arrest you have given an initial plea of guilt. What is your final plea?"

Laye took three long breaths before she whispered, "Guilty."

The collective gasp in the room stole Fere's attention as Dynast Van-Well read her sentence, "Laye; Angle Wing spawn of sire's Olin and Trew of the Ce birth order, you are sentenced to life connected to the neural cycle."

Laye slumped back over in her chair, and Fere couldn't take her attention away from her friend, as chaos in the courtroom burst to life. Chants of tossing her into the Grete rang through the floor, and Fere peered around at the unforgiving Vo-Pess people.

Dynast Van-Well pointed to the door as he met Fere's gaze.

She nodded respectfully and wheeled Laye toward the hallway leading to the prison. Out of millions of their people, only a thousand were incarcerated, and Fere could not accept how Laye had ended up among them. Halfway down the hallway, Fere noticed they were alone, and she placed her hand on Laye's shoulder, her friend startled and peered back at her.

Fere didn't know what else to say, "I'm sorry, Laye. I wish I could break you out of here."

Laye smiled the best she could as she held her friends gaze, "I forgive you, I always will. For everything past, present, and future. I love you more than you can imagine, and I'm sorry."

It was the first time Laye had spoken, and Fere let out a sob, "I love you, too."

Fere heard Gerne open the doors behind her a moment later, and she started moving the chair as Laye turned back around. Discretely licking away the tear that had escaped her eye, Fere turned away from Gerne as he caught up.

He moved ahead of them and opened the door at the end of the hall. Fere moved the chair up to the processing counter, and a technician came over to install Laye's vitals monitor around her arm. When it was snapped on, Fere continued down the hall with her friend.

Gerne read the numbers on the hall, "She's in room 1101."

Fere had a long journey to the end of the hallway where the room was located. When they arrived at the door, Gerne opened it, and inside was a setup similar to their interrogation room. The only difference was the location for the body was protruding from the wall horizontally and not vertically.

Laye crawled up onto the device willfully, and lay down before she met her friend's gaze. Every person they had ever forced into the neural cycle had fiercely fought being put into the machine. Even Gerne stopped and met

Fere's concerned gaze, he seemed disturbed and signaled with his eyes he needed to speak to her outside.

Fere placed her hand on Laye's leg before she pat it twice and meet Gerne outside the door. Gerne kept his trained eyes on Laye until Fere shut the door. He moved in front of the door's window and was silent as he watched Laye just lie there, motionless and without so much as a word.

Gerne spoke toward the window, "What the fuck is wrong with her? She's always been the strongest out of all of us. Something happened to her."

"*Gerne*, do you honestly think our life is good? Laye escaped the Vo-Pess long enough to find herself. That's what a whole person looks like, real strength." Fere pointed to Laye who was still lying still on the device, unbound and unwilling to fight.

Gerne faced the window, "Then why does she seem like she's been broken? She's never acted this way."

Fere was growing sick of Gerne's questions and spoke under her breath, "Why the fuck do you care? You were the one who demanded we find her and haul her home even though her tracking beacon was smashed. She didn't want to be found, and she didn't give away any fucking Vo-Pess *secrets*. She found something far better than we have had on Hyret in generations. She found happiness. I'm not turning the dial to maximum like ordered. Tell on me, or don't, but I'm setting it low. Leem was a monster, and we both know it." Gerne stared at her solemnly and she continued, "She was our wing leader Gerne. She would have *died* for us."

He glared at her and stalked away from the room, leaving Fere there alone in the hallway with nothing but the cameras watching. Fere's gut twisted as she entered the room, Laye didn't look over at who came in. She was still lying motionless, staring at the ceiling.

Approaching the device, Fere gently moved Laye's head to the side and connected the device to the base of her neck, and it lit up under her body. Fere strapped Laye down and she gazed at her friend for several seconds before she squeezed her eyes shut and moved to the controls. Even at a low setting, Laye would go through some of the worst torment their world had to offer.

The device could sense what caused the most psychological pain and would cycle you through your worst nightmares. It ate up your fears and twisted them into terror before feeding them back to you. Fere always avoided looking inside the windows of the rooms in the prison when she brought in targets. She knew what was on the other side, Vo-Pess with their minds irrevocably turned to mush while their bodies lived on. Their life signs usually faded quickly but sometimes it took years before their heart would give out and allow them to die.

Fere stood in front of the controls. She shed a tear as she circled her finger around the dial to the lowest setting. Fere realized Hyret was not her home, it was her prison as she sent the only person she ever loved into an endless, living hell.

Laye felt herself slip into the digital world of the device, and her consciousness awoke in a dark room. She was alone for now until the machine learned what she was afraid of.

There was only one thing she was truly afraid of, and it had already happened. *I am invincible.* She kept her few weeks away from the Vo-Pess secreted far away in a remote corner of her memory as she felt the device prying into her mind. If a flash of trauma surfaced, she knew the programming would cling to it. Keeping her mind on Fere, she reminisced about the time they skipped their training for the day, and they had flown through the trees in the forest south of the city court buildings.

They had been whipped for it, and Laye would never forget how Fere had made a face at her during their whipping, and instructor Sere had whipped them again. Laye laughed to herself and begged her mind to stay positive.

A memory of Leem forced its way in, one of him forcing her to the ground in their living area. He had tapped her armor tab and ripped at her pants as she squeezed her eyes shut, waiting for it to be over, except, she was in the cycle. The memory was real, and Leem was holding her down as Laye whispered, "I know I killed him. I know I killed him," yet all she felt was searing pain as he ripped her flesh.

Her mind shifted, forcing out the memory of Leem. She knew it would cycle back but it was over for a moment. Something told her the device had not been set to the highest setting. She should be experiencing it all non-stop with increased neural output, causing the victim to believe the experience was happening more intensely than the original event.

It would be a week before someone checked, and turned the setting up, Laye's heart swelled knowing it was Fere who had done it. She hoped Fere didn't receive a punishment for it.

Laye appeared in front of Fere with a knife, cutting skin from her shoulder at the demands of their instructor. Fere was sobbing but had not revealed her assigned secret as Laye continued the process. Fere's screams rang through her head as the room became black and empty again.

No sleep, no rest, only the reminders of her past. The

horrible things done to her, and what she had done to others. So, what if she had been commanded to commit the atrocities, she still chose to comply. Laye still believed best thing she ever did was defect, but those memories were off limits. She could never bring them out again.

They are mine and mine alone.

Laye found herself strapped chair with Gerne over her holding a torch, the scent of her burned flesh filled the room.

TWENTY-ONE
SINEX STATION

Orbiting Melior, Mac peered down at the perfectly manicured planet and snarled his lip at their decadence. "Send the access codes."

The guard at the helm nodded and Melior security could be heard overhead, "Access granted, please proceed to the landing coordinates." Mac grumbled, "Take us in. Yarle, you're with me."

The ship set down and the rest of his current fleet did the same, Yarle followed Mac as he lowered the loading bay and made their way to the open doors of Accalia Shipwright.

At the counter inside was a human woman, and she acknowledged Mac with caution. "Voakes Shardlow I presume?"

"You can call me Mac. I need to upgrade my fleet, right now," he demanded as her eyes widened. She was staring into his eyes through his mask, he had no intention of taking it off. The only way he was able to maintain his privacy was to never show his face, and that wasn't changing because of a scared ship salesperson.

Nervously clearing her throat, she blinked a few times before responding, "I am Abril. We have a few options for you, right this way." Mac followed the young dark-haired woman into the hanger where they had several options to view. He approached the newest released UTC issue imperial battleship.

Abril came up beside him and put her hand on the edge of the lift. "This is the same ship the new UTC Empress owns. She purchased this model for the Claudius kingdom's fleet as well."

"How much for fifteen of them? Do you have them available now?" Mac asked as he watched her pale. Abril agreed but seemed skeptical, "Yes, we have plenty available in our shipyard. The cost is going to be over two billion credits."

"Great. I need them immediately." Mac ordered before he added, "Do I purchase weapons from you or at the science and technology station?"

Abril answered as she slid her hands in her pockets, "We can have the armament delivered within the hour, and I can have the ships prepared while we wait. Will you need financing?"

"No." Mac reached into his pocket and handed Abril his credit transfer detail card. Abril, painfully stunned, took the card from Mac, and slowly stepped away to start the transfer. He and Yarle watched as she approached the console and typed in his information. He saw the screen process the transfer and Abril mildly startled as the confirmation codes populated, signifying the bill was paid in full. The K'hornibus had never been known for wealth, so it wasn't lost on him why she seemed surprised.

Much paler than she had been before, Abril came back and handed Mac his Credit transfer card, "Everything went through, and your fleet will be ready within the hour. Follow me and I can provide you with the flight instruction manuals."

Mac smirked at Yarle who was still staring at him like he had some kind of communicable disease. "Do you have something to say?" Mac stopped and stared at Yarle. Shaking his head with his brows raised, Yarle simply answered, "Nope."

If he says one word to me, I am knocking his ass out. Mac caught up to Abril as she approached the front desk. She selected a few options and asked, "We have new holo-tech would you like the manuals in holo form or standard digital?"

"Holograms, and before you ask, I don't want the extended warranty." Mac answered as he handed her his credit transfer card, he knew there would be an upcharge. There always was. She took the card and ran the charge. Abril carefully handed Mac the card back, her hand shook as he took it from her.

"Have you never met a K'hornibus before?" Mac asked as he put his card away. She slowly, but politely, shook her head as she slid the hologram tablets across the counter. That would change, he was tired of his people's hard, secluded way of life. The K'hornibus people deserved more than the dying world they were left with after the collapse of their industrial age thousands of years ago. Their own ancestors had accelerated their planets demise and now their entire world was a wasteland while their system star grew.

Mac and Yarle were led to a lounge and offered a drink as they waited for the ships to be prepared. As promised by Abril, the ships were ready within the hour, and they were being led out to board. Mac had been stewing and tapping his foot, he was sick of Yarle staring at him with a clear air of fear. He wanted Laye back, and this was all taking far too long.

Each crew from their former fleet was assigned a new ship, and they each boarded to begin learning the controls. Their former fleet was made by the same manufacturer, Accalia Shipwright so when Mac turned on the holo-tablet the controls seemed almost identical.

His helmsman Heret reported, "Mac, we don't need training they didn't change any of the main flight controls. Just lower system changes. Where are we going next?" Mac exhaled roughly, this next stop would be interesting, "Sinex station, I have an order I need to pick up. Set coordinates to the Bonted system's third planet. The station orbits the rocky moon."

Heret turned and stared at him incredulously for a moment before he plugged in the coordinates and sent them to the fleet. Sinex was the pirating station, and he had some previous dealings with the owner Benitian.

Laye had not been the first off-worlder Mac had rescued from his backward father's practices. Benitian, a Corvus who owned Sinex station, had landed in his desert with engine trouble many years prior. Mac had made an agreement with him and had found him parts for his ship instead of capturing and presenting him as food to his father. Mac had been lucky he was by himself when he discovered Benitian's ship.

The helm sent the fleet the coordinates, the wormhole opened, and they were approaching Sinex station within a few minutes. Mac pulled up the security access codes he had been given and sent them to the station, and he received a message back signaling to dock at bay 26. After he sent Heret the helmsman the docking instructions, he made his way to the lift and down to the loading bay in the belly of the ship. The ship airlock connected, and the docking arm moved the station loading port to seal around the lower loading bay. When the airlock unsealed, Mac's ears popped, and he shifted his jaw.

Benitian stood in front of the satellites Mac ordered, his big black, feathered wings were tucked behind him as he brushed his hair from his brow, "It's been a few cycles, Mac. You find yourself in some trouble?"

"No. I'm off to make trouble," Mac corrected, and Benitian VanClair slyly grinned back at him.

"That's what I like to hear. I uploaded a rotating shielding program I obtained from the Iungo. I heard the Sarter Queen has access to their transport technology. Let me know if you get ahold of it, I hear it's the best mode of travel and faster than a wormhole."

Mac nodded, "Sure thing. How long will it take to integrate these satellite controls? We need one installed on each ship."

Nodding, Benitian grinned at Mac, "Starting a war, are we?" Mac leaned on the control module in the loading bay and laughed, "Not if they give me back what is mine."

"You're my kind of people, Mac. It's good doing business with you." Benitian moved to grab the box Mac was pointing to. He carefully opened the box, "The neodymium is pure?"

Mac agreed, "It is as pure as it gets." Toying with his lip ring, Benitian reached to close it, "This will go a long way."

"How long will it take to outfit my fleet?" Mac asked,

his insides were clawing at him. The urgency to save his woman was thick on his tongue.

Benitian thought a moment, "I'll move ships around, and we can install three at once. I would say a day or two at the most." Mac reluctantly accepted, "That's not quick enough, but it will have to work."

Pulling a box of neodymium through the loading bay, Benitian signaled his parting with a bow to Mac before he disappeared through the doorway.

Mac exhaled roughly as heard Yarle behind him. "Mac, what are we doing here?"

He turned to find Yarle with his arms crossed. "You'll see."

"I need to know if we're really starting a war. You're acting like father. I thought you wanted change." Yarle accused as Mac approached him.

Mac pointed up the walkway and to the lift. Yarle followed as they heard Benitian's installation crews file in the loading bay and start installing the tech needed to run the satellite.

They rode the lift to the second level, and Mac crossed the common area toward his rooms. The door slid away, and he went inside, the odd metallic furniture protruded from the floor as if it was reaching to the sky. Mac didn't look around his new room but instead turned to Yarle behind him and snapped, "Fine, yes. I am preparing to expose and possibly destroy a hidden world in order to reclaim what is mine. Father wouldn't lift a grain of sand for anyone but himself, we are not the same. You need to learn the difference." Yarle paused before he responded, "How is it any different when the conclusion is the same?"

"Are you challenging me, Yarle?" Mac asked as he took a step forward, putting his face in Yarle's. Silence fell over them as Mac stared into his brother's similar bright lemon eyes. Yarle shook his head no as he took a step back, one thing he would not do is challenge Mac. They were nearly the same size but that meant nothing, Mac didn't hold back, and Yarle never fared well.

"We have new armor, and masks loaded in the ship's bay. Inform the crew and have our gear brought to our rooms." Mac ordered.

Yarle made his way to the door, and when it slid open, he looked over his shoulder at Mac, "I hope you know what the fuck you're doing."

TWENTY-TWO

DIVIDED ANGLES

Gerne stood by his console working next to Fere as she stared at her holo-screen blankly, she had been trying to focus on her intel work all day but couldn't find an ounce of effort. She hadn't accomplished one thing, and Gerne was growing frustrated, "Why are you still toiling over Laye? It's over. Laye is gone. You need to accept that fact and move on."

But how could she? She and Laye had emerged within weeks of one another. They had been together their entire conscious lives, and after Laye had gone missing, she had never been more concerned about anything.

Everyone went into the Vo-Pess academy and then military upon emergence, and classification and placement depended on what wings you emerged with. There were only a few Angle Wing sires, and one was Axit, his spawn included herself, Gerne, and Therow.

Laye had been sired by Trew, a legendary Angle Wing who brought in more useful UTC intel than any other Angle Wing ever. Trew had a statue in front of the capital building, being hailed as the epitome of Vo-Pess ideals. Her assassination list was over two hundred beings long. She had been the closest any Vo-Pess had ever been to assassinating a First Human Emperor.

Trew had sired six batches of eggs, but only Laye had emerged an Angle Wing. They were the fastest flyers in all the Vo-Pess, and their numbers were dwindling despite massive efforts to breed more of them. The Angle Wings were the only Vo-Pess with the genes for their long-lost empathic gifts. Fere felt Gerne's eyes on her and she snarled at him. "What are you looking at?"

"You've been staring at your screen for hours. Do you need to be sent back to training? We have a job to do." Gerne snapped.

Fere huffed under her breath and selected her current assignment, tracking down the Iungo transport technology. Their science teams had not transported anything except plants in their own labs, and when Fere had observed the tech in use when she was on a mission around Melior, she had sent the intelligence tip to their elders. They had ordered her to obtain the technology by any means necessary. She had already snuck inside the abandoned northern UTC base on Portum and found nothing but the installation videos when the Iungo outfitted their ships.

Fere dove into her mind, Laye had also been assigned the project, but she had been given a different route than Fere. Shaking her head at Leem for always tagging along with Laye, she never had a moment alone. She was thankful Pley, her bonded, couldn't get it up any longer, he was even older than Leem. Fere only sired one batch of eggs with him, and after a few years he was too tired to do anything but sit around their home. He repulsed Fere and she avoided him at all costs.

Unfortunately tonight, they had to discuss Fere's next phase of her assignment beginning at the end of the week. She was being sent to the Sarter palace if she couldn't pry the intel from the Iungo records. With what just occurred with Laye? She knew Pley would be furious. It wasn't her choice, the elders were in charge of everything, and they dictated every aspect of the militant operations the Vo-Pess lived under.

There was no mouth that went hungry, but their lives were so constricted Fere lived every day with her chest so tight that some days she felt like she would burst. She stayed so on edge that she often wondered if she would even make it to one hundred. Many of the Vo-Pess were dead before then despite having the genes to live to one hundred and fifty.

Fere dug through file after file in the Iungo system before she was kicked out by their cyber security, "Damn, they're good, I've only been in the files for a few minutes. I wonder if it's a person or a program."

"Kicked out already? You should have been working all along and maybe you would have something by now," Gerne spat, Therow behind them hummed agreeing with the sentiment.

Fere sneered at Gerne, flashing her teeth, "Mind your business."

"You are our business. We are supposed to be an impenetrable unit, and you're still sobbing like a baby worm over Laye, when she betrayed us." Therow defended Gerne and was glaring at Fere when she turned to him.

Narrowing her eyes in irritation at her wing-mates, Fere turned back to her console and didn't look away from her work until the end of her scheduled workday. She didn't say a word to them as she left for her home. At the end of the hall there was a jump ledge, and she headed for it. She heard Gerne and Therow chatting outside their office door as she opened the door to the ledge. She ignored them as her wings peeled away from her skin and passed through her nano-tech armor. Before her wings were fully extended, she dived from the edge and fell for several seconds before she caught the air and flew toward her home.

Fere discovered taking extreme risks during flying was the only control she had, so she vaulted from ledges without her wings extended every chance she could. She took outlandish risks often enough that she had been put under a psych hold four times. Fere shot through the sky and spotted her jump ledge jutting from the side of the building she lived in. All the Vo-Pess except the elders, and the members of the Ven-Well Dynasty received standard rooms.

Her stomach grumbled as she landed on her ledge, and she opened the door to her home without looking up. It had been days since she had been able to eat and before that, when Laye was missing, she had gone two weeks without. It was stupid not to eat, she only received so many rations a day and that was it. Just like everyone else.

Pley was standing at their front door waiting for her, "You're late."

Fere stared at him, there was no way she was late. She had come straight from work, so she checked the time. She was not late, but she knew better than to argue as she approached him. Pley struck her in the face, and Fere leaned against the wall by the door, "I said, you're fucking late."

"I'm sorry." Fere knew there was nothing she could do, so she wasn't saying anything else.

He opened the door and shoved Fere through and toward the lift in the center of the towering building. They rode the lift down to the supply store at the bottom floor, and Fere brushed her hair over the side of her face, hiding the growing welp.

She grabbed the syrup sticks, soap, and water rations while Pley went for a hair trim. Fere stood outside of the door while he finished but didn't look anywhere except at the supplies in her hands. Pley received his payment ticket, and they approached the counter.

Pley handed over their ration allotment code, and the dark green man behind the counter scanned it as he reached for their payment tickets. He nodded to them, "You have additional syrup credits, you'll lose them if you don't use them by tomorrow."

Pley scowled at Fere, "Go buy the number of sticks we are allowed. Why would you pick up less?"

Great, she was in trouble again, and this time they were in public. Could she not do anything right? Pley would probably slam her hand in the door when they arrived back home. She was so thankful his penis didn't work anymore. Sometimes she fantasized about slamming it in a door like he was always doing to her left hand. Her middle finger had been crushed so many times it was just a metal rod, and it didn't bend anymore.

Gerne and Therow had no idea what it was like being a Vo-Pess woman, especially one bonded with someone close to power. Her bonded was the spawn of an elder, and he had always believed he was important, when Fere knew better. *He was just as much of a dung roll as the rest of the Vo-Pess men I know.*

They headed to the lift after Fere brought more syrup sticks to the counter and their rations account was updated. The white hallways of all the buildings were enough to make Fere want to spray paint them in the middle of the night, she would be whipped for it, but the wall would have color for a week until the crews came to make it uniform again.

Fere sensed something, but she wasn't sure what it was. She and Pley were walking down the hall to their home, she wasn't even trying to access any empathic skills. She only had a smidgen of the gift on a good day and Fere wasn't sure what she was sensing. Why now?

They entered their home and Pley went to their bar for a drink while Fere checked her messages. She only had one voice message from Gerne, and she played it. "Someone already noticed the dial was turned down on Laye. You fucking owe me Fere." Gerne sounded furious with her, but she didn't care.

Gerne and Therow had always been like brothers to her. They were the two people who helped Fere and Laye through their first few years of the Angle Wing training.

Fere didn't understand why the Vo-Pess people idolized the Angle Wings when being one was such a curse. There were other intelligence Wing teams, like the Wide Wings who specialized in long distance flight. They were treated similar to the Angles in training and, but they were larger in number.

Pley yelled at Fere from their bar in the next room, "Go back to the supply store, I need a bottle of Clear Nine." She knew damn well he had used up that allotment, and she dreaded having to explain it when she returned empty-handed. As her day grew worse by the moment, Fere understood Laye more than ever. Her face ached, *I would have taken the chance to run away too.*

Fere peered out of her home, and toward the capital in the distance, her eyes focused on the prison wing of the building. She wished she could save Laye, and they could run away together, but she knew that was nothing but a fantasy.

TWENTY-THREE
INVASION

Benitian stood at the loading bay door as Mac prepared to leave for Hyret. "I might be asking too much, but I am just dying to know. Who are you starting a war with old friend?"

Dressed in his new solid black, high-tech shield armor, Mac stared at Benitian as he decided how to explain he was planning to destroy an entire world for one woman. *The perfect woman, my little butterfly.* Mac smirked as he pressed the option to close the loading bay door, "It just depends on whether they cooperate or not. If they don't, I'll blast them all over the galaxy, and maybe you'll find out exactly who it is." Benitian knew Mac had no intention of giving it away, and he disappeared through the doors before the loading bay door shut.

Mac headed up to the bridge, the journey seemed to take an eternity, and he commanded, "Heret, let's move out. Inform the fleet and send them the coordinates I forwarded to your console."

Heret plugged away at his screen before asking, "Are you aware our end point is inside of a nebula?"

"You have my orders, helmsmen," Mac was growing tired of everyone questioning him. *They all listened to my father make endless nonsensical decisions without a word, I don't know why the fuck they choose now to start complaining!* He didn't care that what he was doing was pure chaos, he was a K'hornibus, and no one was taking what was his. The K'hornibus didn't give up without a fight, ever.

Mac was vibrating with anger as the wormhole opened, and his ship fleet moved inside as his hands clenched the arms of the chair he was harnessed in.

Within moments, the new Shardlow fleet poured out of the wormhole and Mac prepared the broadcast message he recorded the day before. He played it to his own fleet as well as pushing out the signal to blanket the Vo-Pess home world. Mac wanted everyone on the planet to see and hear the message. There would be no mistake about his demands.

As the video message began to play, Mac deployed the satellites from each fleet ship from his controls. The video began with Mac standing in his high-tech shining black armor with new silver skull mask on the bridge of the ship, "Vo-Pess, you have something that belongs to me. Your identity has been uncovered, and my surveillance feeds are being transmitted to collection hubs spread over the galaxy. I have deployed satellites around your world designed to turn every electronic you have into a surge explosive, which I can detonate at will. Give me what I demand, or I'll destroy everything you've built. I *will* destroy your world."

Landing coordinates pinged on the helm console as

Mac peered over at his brother. Yarle couldn't help it as he shook his head, and his words slipped under his breath, "Fucking mad man." Mac ignored him.

The ship descended and landed in a grassy area directly in front of what Mac assumed was their capital building. Mac, Yarle, and twenty of his most loyal guard poured out of the loading bay of the ship before it closed back behind them.

A single elderly man stood in front of a monument, and Mac looked up to the face of the statue of a woman who looked identical to Laye.

Approaching the man, Mac furiously pointed to the statue, "Where the fuck is she?!"

"I am Dynast Van-Well, who are you, and what do you want with our planet?" The old man's eyes were darting between Mac and his team.

Mac clenched his fists and resisted the urge to pull the long-range rail gun from his back and blow Van-Well away, "I am Voakes Mac'Kie Shardlow and you have someone who belongs to me. I demand her return!"

Van-Well took a step back and he bumped into the statue behind him, "Who are you speaking of?"

Mac leaned over and growled in his face, "Laye! I demand Laye! You have twenty minutes to produce her, alive, or I will destroy everything on Hyret. I will reveal the location of your planet to every system in the galactic center."

Van-Well tripped over his feet as he rushed inside. A crowd of people had gathered at the windows, and they scrambled away as Mac pushed through the door. The K'hornibus towered over the smaller statures of the Vo-Pess people. Mac stalked through the crowd as Van-Well was addressing what he assumed were the ruling council.

He walked up behind Van-Well just as he was finishing explaining, "...Angle Wing who defected and slaughtered my son."

With a guttural growl, Mac raised his arms and shook his fists in the air above Van-Well before grabbing him by the throat and raising him up as a Vo-Pess wrist spine was shot across the room and lodged in the side of Mac's hard skull. The council members all moved away from their seats as Mac roared at Van-Well, "I should kill you for what your son did to her. Your time is running out, give me Laye, or I will give my fleet the signal."

"You and your men would die along with us in the blast!" Van-Well squeaked as Mac squeezed his throat.

Eyes bulging with fury, Mac brought Van-Well's face even with his own, "Do I look like I'm afraid to die little man?"

Shaking under Mac's grasp, Van-Well conceded, "I need more time. Give me twenty more minutes. I will bring her to you." He moved achingly slow as he set Van-Well down, Mac glaring at him through his mask as the room went unnaturally silent. Van-Well turned to a guard at the end of the room, "Notify the Angle Wing team, and have them bring Laye to the court room. Be quick about it."

Mac turned to his brother who shrugged and looked around the room at all the small people in a multitude of colors. Yarle wanted to go home and finish the business with the Shrout, he still didn't understand why Mac had dragged them all out to the other end of the galaxy over a woman. Mac had plenty of women back home who he could have at any moment, Yarle did too. All their brothers were sought after men being that they were Shardlow. Minutes passed by and Mac seemed to grow more furious by the second. Yarle watched the door everyone faced when he spotted a maroon skinned woman pushing a chair. He couldn't peel his eyes from her as the doors were opened, and she wheeled in Laye who was slumped at an odd angle.

Fere wearily faced Mac and his brother as she moved Laye in front of them. Laye's head was leaned back, and her antennae hung limp behind her head. She was careful not to touch Laye's antennae as she pushed her chair.

Mac took in Laye's state, and he swung around to Van-Well shouting, "What the fuck did you do to her?!" Mac swiftly knelt in front of Laye, and gently lifted her head, being careful not to disrupt her free hanging antennae as he whispered, "Laye? What happened to you?" Fere's heart broke as she watched Mac try to reach her. Mac held her head in one hand as he gently lifted her eye lids, one after the other as he breathed, "Come on, come back to me." Laye blinked and Mac held his breath, waiting for her to respond. His hands shook as she moved her eyes around and blinked a few more times.

Her eyes flew open, and she sat up with a start, "No! No! I didn't open the box! It was shut so tightly. I know you didn't find a way out."

Laye searched the room, and she turned, her eyes falling on Fere, "Fere, what is he doing out of the box? I can't let the program find out about him; you have to help me put him back in!"

Fere couldn't hold it back as she shed a tear, one which Mac noticed, "What happened to her?"

Fere began to answer before Gerne aggressively wrapped his hand around her arm in a reminder to stay quiet. Her mouth parted and Fere searched the eyes of the K'hornibus men standing around Mac, her gaze finally falling on her broken friend as more tears spilled over.

Noticing the hand around Fere's arm holding her back from answering, Mac didn't know what else to do, so he carefully raised Laye from the wheelchair and lifted her into his arms. He turn to the Vo-Pess council, and glared at each one of them before turning to Fere, "Who are you to Laye?"

"She is my best friend," was all Fere could say as her voice cracked. Laye was safe again, and that was all she could ask for.

Mac turned to Yarle, "Take her."

Behind them Van-Well cried out, "You only asked for the one Angle Wing, you cannot have the other female!"

Mac turned to Van-Well, his body moving ominously slow, "And what the fuck are you going to do about it? You returned Laye damaged, and I'm taking another, so I don't blast your world into oblivion for what you've done."

In a move even she was in disbelief over, Fere yanked her arm away from Gerne's grip and she took two steps toward Mac and Laye. *If this is my chance out, and I could have a big, sexy, horned boyfriend, I'm all in.* Yarle gently slid his hand around her arm and she more than willfully turned herself over to him. This was her ticket out of hell and Fere was not passing it up. She took in Yarle with his battle armor and silver skull mask as they moved to the ship, she resisted the urge to lick him and claim him as hers. *I bet he tastes so good.*

Mac led the group out of the court building as Laye pressed herself against his chest, "I need to put you back in the box Mac, the program will cycle, and it will know you're here. It can't find you; I have to hide you; they can't have you."

When they were far enough from the door Fere whispered to Yarle, "Thank you." Yarle was at the point in his confusion that he just didn't care anymore, "I'm going to be honest with you, I have no idea what the fuck is going on."

"I heard that Yarle, shut the fuck up until we're back on the ship," Mac ordered without turning around. Yarle shook his head and dropped his hand holding Fere's arm, she made it clear she was not running.

Aiming for the lift, Mac was heading to his personal rooms, "Yarle you and Fere are with me. Inex, tell Heret to take us home and leave the satellites. If Laye doesn't recover, I'll blow Hyret's electronics for failing to meet their end of the agreement. Make sure he keeps the ship steady, we are not strapping in." *I might blow them anyway just because I want to.*

Behind him, Yarle asked, "Won't they just blow the satellites up when we leave?"

Silently thanking his friend Benitian, Mac smirked, "They can try but it's Iungo rolling shield tech I bought on Sinex. It will take them a long while if they ever do."

The door to Mac's rooms slid open as he approached, Yarle and Fere followed behind. Mac sat Laye on the bed and he kneeled in front of her, reaching up for her hands. Laye saw Fere standing by Mac, "How did you do it?"

Fere didn't understand and moved to sit next to Laye, "Laye you're not in the neural cycle anymore. This is real. Mac and I are real."

"What is a neural cycle?" Mac demanded as he took his mask off and threw it behind Laye on the bed.

Yarle interrupted, "Mac, what are you doing?" Mac

turned to Yarle and narrowed his eyes at his brother in confusion, "I don't give a fuck if this purple woman sees my face, if she wanted to kill me, she would have done it already."

Fere shrugged, and carefully answered Mac's question about the neural cycle. "Its a program they use in the prison. You're tortured with your own memories and trauma. The Vo-Pess use harsh punishments to keep our people from deviating from their duties. The neural cycle is their most extreme measure."

Mac rubbed Laye's hands as she stared at him in an odd way and blinked repeatedly. Laye shifted her attention to Fere, "Did you sneak in my prison cell and change the program? How did you do it? You were always so good at hacking, so much better than I was."

They could feel the ship taking off, and Fere squeezed her eyes shut, "This is real, You're not in the cycle anymore. I unplugged you." Fere tipped her head to Mac that she needed to speak to him and the two moved to the other end of the room as Yarle stood by Laye.

Fere held her eyes on Laye, "She thinks she's still trapped in the cycle. The elder council ordered for me to plug her into the device, and I disobeyed part of my orders. I set the program to the lowest setting. Someone found out and reset the program to the highest setting like the elders wanted. She was only inside for a little over a day that way, I can't believe it's this bad."

Staring at Fere, Mac frowned, "You willfully came with us, why?"

"My life was similar to hers," Fere knew that would be explanation enough as she reached up and touched her own cheek where a deep bruise was healing. Satisfied with her answer, Mac went back and sat down next to Laye. "We are going home to K'hurian. You're safe now."

"No one is safe. The program will find out, we have to get you back in the box. I have to hide you Mac. They can't have you. Your memories are only for me, and I won't let the program take them." Laye peered at Mac with desperation in her eyes, and it took everything in him not to give the order to destroy Hyret.

TWENTY-FOUR
FINDING LAYE

Standing outside the door of his bedroom at his home in K'rin City, Mac leaned against the metal wall waiting for Fere to come and sit with Laye so he could take care of some Shrout business. Fere came toward him from her room down the hallway. "How is she today?"

"No better. She woke up every hour shaking me, and demanding that I hide back in the box." Mac was wearing night clothes, and he had only worn his mask from the ship to his home. It rested on the floor in the entry way.

Fere shook her head, "When we took her back to Hyret, she hid away her memories of you so the cycle wouldn't detect them and use them to torment her."

"You were part of the team who took her?" Mac asked, his full attention stolen by that fact.

Fere looked up at Mac, she had no intention of lying, "Yes. Dynast Van-Well sent her own team to find her. Initially, I was concerned and thought she and Leem had been attacked. I had no idea we would find Leem's body with a hole drilled in his charred skull. I would have done something to lead them off the trail if I had known she defected."

The sound of footsteps down the hallway rang through the metal walls as Yarle approached, "Sorry I'm late."

Mac eyed his brother, "Take the fucking mask off, I don't want you to scare Laye."

"Mac?" Yarle asked, confused at why he was taking his mask off in front of Fere. Mac grumbled as he opened the door to his room, "Who the fuck cares Yarle."

Grabbing his riding leather, he went into his bathroom and changed as Fere crawled into their bed next to a sleeping Laye. Yarle sat in a chair next to the bed and reluctantly pulled his mask off.

Fere couldn't help sneaking peeks at Yarle as Mac left for his meeting. Her people were small, and she was no exception, she hardly came up to the chest of the towering K'hornibus men. Fere understood the appeal, Yarle was strapped with muscle and those masks? Now she was sure if she had been in Laye's position Fere would have done the same thing. *That tall man is something out of my wildest fantasies. Laye is a lucky bitch.* Her stomach turned thinking of Pley and her home. Her face must have told on her as Yarle's mouth twisted to the side before he sincerely asked, "Are you alright?"

Should I tell him the truth? "I will be eventually. I'm just trying to comprehend that I escaped the Vo-Pess with my life," Fere placed her hand on Laye as she pushed Hyret out of her mind. Studying her face, Yarle noticed the dark bruise, and with a chill to his tone asked, "Who hit you?"

"My bonded partner Pley. Or former partner now I guess? Anyway. He can't hurt me anymore," Fere admitted, not meeting Yarle's piercing lemon eyes. Yarle grumbled something about skinning alive and she distinctly heard him toss around the idea that Mac had been right after all.

Laye turned over and sighed loudly before sitting up and startling at Fere sitting next to her, "Fere! When were we here? I don't remember this place. I killed Leem with a drill, he's not real. You're not real either. I just wish I knew where this place was. Did we have a mission here?"

Fere looked around Laye to Yarle, "I don't know what it's going to take to make her come back. She retreated into her mind and locked herself inside." The dry air was scratching at Fere's throat. "May I have some water?" Yarle froze mid breath, his gaze heated her to the core. "I'll be right back."

The door shut behind Yarle and Laye turned to Fere, "K'hornibus have a thing with water, I haven't fully figured it out yet."

That statement was different from the way she spoke before, so Fere kept her talking, "What do you think it means? Should we ask Yarle when he comes back?"

Laye gave Fere a wide grin as she answered in a whisper, "This isn't real, but we can ask anyway."

Yarle came back in the bedroom and handed Fere the glass of water as Fere asked, "Laye and I would like to know the significance of fetching water for someone."

Yarle's mouth parted, and he stared blankly at Fere, he cleared his throat and reluctantly answered, "Presenting someone with drinking water in any capacity is an intimate gesture of care and affection."

Fere peered down at the glass of water in her hands, "Oh." *If that big horny headed man needs a girlfriend, I am right here.*

Drinking it down she handed the glass back to Yarle

and he brushed his hand against hers as he took it. Laye leaned over to Fere and failed miserably at her attempt to whisper, "I knew it. I think he likes you."

Fere's mouth dropped open at the same time as Laye fell back against the headboard laughing. Yarle couldn't help but laugh too. The joy was short lived as she shot up with concern, "Oh no! The program! It can't find out about any of this!" Laye threw the covers off and stood up, Yarle took a few steps toward the door as she frantically searched the room, "How do I put it all back in? How did it escape? I locked it away so tight but why is this all new? Did I forget to hide something and the program found it?"

Fere moved next to Yarle, "This wasn't the place where she was before, she was in an apartment right?"

"She was in Mac's canyon home. Father always sent him to the middle check point, and that's where he had her hidden," Yarle leaned back against the door and watched Laye dig under Mac's bed, pulling out old photos of his children.

Laye opened the box, "I don't understand why there are new things in my head."

"I'll message Mac we need to bring her to the Canyon. He should be wrapping up his meeting soon," Yarle offered as he understood Fere's thought process about Laye.

Fere nodded as Yarle gently touched her arm while he went by her to grab his communication device. Yarle's tail whipped behind him as he sent the message to Mac.

Kneeling in front of Laye, Fere whispered to herself, "How do we wake you up?"

Yarle put his hand on Fere's shoulder, causing her to freeze as he read Mac's message. "He's on his way and says to have Laye ready. He's landing in his courtyard with a transport." Yarle's brow creased as he added, "When the fuck have we ever used an air transport?"

Fere stayed with Laye as Yarle packed up some supplies from Mac's kitchen, and the hover-transport landed in the courtyard just as Yarle went to retrieve them. Yarle moved to one side of Laye as Fere moved to the other and together they guided her toward the front door, Laye seemed like a lost child with wonder in her eyes.

Mac opened the door and scooped Laye into his arms, he was wearing his old mask, and Laye reached up to touch it. "I don't know how to put you back. I'm so sorry Mac. I keep trying, but I don't know how."

He wondered if instead of aiming for her to meet him in reality, he would meet her where she was. "We can figure it out together, like we did before." Laye agreed with a nod as he boarded the transport, Fere and Yarle found their seats behind he and Laye. The transport took off with Inex at the helm, and they headed to Mac's mid-point home.

Mac watched Laye during the transport, and her dazed demeanor terrified him, *have I lost her forever? She is so close, yet so far away from me.* He pulled her closer to him on the bench seat, and she leaned her head onto his chest.

Fere was focused on Laye when Yarle raised his arm and rested it on the top of the seat behind her head. She had a hard time thinking about anything else besides that one place of contact for the duration of the flight.

When they landed, Yarle slid his hand over her shoulder before he rose up and put his hand out for her. Fere wanted to scream in frustration, the terrifying K'hornibus man was gentler than any of the Vo-Pess had ever been, and she had only been around Mac and Yarle for a short time.

Mac carried Laye inside and brought her back to his bedroom as Fere and Yarle stood in the living area waiting. Mac appeared back in the doorway, "She's resting. I have her if you two want to take a break."

Yarle nodded and tipped his head to the side for Fere to follow him as he went outside. "Do you want to walk down the canyon river?" Yarle wasn't sure what else there was to do, and he was glad he offered when Fere brightened up.

Why the hell am I so nervous? When had a woman ever made me feel awkward like this? He was truly beginning to understand why Mac had acted so oddly. There was something about Fere that he found intoxicating, could it be her resilience? She went ahead of him, and he watched her steps, her stride was graceful and full of pep. Her round bottom bounced as she dodged a small cactus, and Yarle found himself wanting to sink his teeth into that luscious ass.

Out of nowhere, Fere squeaked, "Oh!" As she dove for something ahead of her on the path. Alarmed, Yarle took two large steps forward to see what she jumped for. Yarle could have detonated his blood pressure was so high. "Don't move."

"Why?" Fere jumped up with a viper's head pinched between her fingers and the body dangling below, the snakes tail end nearly touching the ground. *She has no idea how much danger she is in,* Yarle put his hands up, "That viper's venom can kill an adult K'hornibus in twenty minutes." Fere smiled, "Oh, poor little sugar baby!" She brought the snakes face around to look at it, and she smiled at its open mouth, filled with fangs. "You're a bad little baby. I need to move you." Fere's wide black wings emerged from her nanotech armor, and she flew into the sky when they spread out. Yarle watched, horrified, as Fere flew down the canyon with the deadly snake and landed about a mile away. *This woman is going to be the death of me.* He slid his hand over his chest where his heart was raging, "She's a fearless warrior, and I will be making her mine." *Mac wasn't out of line after all, I may need to apologize.*

She waved to him as she entered the sky again, the snake no longer in her grasp. She left Yarle rubbing his brow as she flew back.

TWENTY-FIVE

THE FERE SITUATION

After their eventful stroll down the river, Fere followed Yarle up the stairs and he went into the kitchen. Once he removed his mask, he pulled out some food from Mac's freezer and set it on the counter before meeting Fere's gaze. "I don't even know what you eat,"

Fere giggled at him. She licked her lips, *I want to taste you,* "I eat sugar." Yarle furrowed his brow, "That's all you eat?" Fere pursed her lips, she was not elaborating on her inner monologue just yet.

His mouth watered, and it wasn't from the food he was preparing for himself. Yarle had the urge to toss Fere on the counter and find out what her flavor was instead, he knew after her answer she would have the sweetest pussy he ever ate. *I really need to give Mac an apology.*

Fere eyed him suspiciously, "Yes. Why?"

Yarle released a rough breath as he reached over to flip on the heating box and open it. He selected a low temperature before sliding in the tray of frozen meat and closing the door. When he finished, he reached over and opened the pantry cabinet, spotting a box of honey jars.

Yarle picked one up and turned to give it to Fere. Her eyes widened as she took the jar and sniffed it. "We usually ate manufactured syrup sticks back on Hyret. I've only had true honey a few times," her long straw-like tongue unrolled and dove into the natural amber syrup. Watching Fere suck the honey from the jar left him pressed against the counter, trying to hold his length inside of him.

Fere noticed Yarle's hands gripping the counter as she finished slurping up the honey. Fere had a pleading man before her, and he seemed as though he wanted to eat her alive. *If that horny headed man touches me right now, I might yank his pants off.* Mac quietly came out of the room, "Are you cooking something?"

"I put in enough meat for both of us," Yarle answered as Mac sat on a stool at the end of the counter.

They sat in silence for a while before Mac spoke up, "I have a fucked-up idea to help Laye and you two are going to need to go camping or go back home." Yarle and Fere turned to him expectantly, and he shrugged, "You don't want to know. She's been asleep, so I won't wake her, but when she rises on her own, you two need to be gone."

Mac was right, Yarle did not want to know. Yarle noticed Fere's shift in her seat, "Do you want to go camping with me? I would warn you about the sand vipers, but you seem to have already made friends with them." Fere smirked, that viper had been adorable, "Camping sounds great."

"Explain." Mac's eyes moved between the two of them.

Yarle grinned, seeming proud, "Fere picked up a sand viper and relocated it a mile away during the walk we went on by the river."

Mac seemed like he had startled as he turned to Fere, "Are all of you like this?"

Fere laughed, "No, a lot of my people are just in the general military and have normal jobs. The Vo-Pess like Laye and I were born with specialized wings allowing us to fly faster than any other wing type. Other wing types are long range or the smaller precision flyers. When we emerge and our wing type is visible, it pre-determines us to be enlisted in certain groups. Laye and I were Angle Wings, which is part of Vo-Pess intelligence, our training was brutal compared to most."

Mac knew all too well. "I've never seen anyone kill like Laye can." Yarle cringed as he reached up to rub his top horn. "Seeing the Shrout brother with his own horns sticking out of his neck was disturbing."

Fere had no idea what they were talking about, so Mac clarified, "I left for the border, and Laye was here by herself. We had a widespread attack from a clan we're at war with and three of them came here for me. Laye brutally slaughtered them with my knife. I'm not even sure how she had the knife, I keep my weapons locked away."

Fere smirked at Mac, "We can break in and out of almost anything, she probably picked the lock."

Yarle and Mac both stared at Fere before a timer went off on the cooking meat. Yarle pulled it out and prepared he and Mac a plate before Yarle intended to sit on the couch. He passed Mac his plate, and he stayed seated on the stool to eat. Yarle stopped as he passed Fere and sat his plate down before he grabbed a glass and filled it with water.

Fere stood frozen as Yarle reached up and set the glass in front of her before picking his plate back up. *Don't grind on the stool, don't grind on the stool.* She carefully took the glass, and he signaled for her to follow him. They ignored Mac staring, with his mouth open, at their water exchange as Yarle guided her to the couch. When Yarle sat down, he hooked his arm over the couch and gave his brother hand gesture which meant, *fuck off.*

Yarle put his arm around Fere, and she moved to sit closer to him as he took a small slab of meat from his plate and bit into it. She drank down the water as he finished his plate, and he took everything back to the kitchen to clean it before putting it away.

Mac had been staring at the kitchen wall as he chewed his food and Yarle tipped his head for Fere to follow him. "Bedrolls are in the storage closet," Mac called to Yarle before he shut the door.

Yarle followed Fere downstairs and grabbed a bedroll, a pack of travel bedding, and two coats before meeting her outside. The system star was setting and the shadows stretched across the inside of the canyon as Fere soaked up the last of its light. A chill ran over her skin as a cold breeze swirled by her, Yarle had perfect timing as he slid a thick coat over her shoulders. It was so long it dragged the ground and Fere wrapped it around her. She tapped her armor tab, and it receded, she wanted to feel the warm coat.

Yarle noticed her action and took a step in front of her, blocking her path. He had to know what was under that armor as he reached down and took either side of her coat to open it. Fere didn't move as Yarle studied her, she was wearing the long sleeved fitted under clothes she always wore, but she had never thought about how sheer it was until this moment. She knew he could see her every curve and dip, and he softly growled as he reached forward to rub his knuckles over her nipple. Fere was breathless as he leaned forward and sniffed her neck before he brushed his lips under her ear. "You smell too good to be true," Yarle whispered against her neck and buried his face in Fere's loose curly black hair.

Fere wanted to rip her clothes off as she shuttered inside from the contact. She squeezed her thighs together as he tilted his head in the opposite direction of their walk, "Let's camp back this way, I know a place."

Resisting the urge to strip and show him her nude figure, Fere followed Yarle for several minutes before he turned back to her, "This is it. There is a family of jumping juleps nesting around here and they dissuade the sand vipers."

Yarle rolled out the pad and set up the bedding while Fere sat next to the pack and peered longingly at the stars. Noticing her demeanor, Yarle asked, "Do you miss your home?"

"No!" She frowned as she continued, "I hated my life. It was nothing but misery, every day."

Yarle took her hand and pulled her to him before he sat them down on the bedroll with her straddling his lap, "We are going to change that."

Under her coat he reached up and slid his hands in her shirt to her breasts and she moved her hips to grind against his lap. She stole short breaths from the chilled air as her skin wasn't sure what to do with the feeling of his hands on her, her lower belly heated, and she wiggled her hips.

Yarle was giddy over her rocking hips, he slid his hands down to her waist and pushed the top of her pants down. Fere fought for more breath, no one had every touched her like that and she held back a yelp.

Concern began brewing in Yarle and he had to ask,

"Are you new at this? "Fere shook her head and nearly sobbed as she rubbed her hands over Yarle's leather jacket, "No." Yarle's length poured out of its hiding place and pressed against his pants as he understood and whispered against her lips, "You've never had an orgasm have you?"

Fere had heard of them but touching yourself was a borderline crime for the Vo-Pess, she didn't want to answer so she didn't. Her failure to respond must have been answer enough as Yarle rubbed his thumbs up and down the sides of her hips.

"I want you to fuck me." Fere demanded as she raised her hands back to his shoulders. Yarle shook his head and mouthed no with a smirk, "Not yet pretty butterfly, I haven't made you cry for me yet."

Fere's eyes went wide, *what does that mean?* She reeled as she was picked up and placed on the bedding, Yarle was over her and inhaling deeply over her breast before he pulled her shirt up just over her nipples. He licked her nipple once before he leaned up to take off his jacket, then his shirt, before he threw both behind him. His body was magnificent, and Fere gasped trying to wrap her head around how she ended up under this masterpiece of a man. She could have sung when he brought his mouth down on her chest, tasting her everywhere. He gently kissed and tasted her nipples, each one sending a streak of lightening through her. She gasped as she felt his hot breath brushing against her belly as he slid her pants off.

Unable to hold back at the sight of her nude and spread figure, Yarle crawled down between her legs and moved his hands under her rear to lift her up. He kneaded her ass as he ran his tongue against her from back to front, the delighted sound as she writhed, she made Yarle feel like a feral animal, ready to devour his prey. Her taste was enough to make him cum in his pants, she tasted like Fere flavored sugar.

Fere's hips rocked side to side as Yarle pressed his face into her heat, "Oh!" She had no idea what was coming, but it filled her with a contradictory mix of lust and trepidation as she grew closer to a precipice she had never come near before. Yarle ran is rough tongue up and down her nerves and her head lifted to see.

Fere met Yarle's eyes as he cupped his mouth around her nerves and sucked her most sensitive flesh between his lips as he continued to assault her with his tongue.

Trembling, Fere felt him grasp her hips and hold them causing her to come undone. She fell over the edge and leaned back, crying out into the night. Her hips clenched as the pleasure slammed into her, Fere had never felt anything so euphoric. Licking her until she yelped once more, Yarle wanted every drop. He took his pants off and stood over her. "Stand up and extend your wings."

Fere did as he asked, and her black wings peeled away from her skin, stretching out in the darkness. Her beautiful, unique vein pattern was only visible when she shifted her wings under the moonlight. The undershirt she wore rode up with her wings and he pulled it off. He was painfully erect as he lifted her and lined her up with his tip.

Fere angled her hips where she wanted them as he slid her down onto his length. She leaned her head back and groaned at how he filled her, his length seemed to hit just the right place. Fere ground her hips into him, and he slid his hands around her waist to hold her up just so he could bring her back down.

All it took was a few strokes and Yarle's length split in two, causing Fere to straighten, "That's new." He smirked as he ground her down on his length. Her little curvy body was light weight and Yarle was beginning to believe he had found paradise between her legs.

Her black wings extended out behind her under the starlight, slowly flapping back and forth as Yarle pressed into her. The two parts of his length twirled inside, and she felt another orgasm brewing, this time she knew what it was, and a thrill burst through her. She gripped him with her legs and squeezed as she rolled her hips against his length. Her gaze found Yarle's, and she breathed, "Again?" With that his length pulsed, curling forward, and causing her to gasp. When she cracked this time, Yarle spilled over with her, and they both curled toward one another.

Catching his breath, Yarle reached up with one hand and tipped her chin up, "You're too fucking perfect." When his lips met hers, he kissed her with a burning intensity.

TWENTY-SIX
MORNING BELLS

Early in the morning before the system star rose over the land, Laye sat straight up in bed after sleeping since the day before, "Something's wrong with the program."

Mac leaned over her, and he knew what he was about to do would either work and he would have her back, or he would become the most fucked up male in the galactic center. He had already threatened to destroy a world for her, so he was going for it.

"Let's fix it together, my little butterfly," Mac purred in her ear.

Laye whispered, "We have to be quick before the program notices."

Mac shook his head no as he slid his hand over her chest, "I'm taking my time, and we are going to beat the program together."

Laye was visibly rattled and Mac kissed her before whispering over her lips, "I don't give up, it doesn't matter where I am. Even if it's an echo of me in your mind, no box could hold me forever. I would eventually break out and find you. One thing I know the program can't do, is make you feel like I can."

With that, he lifted her shirt and pulled it over her head, carefully stroking the edges of her wings. She shivered under his touch, and he pulled her to him as he leaned in and tasted her awaiting flesh. He licked her along the center of her chest before sucking and licking each of her nipples, Mac felt her thighs rubbing together and held them down. She gasped, and he faced her whispering, "Not yet."

He rolled her over on top of his chest as he lie back on his bed, his hands starting at the top and gently rubbing down her wings. She twitched and whimpered as he traced along the edges, moving with his touch. He sensed when her exuberant shiver was coming, so he grabbed her leg and rotated her around to pull her center to his mouth. Face down on his perfect abs, Laye wrapped her arms around his thick muscled body as he dove his tongue inside of her, her heart sang as he growled against her flesh. *This has never happened before, the program didn't allow this.* Laye felt Mac spread her legs as he licked her along her nerves, giving her a swirling sensation in her heart. Could it be? *Is this real?* Her orgasm crested and she tipped over, shattering into a million pieces as she cried out and gasped with pure confusion. Laye panted as he lapped up the results of her pleasure. *An orgasm would have never happened in the program.* "Mac, is that really you?" She pleaded to the great mother Relit that it was his skin she was touching.

He made a sound she never wanted to hear again as he flipped her around and grasped her to his chest, "It's me. Please come back to me. I need you to be Laye again, I need you to be whole." Laye wrapped her arms around him and sobbed, "This is real? You found me? And Fere is here too?!" She wrapped herself around Mac like a constrictor and buried her face in his neck as she chanted in a whisper, "You came for me."

"Things are different now. I lead the Shardlow's, and we don't need to hide anymore." Mac set his hand on her head and noticed her antennae were coiled back up in her hair like they should be.

He rubbed her arm as he felt her tear slide down his neck. "I would have destroyed everything on Hyret if they hadn't given you back to me. I left satellites designed to detonate all their electronics in orbit with shields, if they try anything further, I'll keep my word and destroy everything they've ever built."

Laye had never known true peace like she did in that moment, and she melted into Mac. He felt her relax and he moved his arms under her to hold her up. He moved from the bed with her and went in his bathroom, turning on his shower without setting her down. He felt the stream, and when it was hot, he led them both under the flow of water. Laye didn't move as he brushed her wet hair from her face.

She had never looked so peaceful. Just like their first intimate encounter, Mac was well aware what he did to have her back was outrageous, but seeing her able to let her guard down and just be Laye? It was worth it, and he would do it a thousand times over.

"I've never been afraid before, not truly. When I saw the feed of my living area was down, I lost my mind," Mac admitted.

Laye sat up straight and stared at Mac, "How the sugar balls did you find Hyret?!"

"When I was sewing you up, I put a tracking bead

inside of your neck," Mac released a deep belly laugh at the surprise in her eyes.

Laye brought her hand to her scar on her throat and felt around, "You put a tracking device in me? I can feel it!"

"It's a rare element that has a harmless radioactive signal. On any other scanner except for one like mine, it shows as a dirt particle. My tracking system utilizes travel wormholes to obtain information on the farther reaches of the galaxy. All my children have them implanted. I had spent almost everything I had left on it when I sent my children to Keru, and I had paid off their tuition and living expenses." Mac grimaced with the memory of the bill to send them all away to school and then finding out the cost of the tracking devices. He had to pick up side jobs to make up for it.

Laye gave Mac a soft smile as she rested against him, "The Vo-Pess put an electronic tracker inside of my shoulder when I emerged. I dug it out and crushed it when I defected. Now that I have yours inside of me, instead of feeling trapped like before, I feel cared about. There is truly a fine line between control and love." *Did I just say love? Oh no. I am not opening that can of syrup.* Mac turned the shower off and tried to wrap a towel around her, but she shook her head, "Are Yarle and Fere here?"

He shook his head no and she grinned and wiggled her legs to be let down. The folded creases where her wings rested against her skin never dried well if she didn't shake off, so Mac wrapped the towel around himself instead as he followed her to the shop down the stairs. She stood in the center and released such a monumental shiver her feet left the ground, and she landed with a plop when it was over. She had sprayed water in a circle all around her. "I would always rather shake off than use a towel."

Mac couldn't help but admire her as she stood in front of him, and when he sat on the stairs, she crawled into his lap. Her mind seemed to have been sorted, but she admitted, "I might lose my grip again and there is no telling when it will happen. Many of our people end up with memory problems as we age, sometimes I think it's how the Vo-Pess live. I don't ever want to be trapped in my own mind like that again, but if I do? I am so thankful I have you. I know you will take care of me."

"I'll do anything for you." Mac pulled her leg over his lap, so she was straddling him.

Laye rested her forearms on his shoulders, "How did you talk your father into stepping down?" Mac slapped her on the ass and grinned, "I shot him."

"Oh." Laye should have known that. It finally dawned on her then, "Wait, so you really are the one in charge now?"

"That and I found out my father was hoarding trillions of pounds of neodymium deposits around our southern pole," Mac explained, and he watched her face change as she did the math in her head.

Laye stared at Mac and blinked repeatedly, "Oh. When I thought I was in a Melior made ship that was real right? Those ships are outrageous and with a combined fire power it would be enough to decimate the surface of a world. You showed up with how many ships?"

"Fifteen," was all Mac said and Laye deadpanned him.

Licking her lips she whistled, "You could have smashed Hyret into the size of an asteroid with all those magnetic charges."

"Like I said, I'll do anything for you," Mac growled as he ground against her.

Laye rolled her hips against him, and she could feel

how hard he was for her underneath his towel. Straddling him, she reached down and pulled his towel off and lined herself up with his tip. She slid down until she seated herself, and he groaned as he wrapped his arms around her. Laye lifted and slid down few strokes when she felt him come undone inside of her, his length separating and rolling.

Something is different this time, Mac leaned up and kissed her forehead as he moved inside of her. The way he was looking at her, Laye could have sobbed aloud. She moved her hands from his chest to his face, and he leaned into her touch, she felt herself beginning to tip over and she didn't want this moment to end.

She felt him curl up inside of her and Laye came undone, crashing into another fit of pleasure. She shook as it took hold and moved through her. Mac squeezed her hips as he poured inside of her, his release pulsed, and she reached for breath as her pleasure crested with delightful heat.

Laye spread out and rested against him as they remained joined. she could hear his heart, and she memorized the way it beat. She was spent, and she felt him lift her up off him and carry her to his bed.

Mac brought a cloth to clean her before laying on the other side of her. He was still reeling over having her back, and he couldn't take his eyes away, "You do something to me, it's like an addiction. I can't ever get enough of you, and I find I don't care what part you share. You make me want to change things on my world." Laye gave Mac a wide, dazzling grin. "What are you changing?"

"I had a meeting with a few Sarter Kingdom representatives when we arrived back on K'hurian about buying terraforming equipment from the Queen. The only problem is the Shrout will cause disruptions for the people working on the terraforming. We can start in K'rin City, but the Sarter Queen has asked that we eliminate the problem before we proceed with the rest of the planet."

"You need to assassinate the Shrout leadership and take over their territory, so they don't interfere?" Laye was all ears and ready to form a plan.

Mac smirked at her piqued interest, "You are going to rest for a little while before we do anything about the Shrout." Laye curled up and Mac wondered if he would get any sleep as she ground her ass into him.

TWENTY-SEVEN
ANTENNAE

Fere and Yarle opened Mac's door and quietly went inside as Mac stood in the kitchen preparing himself a meal. Neither of them wanted to ask.

Mac didn't look up from his pan of snake meat. "Laye is much more of herself. She woke up confused, but it only took her a few minutes to regain her clarity."

They relaxed with the good news. Fere sat on the stool and held her nose over the scent of the meat as Yarle stood close to her, close enough he was making contact. Mac turned to hand Yarle a plate, certainly noticed how close his brother was to Fere. Yarle seemed to be moving quickly, Mac bit his lips together. *I can't really say a damn thing but, I will anyway because it's Yarle. He was just supposed to entertain Fere not fuck her.*

When Yarle took the plate from Mac, Fere followed him to the couch, and they sat down together. Passing Yarle to check on Laye, Mac aggressively patted him on the head, "Fuck you, Yarle." He could hear Yarle clear his throat behind him as Mac went into his room and shut the door too fast to hear the rebuttal.

Laye was sitting in the middle of the floor with her legs crossed and eyes closed. She held her hands up even with her extended antennae. Mac knelt down in front of her, "Your friend is here."

Laye kept her eyes closed as she smiled, "I felt her when she was outside, and I could sense when she came inside. She is happier than she's ever been. I just need a few more minutes."

It struck Laye she had forgotten to tell Mac about how she could sense him, and her eyes flew open. "Can I try something with you?"

"Anything," Mac offered as his brow creased in concern.

She reached her hands out, and placed them on either side of his face, guiding him down as she sat up on her knees to bring her forehead to his. Laye closed her eyes and reached for Mac's horns with her antennae and her empathically sensitive tendrils wrapped around them.

Closing his eyes, Mac sucked in a tense breath as he and Laye connected on such a level he felt she had exposed his soul.

Laye was overjoyed as she whispered, "It's working, I can feel you."

In a rush, Mac felt her in the same way. He was overwhelmed by the gratitude she had for him, this woman was ready to do *anything* for him. Just like he had done for her. She truly was his perfect match, and he sucked in quick breaths of air trying to process her complex feelings.

"Breathe slowly, like you're meditating. I have substantially more emotion than a typical Vo-Pess and likely more than most creatures in the galaxy. I've never been able to allow it to exist before, and I understand it is a lot of brain chemistry happening. I know I am overwhelming, if you need to stop." Laye offered, but she was already feeling him calm.

Raising his hands to her shoulders to hold her in place, Mac did as she suggested and inhaled slowly. "No, you're not overwhelming. You're fucking perfect. I swear I can feel your soul. It's like a stationary, raging cyclone. All around is chaos, but you have a calm inner eye. I know that's where you hid all our memories. I can feel some of them still left inside of the box you created to hide them in, or are those your hidden moments now? The ones you treasure, no longer hidden, and now tucked in a safe place. Everything that makes you who you are is perfect. Don't ever hold yourself back again."

Laye whispered, "The inner calm space is only there because of you. It's the calm you gave me, that little bit of security. That's where I hid everything. You gave me something to build on, something solid and immovable."

Laye could feel Mac swell with affection at her words, and she felt a pang of guilt for tapping into his emotions without asking when they had been in the mountains. "What's wrong?" Mac sensed it as the feeling occurred.

A flash of sadness fell over her as Laye admitted, "When we returned from the mountains, you fell asleep, and I may have felt up your horns with my antennae."

She felt something raucous brewing, and her antennae flew away from his horns just as Mac roared with laughter. Laye bit her lips together as Mac wiped his eyes. "I think that's the most ludicrous thing anyone has ever said to me."

"Did you manage to forget what I did to you when I

brought you to my father's home?" Mac stood up and helped her from the floor. Laye shook her head as she opened the bedroom door, "Do not act like that wasn't the right choice."

Mac slapped her ass, and in the living, room was Fere standing by the couch with Yarle nowhere to be found.

Laye fell into Fere's open arms, and the two squeezed one another like they had been apart for years. Now that they could allow their guard down, they felt one another and connected in a whole new way. Fere whispered, "You're strong today, I think you're enhancing my own sliver of a gift."

Mac noticed both of their antennae popping up and down out of their hair as they embraced. He reached up and rubbed his horn, those were some incredible antennae. His hand was wrapped around his horn when something struck him, "You can regulate the flow of what goes in and out of those antennae right?"

The two Vo-Pess women seemed to flip a switch with the question, they both turned and Laye nodded. Their understanding that his question was business without explanation was fascinating. He marveled at their ability to flash into action.

Now his heart squeezed for an entirely different reason, he had not even considered the fact that he had just stolen two of the most skilled assassins, likely in all the galactic center.

"Angle Wings are sought after as sires because we are fast, and we carry the empathic genes. We are expert inter-rogators. Fere can do everything I can do, except project her gift." Laye explained as Yarle came in the door.

"I'm better at math," Fere interjected. Laye fluttered her

lashes as she rolled her eyes, "I knew you would say that. I failed *one* math class."

Mac signaled for Yarle. "Fere, I want you to see if you can sense Yarle's emotions through his horns. Can you do that for me?"

Beaming to help, Fere nodded as Yarle curled his lip, "What?"

"Kneel down," Mac pointed to Yarle, and he gave Mac a side eye as he reluctantly complied, sitting back on his feet.

Fere got on her knees and sat up, so her face was even with Yarle's, his eyes were brimming with concern. She smiled and assured, "I won't hurt you."

I do not believe you. He had seen what Laye had done to the Shrout brothers who came for Mac, and these two women frankly scared the sand devils out of him. She closed her eyes and Yarle tried to stay calm as she wrapped her antennae around his horns. He worryingly peered up at Mac who pointed at him to pay attention.

Yarle snapped his eyes shut, and that's when he felt her, like a soft song entering his mind. He relaxed his shoulders and was in awe of how delighted Fere was feeling, her heart was pure and kind. Inside of her was a vast, turbulent sea with a small tropical island off to one side. The island seemed to be her sanctuary, it was cheery and full of life.

He was thankful he folded, and Mac had brought them all to this point. Yarle had never cared about women or relationships before, and he sensed himself shifting. He hoped Fere understood how badly he wanted her.

Fere was giddy as she felt everything Yarle was sorting through when she felt something click into place, like a key opening a lock. She gasped as the room became wider, her gift reaching much further. Fere could feel Laye standing nearby, and that was something she had never been able to do.

Her heart pounded and Yarle held back a startle as she realized she had her pathway wide open. Fere unraveled her antennae and stood up. "I think something just changed, I can feel Laye, and our antennae are not touching."

Yarle rose from the floor and stared at Mac like he had changed his life.

"You can?!" Laye nearly hurdled out of her skin. They had been working with Fere on projecting her gifts for their whole emerged lives. Fere nodded, and her eyes went wide, "I can feel you without trying."

"Regulate it like in training, lift the bridge," Laye instructed as she nearly burst with excitement.

Smiling, Fere agreed, "I have it."

"We are willing to do whatever is needed to secure the planet so you can begin the terraforming project." Laye met Fere's eyes and Fere whole heartedly agreed.

Mac looked down at the two women like they were the most priceless thing in the universe. "We are waiting on some supply shipments before we begin planning. I want you two in charge of the invasion because that's exactly what this will be. We need to make all the territories one, and there is only one way to achieve that on K'hurian. There are a few smaller territories up north, but they are nomadic, and they will remain untouched. Our only concern is with the Shrout. We will begin planning next week after we rest. I have plans for the four of us back in K'rin, the transport is ready when we are."

Laye and Fere grabbed one another, each of them so filled with hope and delight their bodies wildly vibrated, and they lifted off the floor.

Yarle stood stunned while Mac laughed and slipped on his mask. "I will never get bored of that."

TWENTY-EIGHT
THE CALM

They climbed aboard the transport and as they flew toward K'rin, Laye had to resist the urge to press herself against the glass window.

The open sky above K'rin was bustling with hovering construction equipment. Flying cranes moved large concrete walls, and construction workers buzzed around the structures like bees.

"Please tell me we are going to have a tour of your plans, I'm dying to know what's going on down there," Laye admitted as she leaned up as far as she could so she could see out of the window as the transport angled up and over the tall wall around the city.

Mac turned her toward him. "How did I know you would have questions about everything?" She returned a bright smile.

A transport dropped through the atmosphere towing what looked to be a building sized block of ice down into a rounded structure, and Laye bent herself around trying to see it, but finally gave up and stood. Steam surrounded the ice as it descended through the sky.

"I hired the Sarter Kingdom to tow a small ice moon through a wormhole, and it's being divided up in orbit. The ice will be delivered to our reconstructed reservoir, and it will provide us plenty of water to begin enclosed city terraforming. We already have shielding up to reduce water loss in the air as we irrigate our city crop lands." Mac explained as the transport landed in his courtyard.

Two guards carried in crates, which Laye was sure she could fit five of herself inside.

His front door was wide open, and a beautiful Annulos woman was standing in the doorway. Her hair was jet black with white stripes, and she had a solid white face with black arcs around her eyes. She wore a fitted black suit and heals, her bushy black and white striped tail was held to the left behind her. The poised woman held a tablet in her arm, and she was plotting away on it as they approached, "Good morning Mr. Shardlow, please excuse the mess. I have your deliveries being sorted. I just received word the crews have wrapped up on the demolition of your father's home, and they are beginning construction on the capital building. Your temporary Sarter city manager will be here by the end of the week at the latest. Your command center assembly is well underway and ahead of schedule, it should be operational by tomorrow. The surveillance satellites are being deployed tomorrow afternoon, and your most recent border report has been forwarded to you. It seems as though the shielding you had delivered has deterred the Shrout attacks, and you haven't had an injury since. Oh, your daughter Mere broke her arm, but she's fine, and it's already been repaired. She was on an amusement ride, and that is all she would admit to."

Mac nodded to her, "Thank you Cicilo. This is Yarle my first brother, and this is Laye and Fere."

Cicilo bowed to them, "It's a pleasure to meet you, I am Mr. Shardlow's new assistant."

Laye felt Mac put his arm around her and guide her inside, Fere and Yarle followed. The metal walls had been painted, and all the old simple furniture had been upgraded, his house went from almost garage chic to looking like a modern, high-tech home. Holo-screens were being mounted on the wall as Mac led them to his kitchen where some of the oversized crates were being unloaded. He took a box out of one of the crates and opened it, presenting it to Laye and Fere. It was jars of honey from all over the galactic center, each label had the planet and type of bee on the side of it. Laye and Fere nearly squealed as each took a jar and devoured the honey inside while Mac and Yarle watched and waited for their approval.

Yarle shifted on his feet as Fere leaned into him as she finished the honey, "That was the best thing I've ever eaten."

"Yet," Yarle couldn't help but correct her.

She pursed her lips as her cheeks warmed, she was much shyer about her sexuality than Laye, and something told her Yarle loved it.

Mac led them back through his living area, and down the hall to the rooms in his home. "I had Cicilo order you and Fere new clothes, they're in my closet. Wear something comfortable that you can get dirty."

Fere grabbed Laye's hand and dragged her into Mac's room to his closet which had previously been bare of anything but a few sets of leather pants and jackets with some under clothes. The two women stood in the doorway and admired all the hanging clothes before they each picked a side to start on.

Laye pulled a dress out and noticed the two slits down the back. "Mac?" She had to know.

He darkened the doorway with this massive form, "Yes?"

Laye turned to him with the dress and asked, "Did you have clothes made so we can use our wings?"

"I told Cicilo about your wings, and she changed the patters on the particle replicators," Mac explained as he leaned on the door frame. Laye could see his eyes roaming up and down her figure as he spoke, even through his mask.

The two simultaneously replied, "That was thoughtful." After a giggle over saying the same thing at the same time, they returned to digging for clothes for the day as Mac sat down in his chair next to the closet.

Yarle pulled his mask off, and he tossed it on Mac's bed. "It's hard to believe father was hiding so much wealth."

"Scouts found more neodymium in a moon around our gas giant." Mac pulled his mask off and set it in his lap.

Yarle stared at him, "How much?"

"Half of the mass of the moon is neodymium, and it's on the line of proto-planet. After Sarter taxes, that's enough to *buy* us a new home world, plus some." Mac explained as he tapped Yarle's mask with his middle finger.

Yarle whistled, "How did we not know this before?"

"Do you remember when Father had the reports done on the sands? The deep samples he had taken all over the desert?" Mac asked.

Yarle agreed, "I remember, I had to oversee a delivery to one of the drill pads."

"Our planet has high copper concentrations just like we do in our bodies. It blocks most scanning equipment, and Father was hoping to find more sought-after elements, so he spent a fortune on drilling samples. He's been doing this since long before we were born." Mac explained, *I would've killed him a long time ago if I had known.*

Laye popped her head out of the closet, "I bet copper blocks empathic signals too. I can easily sense Cicilo but never a K'hornibus."

"What do you sense from Cicilo?" Mac asked, he had not thought to evaluate her.

From the open door of the closet Laye laughed, "She would do anything for you, including fuck you."

Mac coughed with the unexpected admission, "What?!"

Laye and Fere giggled in the closet as Mac came around and stood in the doorway, "What is that supposed to mean?"

"I don't blame her. I like her, you should keep her on your staff." Laye shrugged and patted Mac on the side of his thigh before she went back to outfit hunting. Mac wasn't sure what to say, *my woman isn't threatened by anything.*

After a long while of sorting through their new clothes, Laye settled on a simple grey t-shirt and fitted black pants with boots. Fere wore a white sleeveless low-cut shirt with a pair of fitted black pants with short boots. They decided since construction and development were all over the city, they didn't want to dress up.

They boarded the transport, and Cicilo sat in the front seat. Mac and Laye sat in the middle row and Fere and

Yarle climbed in the back. As they took off, Mac pulled Laye close to him and slid his hand between her legs.

Cicilo turned around in her seat with her tablet in her hands. "First, the building to our right is where the new galactic market is being built. It should be completed in a few weeks. Companies from all over the center have already inquired about purchasing retail space. Next, on the left, the new capital building is being constructed where the fifth house of the Shardlow clan once resided. This is in preparation to form a balanced government and send official diplomats to the Sarter Kingdom's council to elevate K'hurian from Sarter territory to a recognized Sarter world. On your left is a social services center where the people of the city can obtain everything from food and water to housing and medical care. Last, we have the K'rin city Shardlow ruins where we will be landing."

The transport set down outside of a barrier surrounding mud buildings. Mac helped Laye out as Fere and Yarle followed, while Cicilo remained in the transport working on her tablet. They passed through a security door and Mac led them into the ruins. The remaining half of a stone building was directly ahead of them, the sound of bells and chimes rang out in the city. Mac stopped and turned to Yarle, "I never thought I would hear the celebration bells again."

"Not when father was alive. You're fixing things, and they finally have hope." Yarle wrapped his mind around the concept of their people caring about them instead of hating them. *We might not have to hide anymore*, he rubbed his hand down the side of his mask. *Wouldn't that be the day?* She and Mac could just be themselves and not have to protect every inch of their lives?

Mac stepped down into the ancient home. "This is over

two million years old when our people finally stopped roaming and settled down. We spent forty million years roaming this planet, two million years building up to a space faring civilization, just to destroy it all over time and our planet along with it from greed the moment we ventured into the galaxy. The high metal deposits here spawned heavy industry which destroyed our environment. K'hurian's average temperature has risen more than thirty degrees over the last hundred thousand years and most of our water evaporated into space. Eventually the only two families with any money left were us and the Shrouts. Both territories have an aquifer, which is drying up, and we've been fighting over the last of the water ever since our planet began its steep decline. When things became bad here, the Shardlows used to gather to pray to the sand and the system star to provide for them."

Mac traced the edge of a broken piece of pottery as he crouched by what was once a fireplace. "If you look closely at the art, you can see all the plants and animals we no longer have. Besides the coastlines, our former environment resembled a flourishing desert with separate seasons, not the wasteland it is now. The Sarter Queen informed me they still have the seeds and millions of genetic samples from our former wildlife, fungi, and plants, she is willing to help us fix our pile of dirt and restore what our ancestors destroyed. We just need to unite our planet."

TWENTY-NINE
SURGERY AND SEX

Fere startled and shot out of bed, her feet landed on the floor silently, and she twirled around ready to fight whoever had snuck up on her. *Wait. Why am I naked? What is happening?*

She heard heavy breathing in the dark room, and Fere crepted toward it, *someone is sleeping in this dark room.* Crawling toward the form on the bed and peeking over at the large person, the last few days came crashing back into her mind, and she slumped against the side of the bed.

It's just Yarle, I am on K'hurian. She was free from the Vo-Pess. Her breath caught as she slapped a hand on her shoulder, she forgot all about her tracker and kill switch.

Fere sprang onto Yarle and shook him, when she saw his eyes open, she demanded, "Get a knife now! We need to dig the tracker out of my shoulder. It's also a kill switch and they can pull the trigger."

Her words caused Yarle to move faster than he ever had in his life, he nearly threw her to the ground as he tore out of the bed in a flurry. He grabbed his knife as Fere turned the light on, she pointed to where it was, and he felt around for it. Not hesitating, Yarle sliced down her shoulder, and Fere was unfazed. Her clear blood ran from the wound as Yarle reached in and pulled the tracker free.

The device had long wires that slid out behind it, and Fere scowled when the last of the wire was out. "Thank you. I woke up from a dream, and I was disoriented. I saw you sleeping, and when my mind caught up, I remembered my tracker."

Fere's blood was running down her arm, and Yarle shook his head trying to wake up as he grumbled, "Fuck, I need to call the medic."

Checking her wound, Fere shrugged, "That's not bad at all. I'll be fine. I just need to hold a cloth to it."

Yarle closed his eyes and pinched the bridge of his nose before he turned and set the tracker on his side table and picked up his tablet. He typed a message to the guard to have their medic come to his room.

"You really don't need to call for someone. I've had so much worse with no medical care, I promise I'll be fine. It doesn't even hurt," Fere tried to reassure Yarle, but all he did was shake his head at her.

When he sent the message and tossed his tablet back on the table, Yarle slid his arm around her nude form, tugging her to him, "Your old life is over. You're not going to live that way here."

The chill of the room pebbled her skin as he stepped away and found a robe for her. He slid it on her right arm and tucked it under her left, wrapping the rest around her and tying it. Yarle was doing everything he could to avoid thoughts of losing her, *she had a fucking kill switch?* The Vo-Pess seemed to grow worse with every revelation. *I thought my father was the worst, he never compared to the Vo-Pess.*

A knock at the door had Yarle turning to answer it, and a smaller male K'hornibus came in with a small basket of supplies. "Iker, can you sew Fere's arm?" Yarle asked as Iker narrowed his eyes at the wound. Iker raised his eyebrows in concern, "Was there a reason you were digging in this woman's shoulder with a knife in the middle of the night?"

Yarle pointed to the tracker, and Iker nodded without further questions.

Iker took out a device Yarle had never seen before, "Wait, what is that? Are you not stitching it?"

Frowning, Iker turned to Yarle with the device that resembled a torch, "It's a dermal bonder. It has glue and an amino acid complex to promote healing. She should be healed in two days at the most."

This new level of tech and resources was something Yarle would need to become accustomed to. Yarle moved to sit on the bed, and he watched Fere as Iker repaired her arm.

Iker bowed to them before he stepped out and Yarle tugged Fere onto his lap. Fere leaned onto him and reveled in his warmth, "I'm not sure I can go back to sleep."

Yarle yawned, and she closed in, staring at his mouth with her eyes wide with intrigue, "What was that?"

"A yawn? Do you not? Oh, you're a butterfly. I guess bugs don't yawn." Yarle couldn't help but laugh a bit. Yarle wanted coffee and leaned back to reach his tablet on his bedside table behind them, "If we're staying up, I need coffee, do you want some?"

"I've never tried it," Fere was intrigued. Smiling as he fought to keep his eyes open, Yarle couldn't wait to introduce her to his favorite thing in the galaxy, he lived on coffee. Yarle ordered two, one concentrate for himself and a mild version for Fere. He felt so sleepy he laid back on the bed, and Fere curled up on top of him. If the lights had been off, he would have fallen asleep in matter of a few breaths. He must have dozed off anyway because woke with a start when he felt Fere slide off him to answer the door, it was Cicilo with the two coffees. She bowed to Fere and closed the door behind her.

Fere presented the two drinks to Yarle, and he took his from her, the smell of the steaming drink wafting by his nose. He could feel himself waking up with just the nutty, wholesome scent. *What time is it?* The clock read three in the morning. They had some time to waste and Yarle wanted to get to know his woman better. His woman, he liked the sound of that.

"Tell me about you." Yarle ran his hand up her back and slid his arm around her pulling her toward him. He fought with the fabric of her robe for a moment before he had his hand inside, and the way she curled next to him. She had a roundness to her middle he couldn't resist. She hadn't answered yet and Yarle growled in her ear as he ran his hand over her belly as his other hand squeezed her ass, "I like all of this, you're so soft. Your body was made for me, I need to know if your mind was too."

Fere knew K'hornibus women were similar to the men with their trim, hard form. Beings who developed from reptiles rarely had varied body types. Pley had constantly complained about her figure, but she was just built with a little more. Yarle's hands were roaming the curves of her figure, and she had never felt so beautiful. He paused, "Fere?"

She had forgotten the question, and had to think. "I never really had the chance to build a version of myself I could call my identity. I was always just an Angle Wing."

Yarle scowled as he reached across the bed for his coffee resting on his bedside table, Fere still had hers cradled in her hands. He drank his coffee and set it down before resuming his exploration of her figure.

He was moving her around, and she nearly spilled, so she finished her drink before setting the cup on the floor at her feet. *That was a little gross, but I also kind of liked it.* Yarle grabbed her hips and wouldn't let her up from his lap.

"Nope. Take this off I want to see you." Yarle pulled at her robe, and she moved so he could pull it from between them. He stood up with her and set her down in front of him before he scoffed, "Damn, you're a lot shorter than me. That won't work."

Yarle lifted her up, so she was standing on the bed, and her face was even with his. He held her shoulders as he looked down at her in the light, his mouth watering. She was all curves with full round breasts, Yarle reached around to her rear before he squeezed her just under her hips as he hauled her against him.

Yarle breathed against her lips, "Tell me about your favorite's. It can be anything."

Fere felt Yarle lay her back on the bed as he leaned over and he kissed her under her chin before he kissed her throat. She could barely form words, "I like animals, I've always wanted a pet bird."

Yarle's hands cupped her breasts, his thumbs gently moved over both of her nipples. She inhaled in quick breath as he leaned down and took her dark maroon nipple into his mouth. "What do you want to do with your time now that you're free?" Yarle asked before he lifted her legs to spread her wide for him. Yarle licked his lips as he looked down at her, "Fere?"

"Oh, I want to travel for fun. I never had a chance to

enjoy myself before. I saw so many worlds, but I always had to stay hidden." Fere words cut short as Yarle buried his face between her legs.

Fere arched off the bed as Yarle tormented her, licking her line of nerves before pulling away, then starting over. She was panting when he finally held his rhythm, her hips trembled, and she felt an unnatural thrill burst through her. Her legs clenched around Yarle's head so tightly he thought it may burst, *what a way to go*, as he buried his tongue in her deeper. A high-pitched tone came from Fere as she dove over the edge, writhing as her release spilled over. Yarle smiled with his tongue still on her, he took his time licking up every bit of her pleasure. Her heart was racing as his hard body crawled over hers, and his length was out and ready for her. She moved her hips up to accept him.

Yarle slid into her, and she seemed to disappear under him as he did, he breathed, "You're so small." He grabbed her hips and flipped them over, so she was riding him, and she nearly vibrated as she ground down onto him. Fere felt him split, and as his length rolled around inside of her, she felt another rush of energy blast through her. The electric sensations built and she felt herself flying inside as his length seemed to shake. *Or is that me? Oh fuck!*

Yarle grasped her hips and holding her down on his length as she began an exceptionally lively shiver. Her inner walls vibrated around him, and he came with a guttural moan. Fere broke apart again, and she leaned back trying to suck in a breath and willed herself not to shake again.

Her orgasm crashed into her just as another all-consuming shiver burst through her, Yarle yelped as he tried to pull her off him. He caught his breath as he held her up and away from him, he laughed like never before, "We need to be careful with you and coffee, it contains caffeine."

Fere's eyes went wide with his words, "OH! That's why I feel so hyper?! Oh, sweet honey hell, I'm about to shiver again."

Just as she finished forming her words her body vibrated violently, and she squealed, her voice sounding like she was speaking into a fan. Yarle tensed as he tried to set her down on her feet, but her feet left the floor as she continued the blurring shake.

Fere burst into laughter as she finally willed herself to quit trembling, Yarle rushed into his bathroom and emerged with a glass of water for her. She drank it and handed the glass back as she shook her head, "I don't know about your coffee, that drink turns me into a living vibrator."

THIRTY

ONE STEP FORWARD, TWO STEP BACK

Once she had come down from the initial coffee high, Fere sat on the floor and Yarle sat down with her. He took her foot in his hand and rubbed it, she leaned her head back, and wanted to fall over, or moan, or maybe both.

Touch wasn't a thing where she was from, and she had always been desperate for it. His hands moved up her leg, and he kneaded her calf, *is he always like this?*

If I make any sort of sound without words, I will sound like I'm having the best sex of my life, she had to ask, "What did I ever do to deserve all of this? I was a terrible person. How could I be rewarded for all the despicable things I did?"

Yarle leaned forward and kissed the inside of her ankle, "You've never done a thing wrong. You've never had choices before." Picking up her other foot, he repeated the process. This was a perfect man, *so what is the catch? There is always a price to pay.*

A feeling passed over her, a great sorrow. She raised her antennae and Yarle stared at her before grabbing her robe and handing it to her. She focused on the feeling when they heard footsteps running down the hallway.

They could hear a knock-on Mac's door, and when he opened it, they could hear Cicilo clearly. "There has been an explosion. A Shrout man entered one of the old temporary shelters for your most needy residents. He had a gas bomb on his body and it fully detonated, spraying all its toxic gases and leaving twenty-six people dead, and over thirty injured. More deaths are expected. It was mostly elderly, women, and children."

Fere slid her hand over her mouth as she reached for Yarle, his face was helpless and distraught as he lifted them both from the floor and stood her on her feet. She put on her robe, and he pulled up his sleep pants before he swung the door open.

Cicilo and Mac were standing in the doorway, and Laye was tying a robe around her in Mac's bedroom. Mac's arms were folded, and he glowered, "Everyone dress and meet me in the kitchen in ten minutes."

Fere and Yarle turned back into their room, and behind him, Laye went straight into her closet. They all filed in the kitchen a few minutes later, Fere and Laye were both in their nano-tech armor. Mac and Yarle were dressed in their riding leathers, Yarle's jacket was open, and his shirt was untucked.

Mac sipped a steaming cup of coffee and sat down at the table next to Laye, and Yarle sat on the other side of him. Yarle pulled a chair out for Fere next to him. Lying on the table before them was a holo-gram projection mat, and Cicilo turned it on with her tablet as she sat down at the end of the table.

The Shrout territory map popped up and Laye stood to

study it, Fere not far behind. Yarle suggested, "I think we need to put these two in charge of our strike."

"Cicilo, send my guard commanders out to collect those on standby. We are introducing my new generals." Mac leaned toward the table, watching Cicilo raise her eyebrows.

"May I ask what species Laye and Fere are?"

Laye lifted her gaze to Cicilo, "We are Vo-Pess. Our world and people are not known to the rest of the galaxy."

Cicilo was clearly stunned, "May I ask for personal reasons, what do you evolve from?"

"Butterflies," Laye answered. Confusion was written on Cicilo, but she did as instructed, informing Mac's guard. Beings evolved from insects were not common, even in pre-space faring species.

Looming over the map, Laye asked, "Is this interactive?"

Cicilo didn't look up from her tablet. "Yes, you can manipulate the image with your hands. Mac, we've just received word of another attack on the border. The Shrout dropped gas and explosives on the west checkpoint, but there were minimal casualties, their shielding held."

"Fuck. We need to end this," Mac grumbled as he watched Laye and Fere wordlessly coordinate their planning.

Laye turned to Mac, "You're not going to like this."

Mac gave her a side eye, "I was watching you. We're moving at night and storming the two Shrout homes?"

Laye and Fere nodded, and Laye added, "We need names and the locations of their rooms in the two homes. We need imagery of their floorplans, and I want all their routes plotted out. I need to know who has children and where. I need pictures of family who are not targets. This city is adequate for small infiltration."

Mac lifted a brow at Cicilo across the table, and she briefly nodded as she wrote down what Laye requested. She created a destination address for the information and sent the request to Mac's brothers in charge of the guard.

Cicilo rose from the table, "I set up a destination address for Laye, I'll be right back with communication tablets for Laye and Fere. Mac, your brothers are all dying to know who their new general is."

"Tell them they've already encountered her. We went to her planet to bring her back when her people took her from me. Call them in, we will set up temporary command here, and as information comes in, we will provide them with updates to our plans." Mac explained, Cicilo nodded as she stalked off down the hall, her heals clicking with each step.

Laye and Fere continued to stew over the image before Laye narrowed her eyes at Mac, "What would you do if we weren't here?"

"My father would have bombed them. Without highly skilled operatives like you two I would have been stuck with the same option," Mac admitted. Laye scanned her eyes over the holo-gram as she understood. Mac continued, "I want to do this clean. I want minimal deaths because I need to usurp the territory leadership, and in order to hold it, I'll need to be damn convincing that I can bring positive change. If I go in guns blazing with an army, they won't believe I'm capable of change."

Several locations updated on the map as Laye's requested information poured in, and Cicilo came around the corner with two tablets. She handed one to Laye and the other to Fere.

Mac's front door opened and three of his brothers walked into his kitchen.

Inex leaned against the wall, "You're making the butterfly the general?"

Laye smirked at him, "Did you really think your new leader threatened an entire planet for *just some girl*?"

"You're a dum…" Laye stepped on Mac's foot under the table to stop him from finishing his sentence.

Inex replied, "Fair enough. What's the latest update?"

Laye glared at Mac, and he shrugged when Yarle met Mac's line of sight, and he creased his brow. *Did Laye just make Mac shut up, and he complied?* Yarle was really beginning to like these bold little butterflies.

"Our first job is creating a target list and establishing rank of importance. We are aiming to build a target list *and* a no kill list, and everyone going in needs to study the faces and names. We are memorizing floor plans and schedules. We strike when we know each target is asleep, we are performing coordinated silenced assassinations. Simultaneously, we are relocating everyone on the no kill list out of Shrout territory and into K'rin city. I need the best of the best on these missions. Fere and I will take out the main Shrout targets while the rest of the teams will take out the remaining loyalists and ruling Shrout family members lower on our target list. We set a date when we finish compiling information," Laye ordered, Inex nodded along as she instructed.

By the time she finished speaking, no one in the room doubted why Mac had put her in charge. Cicilo seemed star struck by Laye and slowly disappeared into the next room, focusing back on her work.

Mac's stomach grumbled, and Yarle went to make them a meal, "Sit down, Yarle. We have someone bringing food in a few minutes." Like clockwork, two minutes later several guards brought in a table and plates of food. Mac and Yarle ate, and when they were finished, they went back to assist Laye and Fere.

Hours rolled by as they compiled the information as the rest of the Shardlow brothers showed up to assist. Around mid-day, Mac slid his hand over Laye's ass, and leaned over to her ear, his breath hot against her skin, "We are taking a break." She leaned into his touch and nodded, following him to his bedroom.

Mac closed the door behind him and moved toward his bed. "Watching you boss my brothers around has had me hard for hours, take your fucking clothes off." Wetting her lips in anticipation, Laye tapped her armor tab. It receded, leaving her in her underclothes, which she began peeling off. Sitting on the end of his bed, Mac watched her as she undressed, "You may be leading my invasion, but in here you submit to me. On your knees."

She could have orgasmed right there, Laye fell to her knees as Mac sat in front of her. Laye unblocked his pants and could feel his hard length was already out and ready for her. Her mouth watered as she freed him. Laye took him into her hands and opened her mouth, drawing all of him in. He made a deep, sensual sound in his throat as she could feel his length split. She stroked him as she felt his dual length twirl in her mouth as it rippled along the sides. The way his hips moved, his deep breaths, and his flexing muscles above her. It left her so turned on she felt heat form in her low belly, and she was so wet it was threatening to run down her leg.

Mac curled toward her and as his swirling sides slipped from her mouth, his cum slapped her in her face and neck. "Damn, I didn't mean to do that. Keep your eyes closed, I'll guide you to the sink."

Laye couldn't help but laugh, she could feel his slimy hot cum dripping down her face, "Why the hell does your species spill so much cum?"

"We can have up to eleven eggs per batch, I guess we need a lot of sperm to make that happen," Mac explained as he wet a towel and cleaned her up. Mac huffed as he spotted some cum on top of her head. "It's in your hair, I'll start the shower."

THIRTY-ONE
PREPARATIONS

The next evening as the system star set, Laye stood in front of the remaining Shardlow brothers and the best of their guard giving her final orders. "Tomorrow night we make our move. You each have been given a list with your target's information and locations. If you fall, you have sensors to notify the rest of the team. Remember, we will assume each fall is a missed target and command will add additional targets and locations to the remaining guards. All information and communication are accessible on a screen located on the outside of your forearm. Your new masks are outfitted with automatic night vision shift in case you are caught, and the lights switch on. The masks also filter the air, protecting against gas attacks. Your new Sarter Kingdom issued armor has shielding which can deter rail gun rounds shot from a distance, but in close proximity, the armor's protection is substantially reduced. Do not rely on the armor; rely on your training. No kill targets will be rounded up to the cropland, and once the territory is secure, we will send transports to retrieve them. If they need to be sedated, you have a spray sedative on your belt that works instantly if sprayed directly onto the face. We will be traveling by stealth air transports, and we are dropping down into the Shrout compound. You will be placed on the roof where your targets are located. Expect heavy fire and losses. Make arrangements as needed, we are invading the north so the Shardlow's can repair the planet. This sacrifice will be for your future generations."

Mac, Yarle, and Fere stood behind Laye as she spoke, Mac couldn't help but burst with pride. He had gone with his instincts with his little butterfly, and *now she will help me repair my world.* Mac watched his brothers, and the best of his guard stand at attention, accepting her as his general. They would understand better when they witnessed her in action.

The guard dispersed, and Mac finally had an empty home, save Cicilo who was busy in his living area at her makeshift office. He would construct a new home after everything else on his top agenda was completed, so they would make do until then. *I can't imagine being selfish and building my own new home at a time like this.* His memory moved to his father, and he cringed, no one else was ever above Voakes and Mac was set on changing how the K'hornibus functioned. Their old ways had never paid them any favors and the change began with him.

Mac and Laye went to his room for some rest while Fere and Yarle did the same in Yarle's room. When Yarle's door shut behind him, Fere was already climbing into bed. They needed as much rest as possible, and Yarle slid in next to her. Fere felt his arms wrap around her and tugged her close to his hard, warm body. She could let her walls fall with him, and she didn't have to protect herself anymore. The comfort she found in his embrace was something she never wanted to give up and she wiggled closer to him.

Above her head, Yarle mumbled, "If you don't hold still…"

They were supposed to be resting. Yarle's hands moved to her hips, and he pressed his bulge into her ass before grinding against it. His hand reached down between her legs, grabbed her thigh, and turned her on her back to face him.

"Two steps toward you was all it took, and now I have a life of my own. One I chose. No, I won't hold still. I'm going to grind my ass on you until I can't, or you don't want it anymore," Fere spoke bluntly. She had no idea if she was the right woman for him or if she was just right now. She couldn't be upset if he just wanted her body. Fere would gladly give it to him for what he did for her. She wanted to give him everything even if she hardly even knew him.

Yarle stared at her motionless before he corrected, "Or until I don't want it anymore? You're my superior in every way, I'm the one who should be hoping you will still accept me once you realize your worth. I am far from a humble man, even now I feel the urge to selfishly mark you as mine. To claim you and keep you before you find out what kind of man I am."

"Stop acting like we are not both filthy, rotten murders, because we are," She paused a moment and tapped his chest with her finger. "What kind of man are you?" Fere asked as she slid her hand up his muscled arm, his skin so different than her own but still so similar. She loved the way it felt under her palms, the way the ridges of his scales moved under her touch on the back of his arms.

She could feel his thick, powerful form leaning over her own, and he whispered over her lips, "I am the second son, and the atrocities I've committed were by choice. I uphold Shardlow law with an oath I'll never break."

"That's what you do, not who you are," Fere corrected.

Yarle gently bit her lip, "Are you asking me if I would destroy a world for you? The K'hornibus are territorial beings, we will always come for what is ours. At any cost."

Fere leaned her head to the side and showed him her neck. "Then make me yours."

Thrilled beyond what he could contain, Yarle all but yelled as he growled and he bit into the skin above her shoulder, leaving the marks of his sharp teeth. A drip of her blood trickled out, and Yarle leaned back to open the drawer in his bedside table. He rummaged around and pulled out a box, "I planned to wait until tomorrow, but now works."

He had spoken to Mac about the tracker he had used in Laye and his children and Yarle had Cicilo purchase him a set. Pulling one of the rice sized tracking beacons from the box, he held it up to her.

"Is that how Mac found Laye?" Fere asked. Yarle nodded, and she narrowed her eyes at him. "Well, what are you waiting for?"

He scoffed under his breath and slid the tracking device into one of the puncture marks he made in her shoulder, "I had a whole speech planned for this. You had been controlled and trapped before, I wasn't assuming you would take this lightly."

Fere turned back to him, and explained, "Obedience and submission are all I've ever known, and it was at the hands of people who chipped away at me. I was nothing but a tool for them to use and throw away when they were finished. I had no choices, no one cared about my wellbe-ing, and I was demeaned for any and every mistake I have ever made. I have spent my life feeling empty and yearning for so much more, to be able to grow as a person. To be more than just a killer, spy, and interrogator. I want to just be Fere, I want to figure out who that is or who that might be one day. I want safety, and I want someone who cares watching out for me. I need someone to wants to set me free but will always be there keeping me safe. I used to jump off ledges before my wings had fully spread, daring myself and testing my limits every chance I had. The high of the free fall was sometimes the only thing that would get me through. All I ever really wanted was for someone to catch me, to be my safety net far below, but no one was ever there. Every time I fell, I always had to flap my wings in a rush to avoid slamming into the ground."

Yarle bit his lips together before he admitted, "When I was a kid, I used to weave nets and catch butterflies." Fere smiled at him sweetly, but he smiled wide enough to show all his teeth as he confessed, "I used to catch them and eat them."

Her eyes went wide as he leaned down and licked her nipple, wrapping his lips around it and twirling his tongue over the tip. He licked her down her maroon curvy body as he pulled her up the bed and spread her thighs. Reaching his hands under her rear, he lifted her hips to devour her center.

With his horns jutting behind his head, which was conveniently between her thighs, she curled up and reached with her antennae to touch the tips to his horns. Yarle grunted into her heat as she sent the way she felt into him. His licking became deep and slow, driving her further into ecstasy. He snapped up and shoved pillows under her before angling his horns so she could reach better. He resumed his delicate work between her thighs as she made the connection, allowing him to experience what she felt and giving him the ability to decipher exactly what to do and when. He wrapped his arms under her plump ass and made himself comfortable, he was sending her feelings of longing but in a torturous sense. Yarle wanted her to beg, he wanted to see her shake in desperation. His rough tongue against her row of nerves moved slightly faster, and she felt as though she would burst.

As Fere began to tremble, he growled against her flesh, and he sent her feelings of satisfaction. She was exactly where he wanted her, breaking a sweat and panting. He kneaded the crease of her hips with his thumbs, and she nearly came undone with his sincere love for the softness around her hips and belly. Yarle began running his tongue up and down her center faster, taking her so much closer.

She squeezed her eyes shut as she felt herself near the edge, the cresting overflow of pleasure was steady as it moved through her. The way he had her body curled around his head, she couldn't move as her nerves flared and pulsated. He kept going, taking her further and drawing out her euphoric pleasure. He didn't set her down when he pulled his mouth from her, but instead kissed along her inner thigh and up her hip. He gently bit down on the softness of her lower belly above her hip and licked the flesh between his teeth as she felt pure joy from him.

He slowly set her down as he kept his head resting on her stomach, right under her ribs. He didn't want to stop feeling her inside and out. He ran his fingers down the valley of her hip and brushed his hand all the way down her inner thigh to her knee and back up. The sensation made her muscles jump and he revealed in it. She sensed his growing need to sink himself into her, and she pulled her antennae away. He rolled his shoulders before he moved over her, his lips hovering over hers as she felt his length brush against her entrance.

Keeping his eyes locked with hers before he kissed her, she could taste her own pleasure on his lips as he claimed her mouth. When he slid himself inside of her, she watched his large body move up over her, and he grabbed the headboard above her. Fere ran her hands up his chest and whimpered as he began moving inside of her. "You feel like forever," Yarle mumbled as he thrust deeply, and his length split in two. Fere sucked in breath as she felt his dual length begin to roll.

Above her, Yarle peered down, "Breathe deep and hold it in." She did as he asked, and felt herself accept more of him as his length began flitting at the tips. Fere felt herself come apart as he demanded, "Inhale now." Fere pulled in a deep breath, and she felt her orgasm spread from her center as he reached down to grab her hip and ground into her.

With a long, draw out growl, Yarle came inside of her. Holding the headboard, he leaned down as he slid out of her, kissing her before smiling against her lips, "Now let me sleep, you fucking temptress."

THIRTY-TWO
ASSASSINATION

Mac kept his eyes on Laye as she slipped on her underclothes before she tapped her armor tab. He had been up for over an hour watching her sleep.

Laye came toward him, he was already dressed in his armor and his mask hung from the arm of his chair. She slid onto his lap and rested her forearms on his shoulders, bringing her face close to his. Mac ran his hands up her sides and wrapped them around her, pulling her closer as he whispered, "I believe you have taken my heart all for yourself, little butterfly. When I bit you and marked your flesh, I claimed you as mine. Do you know what that means?"

Laye answered, "I knew exactly what it meant when you did it. I know the K'hornibus mark their women."

Mac smiled and corrected, "We mark our woman, singular. We only mark one woman. The one who possesses us, in our mind, heart, and body."

She held his gaze as she wrapped her hands around his neck. "Like a bonded partner?"

He shook his head. "More than that." Laye grinned and kissed him before she sighed, "We have a planet to save."

"That's not for several hours. We didn't sleep in as long as we planned, and we have a little time before we're needed," Mac explained as he felt her thumbs run along the sides of his neck.

He shivered and resisted the urge to toss Laye across the room, "I still don't understand why that keeps happening."

"I think you needed affection more than you realized," Laye explained as she ran her hands down his chest. The profound love he held in his eyes for her made her crumble, and she found herself swelling inside with the same feelings for him. Something deep inside of her fluttered, and she became overwhelmed with a rush of euphoria when it settled in her mind that this man may truly *love* her. The kind of love that caused men to conquer worlds. The kind of love that was consuming, but freeing and light, unconditional, and safe.

He leaned into her warmth as she asked, "You've never had anyone be soft with you, have you? We seem to come from unforgiving backgrounds where sharing feelings isn't acceptable. We change that now. I think, I love you. I think I have loved you for a while."

Mac smirked, "You're right. I thought I simply had an obsession with you, but my compulsions can't be explained by any concept other than love. I love my children, but I have never loved a woman before you. I didn't know I could. I would have burned both of our worlds to have you back because of what we have, right now. You are my world now, where we are doesn't matter as long as you're there."

Laye sank into him and he wrapped his arms around her, holding her close. They remained this way for a long while, until Mac saw the clock, and it was time for them to begin floor plan drills before the mass assassinations later that night. Their drop was scheduled for midnight.

Mac whispered into Laye's hair, "It's time to be a spy again, my little butterfly."

She breathed in his scent before lifting up from his chest and kissing him, "Let's go." As Laye crawled off his lap, he missed her warmth and had to resist the urge to pull her back to him.

They left his room around the same time Yarle and Fere emerged from Yarle's room. Although angry in the moment, Mac wasn't sure he had ever seen his brother so peaceful. Their lives had been filled with nothing but war since they were children, to find a bit of peace in the chaos was more than Mac could have ever hoped. What had they found in Laye and Fere, he knew how lucky he and Yarle had been. Yarle clearly cared for Fere, and Mac decided if his brother behaved, he wouldn't intervene.

During the day, the Shardlow brothers and the guards slowly trickled in, one after the next. Mac's living area was soon filled with chatter about routes and targets. Mac beamed with pride when he saw how much they had already memorized, *they are listening to Laye and accepting her*. They were changing every aspect of their lives, starting with this mission. This was the beginning of the end of the thousands of years of war thier planet had been scarred by.

Night fell over the land, and Laye checked the time, "We have two hours before we head out. Make your calls."

A few of the men stepped out and some stayed inside to make their calls. Some didn't call anyone.

When the time rolled around to eleven, Laye whistled, "It's time, line up for your weapons." Cicilo had laid out rail guns, knives, and masks for each man by the door, and they took their weapons as they moved outside and lined up to board their landing transports.

Two stealth transports landed on the street in front of Mac's home and team two filed out and into the larger transport. Laye, Mac, Fere, and Yarle climbed in the smaller transport as Cicilo approached with her tablet shining brightly in the dark night. Mac turned to Cicilo, "Is Berem here yet?"

A transport dropped down from the sky and landed next to theirs. A K'hornibus man stepped out and walked over to Mac. "Thank you for leaving your studies. This shouldn't take long, and you can go right back." Mac explained.

His son lifted his mask, "Is this Laye?"

Laye waved from her seat next to Mac, "I wish we could have met under better circumstances."

"I think meeting you now, as you're on your way with my father to save our planet, couldn't have been a better time. I am proud to serve my family, father, I will gladly do what is required of me." Berem declared as Mac took in the man his son had become.

Berem bowed to them, and he followed Cicilo inside as the transports silently lifted off. They would have a long journey over the desert and through the war zone before they would be able to drop on their assigned roofs.

Mac zeroed in on the Shrout tower and pointed it out to Laye as he unbuckled his harness and picked up his drop line. Laye did the same while Fere and Yarle followed.

They were each seated facing out toward the door so that when the door opened, they could all leap out at once and belay down.

Mac spotted the roof they were aiming for and prepared himself. Battle was unpredictable, and this was all new ground for he and his men.

The doors slid open, and he turned to look at Laye one last time, her hair was whipping in the wind as she reached up to tap her face shield. He watched her face disappear under a flood of nano-machines, all linking together to protect her.

The tiny light blinked on the floor, and they each belayed down ropes anchored to the transport as the other team did the same on an adjacent roof.

When all their boots hit the roof, Mac tapped the screen on his wrist, and the stealth transports flew away to wait for them. After setting down a bag with a flare inside in case things went awry, Laye signaled to follow her as they approached a door at the end of the roof. Placing her hands on the door, she felt for vibrations before she put a lock breaker up against it. The tech had the lock clicking open in seconds and she turned the handle to open it.

Mac grabbed her and put his body in front of hers as a blast went off. Laye stood stunned as her nano-tech failed, and her armor fell in a metallic heap on the rooftop. She shivered a bit in the chill of the night, all she had on underneath was her sheer underclothes.

"The door was rigged with an electromagnetic pulsation bomb. All our equipment is dead," Mac explained as he took his mask off to poke the eyes out so he could see.

Yarle did the same and they replaced their masks just as someone came around the corner into the roof access room, Laye charged him and had a knife in his gut within seconds. As he fell, she sliced across his throat, and he landed face down at her feet. Laye turned back to the team. "We need to move. This mission isn't over."

They heard screams from the tower next door as Laye took off into the building and Mac, Fere, and Yarle followed. The team moved down a long hallway and reached a set of stairs, they were met with heavy gunfire from old fashion explosive projectile guns. Mac growled, "They knew we would be coming with tech."

In front of him, Laye peeked around the corner and signaled two men on the left and one on the right. She looked one more time before dropping down and bringing her wrist within her line of sight.

Laye leaned forward and shot one of the K'hornibus in the eye with her spine. He cried out, and it provided the perfect distraction. Laye and Fere used the walls, bracing on either side as they leaned forward to run down the stairs, aiming for the two remaining men.

With the angle of their entry in the room, they came down with great force on their targets. Laye struck the standing man in the neck with her knife nearly decapitating him, while Fere gutted the kneeling one, both men hitting the ground as they absorbed Laye and Fere's impact.

Whistling, Laye signaled the way was clear as she picked up one of the guns and tossed it to Mac. Yarle followed suit and collected one of the guns up as he passed over a body. Each downed man had several.

Moving from one room to the next down the hall, they found each door locked down. Laye shook her head and waved the team on. She and Mac needed to take out the elder Shrout named Grett first, and his rooms were at the end of the hallway while his first son was the door before.

Fere and Yarle stood at the Shrout first son Harec's door as Laye and Mac made their way to Grett's door. Laye signaled to Fere, three, two, one.

Laye and Fere each spun and kicked down the doors in front of them as screams burst from the rooms. Grett stood in the corner of his room with a teenage K'hornibus boy, the boy was horrified as Grett moved him as a shield with gun at his side. Laye, in nothing but her underclothes, demanded, "Let the boy go, and fight me like a man."

Mac stood behind her with the old gun lifted and pointed at Grett's face. "You heard her, why don't you fight her, Grett?"

Grett raged, "Fuck you Shardlow! You won't take my territory so easily. We knew you would be coming!" The young boy shook his head and tried to pull away from Grett.

Mac tilted his head to the side as he realized what they had walked in on. "Laye, he was abusing the boy." He watched Laye clench with fury as the boy's eyes pleaded for help, giving her all the confirmation she needed. Laye moved like a flash of light, shoving the boy onto the ground as she slammed her knife into Grett's face through his chin. She yanked her knife out as Mac lifted the boy from the ground. "Get under the bed and stay there until someone comes for you. Don't make a sound."

The boy dove under the bed as a shot rang out from the next room, and Mac and Laye sprinted down the hall. Laye arrived first and Mac heard a crash before he rounded the doorway. Yarle was on the ground cradling a wound in his lower gut as Fere was wrestling with Herec who had a gun in his grip. Mac tried to aim as Laye swarmed Herec. Fere was able to pull her knife from her belt and she drove it forward into Herec's side. When he hit the ground, Laye yanked his head back and jammed her knife down into his throat.

Gunfire erupted behind Mac, and he spun, aimed, and fired on the Shrout guards pouring up from downstairs. Laye and Fere bolted from the room to the opposite wall and stopped, stacking themselves one over the other and ready to fire with their guns raised. They didn't hesitate as they opened fire on the advancing guards and began taking them down as Mac provided cover in the doorway.

Behind him Mac could hear Yarle groan, and Mac demanded, "Apply pressure! I don't care how bad it hurts, stop that blood flow." Yarle made a gagging sound as Mac shot three more guards. He tossed away his gun as Laye fired her last round.

Fere checked her weapon, "I have two left. We need to move. We have four more targets downstairs. Mac, you stay with Yarle and get him to a transport. A bag on the roof has an emergency flare the pilot will be waiting for."

Laye and Fere ran for the hallway and Mac turned to his brother to lift him from the ground. Yarle tried to push Mac away and demanded, "You're their cover! You can't Mac! You need to go with them!"

He had to trust that they would make it, as he lifted his brother from the ground, "Mac, no!" Yarle grabbed his gut, and doubled over as Mac helped him out of the room and up the stairs to the roof access room, "Trust them. They are the best in the galaxy, the Shrout are no match."

Male K'hornibus screams blasted down the hallways as Fere and Laye burst into the room of their next target, Grett's second son, Kaim. A nude K'hornibus women had been forced in front of him, he had a knife at her neck as another woman cowered in his bed.

Fere hopped to one side as Laye whistled and jumped

to the other. Kaim shifted his head back and forth as the two attacked from either side, Fere planting her knife into his neck as Laye knocked his knife away.

Laye pointed to the closet, "Hide and don't come out." The two women forced their bodies into the small space as Laye and Fere moved to leave Kaim's room. The transport landed on the roof as a door at the end of the hall on the second level swung open, and five horned and furious guards came running toward them.

Fere aimed and shot her last rounds, taking down two of them as the rest sprayed the area with bullets. In an attempt to trick them into waste more ammo, Laye pitched a piece of clothing from the floor out of the door, and as they unloaded, she heard the distinctive clicks of empty chambers.

Laye and Fere ducked low, and ran out of the room just as the first guard reached the doorway. They slid to a stop on the other side of the men, and they each jumped onto a man, driving their knives into their throats. The last man standing tried to lift his gun to Laye as Fere aimed and threw her knife into the man's shoulder. Laye ducked as he shot, but missed, before she rolled toward him and jammed her knife into his thigh. Fere jumped onto him and yanked her knife out before running it across his throat.

As the body fell, Laye was already running for their next target, and Fere was not far behind. Laye heard the door click open, and their target was marched out by a young woman with a gun to his back. The K'hornibus woman, wearing nothing but tattered sleep clothes, nodded to Fere and Laye from behind their target Jeun. Laye smiled at her as she charged forward, and pounced on him, her arms crossed in front of her before she swung them apart, slicing her knife across Jeun's exposed neck.

"Hide, now." Laye demanded but the girl shook her head. The young woman handed Laye the gun in her hand. "I can help you."

"Why would you do that?" Laye questioned. The woman scowled and spat on the floor, "Do you think I want to be here?"

"Good enough." Laye admitted, she appreciated the sentiment. The woman pointed to a door down the hallway. "There are guns in that room. My name is Tupol, and I can shoot." Fere and Laye nodded, and Tupol followed them to the door.

Laye checked the ammo as Tupol pushed by them and reached up above the door producing a key. The door swung open, and they found several loaded guns in a row by the door with a locked gun locker across from them. They all had a gun in each hand as they ran in a line to the stairs, and Laye threw over her shoulder, "We only have three more targets. First, second, and last door when we make it down the stairs." A guard appeared around the corner and Laye hit him between the eyes before he could lift his weapon. The three women went around his body, and as they reached the bottom of the stairs, four guards came barreling toward them.

After Laye struck the first guard in the leg, he tripped the other two as he fell. Reaching around Laye, Fere shot two of them in the head as Tupol hit the man on top in the back.

They rushed for the first door, and Laye opened it but found the room empty. She tried to not let discouragement set in; *we can complete this.* Their last targets had ample chance to escape with all the time it had taken them to reach this point, but she wasn't giving up. They wasted no time and moved to the second door, finding two of their targets inside with weapons drawn.

Laye ducked and yanked Tupol down as Fere rolled across the doorway. Laye had seen their position and didn't even look as she peppered the area with gunshots. No one shot back, and Fere peered in, giving Laye the signal the two were dead. They moved to the last door and found it locked, so she prepared to kick it down when Fere grabbed her.

A blast ripped through the door, and the three ducked before a man came out into the hall with a massive weapon on his shoulder. Fere spun and sliced across the back of his ankles as Laye shot him in the gut. Tupol caught the large weapon before it hit the ground.

Laye held her hand up to her ear trying to listen, she had no way to know what was happening in the next building. "Tupol, run to the roof and see if the Shrout tower is secure yet. We need to barricade the doors and move the no kill targets to the roof for extraction in case they were overtaken. They knew we were coming, and we have no idea what happened over there." Laye instructed and Tupol took off as Fere ran to the doors at the end of the hall and locked them before she began pushing furniture in the way.

Laye ran to the opposite end and did the same as Fere, blocking any access. The two ran for the stairs and scaled each level, yelling, "It's over, move to the roof for rescue!"

Laye found Tupol on the roof, who was squinting at the tower, "It looks like your people are almost through the building, but there is only one transport and it's hovering back that way," Tupol pointed to where the larger transport was hovering on the other side of the tower.

There was no sign of Mac or Yarle, and with one of the

transports gone, Laye began to worry about Yarle. Mac would never have left unless Yarle was dying. Laye turned at Fere who already knew, the terror behind her eyes was unmistakable.

Within minutes all the no kill targets were rounded up on the roof awaiting transport, but they had no way to give the signal that they needed off the roof since the flare was already used.

"We need some cover, Tupol can you help us out?" Laye asked as she tapped the helpful K'hornibus woman's shoulder. Tupol ran for the door to find a fire source as Laye heard gunshots from an open window in the tower. Laye asked the no kill targets, "Has the tower been quiet? Did they have the same blast?" The young boy answered behind her, "There was only one bomb, I heard them talking."

Laye turned and grinned at the boy, "Thank you. That's very helpful."

The team in the tower still had masks, rail guns, and working armor. Laye took a breath of relief as she watched the ground floor of the tower light up and one of her team members came outside.

Laye called down to him from the rooftop, "Are we clear? We have no tech, and we need off this roof with no kill targets."

He raised his eyes up to her, "We just cleared the tower. Sending the transport to you now."

Laye yelled to Tupol, "We made contact, come back!" In seconds, the transport was lowering, and a lift was dropped down, all the targets were loaded first. Tupol came out and rode up with Laye and Fere.

Fere climbed into the front seat and located her tablet before she put in a call to Cicilo, "He is in surgery. He is in orbit on the Sarter Queen's emergency medical ship. We are sending the transport back for you, and it will take you directly to the Sarter ship."

"No word on his condition?" Fere was distraught, she could hardly concentrate enough to speak. Cicilo went silent for far too long before she finally replied, "I'm sorry, no. The transport will be there in fifteen minutes." Fere handed the tablet to Laye, who tucked it under her arm as they landed in the empty crop field. Jumping down from the landed transport, Fere began pacing as Shardlow guards came out of the tower with their no kill targets and guided them to the field. Inex approached Laye, "Where are Mac and Yarle?"

"Yarle was hit. Mac must have known it was bad, and he probably called the Sarter Queen on the way back to K'rin. Sounds like the queen sent her personal emergency ship, and Yarle is aboard in surgery."

THIRTY-THREE
THE QUEEN

A transport they had never seen landed in the field, and a Sarter was at the helm. The door slid away, and a regal dressed Sarter stepped out, his garments flowing. Stunning jewelry adorned his ears, neck, and wrists and it vibrantly sparkled in the lights of the transports.

"My Queen has requested both of you." He waved for them to board the transport.

Laye threw her hand up, "I need a moment." Running to Inex as he loaded the no kill targets into a transport, Laye yelled, "I'm going with Fere, follow the plan. If anything happens call me."

Inex raised his arm to her, and Laye turned back and ran to the transport, she jumped in next to Fere as the door closed. In seconds they were in the air and taking off for the ship in orbit.

The Sarter man angled around from his seat in the front, his expression gave no indication of his feelings in his expression, but Laye could sense a guarded fear. "My name is Mr. Zillien Pinth of the third house of Nimroute. I prefer Zill. I am the Queen's liaison. Mac Shardlow sent a distress call to the Sarter Queen about his brother. Yarle is alive and in surgery, Mac has requested his status remain private until he is able to discuss it with you in person. We understand Fere is his significant other?"

Fere swallowed roughly before she nodded, "Yes."

"You will be escorted to the family waiting area, and when Yarle is out of surgery you will be allowed to sit with him. Laye on the other hand, we have questions, and we are certain you have the answers." Zill's tail flitted between the V in the seat as he faced forward.

Fere and Laye met one another's eyes over Zill's last statement, and Laye shrugged, "It's time." Laye knew exactly who Zill was, and his reputation was well known. He was as lethal as he was beautiful. He was relieved to a degree that Laye rested back in her seat to force a calming breath, she hadn't realized how overwhelming his emotions had been.

In the front, Zill tilted his head to the side slightly, just enough that Laye noticed. He slid his tablet into his lap and turned the brightness down, he was likely notifying the ship that she would be compliant and to stand down.

The ship came into view, and she looked down at herself and over to Fere. They were practically nude. They both had thin underclothes on and both of them were soaked in sweat from all the running they had just done. Laye pursed her lips, *sugar tits*. She would strut onto to the Sarter Queen's ship with her breasts practically on full display, and she would own it.

The ship docked at the enormous, sleek ship. Laye didn't see a wormhole port, and she wondered it if was because they had the Iungo transport tech. The seal locked and they rose from their seats. Laye sighed at her dirty feet and tried to brush them off on the floor mat. She looked up to Zill staring at her with his arms crossed, frowning. "Sorry. I'm a little dirty," Laye explained as she assessed herself in the light. She had never cringed so hard in her life, she looked like she had been run over by a rock transport, and her own scent hit her nose with vengeance. It was as if her body had soured, and she shook her head at that damn electric bomb and her old suit. The Vo-Pess had designed it well because it had apparently been whisking away sweat. *Oh good, now Zill just thinks I'm gross.* Laye snarled a bit, but she kept her head high, as she and Zill moved down a long hallway with beautiful, swirled patterns on the walls. The glowing ceiling overly illuminated the space and Laye had to squint before her eyes adjusted.

Zill stopped and a door disappeared into the floor, "This way for Fere." When Zill saw Mac, he held the door from closing and nodded to Laye that she could step inside first.

Laye spotted Mac inside, and her heart sunk. Mac was a wreck and upon seeing her, he dropped his shoulders a bit.

Fere ran into the room toward Mac, "What's going on?"

"The bullet hit a main artery, and he was bleeding out. He died on the way up to the ship, but they revived him and they're still working. The only thing I know is they have blips of brain activity, but that could mean anything." Mac explained to Fere, his gaze sorrowful.

Beside Fere, Laye felt the air shift as Zill approached her. "It's time." She complied and followed him, giving Mac a small wave before the door shut. Following Zill, he led her further down the hall before turning to the wall.

She said a prayer to Relit and begged the wind spirits to guide her.

"She's ready." Zill seemed to be speaking to the wall until it opened to reveal a large room. The room was decorated with plants and small trees, and at the back was a Sarter woman with a sleeping robe on. She was sitting on a bench and pulling weeds from some of the pots. "You may have a seat," Zill instructed as he pointed to a metal garden chair facing the bench.

Laye sat down as the woman turned around and gave Laye a small grin. "Thank you, Zill." The Sarter woman assessed Laye intently as Zill made his way out.

"My name is Destry, and you are Laye?" Destry asked as she continued to evaluate Laye.

Feeling no fear and an odd sensation of acceptance from the queen, Laye nodded, and smiled, "Yes. I'm going to guess you are the Sarter's Queen?"

"I am. You can call me Destry, though. I only play queen when it's necessary and today it seems, it is not necessary." Destry brushed at her sandy hands and when she did, she noticed Laye's dirt crusted feet even though Laye tried to hide them under the chair.

Destry laughed under her breath before she brought her attention back to Laye, "How did you manage to flip K'hurian's internal power balance so quickly? I am simply astonished at how fast Mac was able to pull off what I requested of him. When he arrived with his dying brother, we helped him with no question. That was what he called us to do. But when he said, it was over, that the Shardlow's had usurped the Shrout territory? Well, my dusty friend, that information makes me rise out of bed in the middle of the night. That is some delightful news, yet unbelievable, considering he had also revealed that none of the civilians lost their lives. Now that, that bit of information was intriguing and outrageous considering who I was speaking with, but I didn't want to doubt Mac. I simply asked, did you have help? Mac, knowing his next step is negotiations with me, told me to request you and I have a chat."

Laye twisted inside as she felt herself betraying all the years of torture she had endured over ensuring she would uphold the Vo-Pess greatest secret of their existence. *Honey butt, you're safe here, just tell the nice, dirty woman the truth.* Laye squeezed her eye shut as she fought her conditioning, "I am Vo-Pess. I come from a hidden world. Fere and I were both part of the Vo-Pess intelligence. Our world is run by our military, who took over when our ancient home planet fell to the First Humans, back when they still used Janus as a secret base for sending their dirty little virus all over the galaxy."

Destry cleared her throat and feigned calm. "Oh? What creature do your people evolve from?"

"Butterflies," Laye answered as she watched Destry sit up. She could pretend to be calm all she wanted on the exterior, but Laye knew the truth. Destry was coming *unglued* with excitement. Peering around the room, Destry spotted her tablet, and moved to pick it as she asked, "Do you still have wings?"

Laye stood up and lifted her shirt as Destry returned with the tablet. "Yes, I have wings. They fold against my skin when I don't need them," Laye answered and Destry studied them closely before Destry sat back on the bench.

Holding her tablet to her chest, Destry asked, "Can you show me your wings?"

Laye agreed, and she spread them out, slowly peeling them away from her skin and pulling them out from under her clothes. Her shirt lifted as her wings rose and filled out. They were solid black, bending down slightly at the tips with matching vein patterns on either side.

Destry studied them with delight and awe, admitting, "I was aware of your species previous existence. I was not aware you still existed. I am, by nature curious about biology. Unfortunately, we don't have time for that right now, and my kingdom demands further questions are answered."

Laye smiled and nodded, "I understand." She pulled her wings back against her skin and sat down in the chair.

"I know it was you and Fere who managed to take out the Shrout targets with almost no civilian casualties on the mission. Do you understand how valuable your skills are in the galactic center?" Destry asked, still holding her tablet tight to her chest.

Laye understood perfectly, "You want to be able to hire me? In exchange for what?"

Destry didn't waver as she demanded, "I want the option to call on you in a pinch. You will just have to trust that I won't abuse it. It will be limited to crisis with world or galactic ending repercussions. We want to trust Mac, but we are far from stupid. He is still a K'hornibus, and they have not had a strong historical record of peace. If we had the option to call on you, my council would be much more inclined to allow K'hurian into the Sarter Kingdom as a voting member. I won't reveal you, I will simply explain that I have obtained a highly valuable asset or two."

Destry was leaving something out, an important piece to this puzzle. Laye thought a moment before she asked, "What current job do you need completed?"

Destry tapped her tablet as it sunk in that this woman was the real deal, someone who could take out the most wanted woman in the galactic center. "I have one job that I think might interest you. It's an assassination."

"Fausta?" Laye asked, her heart slamming against her chest with delight.

Destry's interest in Laye piqued even further at her correct guess. "Yes. I want you to find and kill Fausta Urus III of the house of Venus. I will give you whatever resources you require. This is going to be a joint effort with the current UTC Empress and King of Aduro, Livia Claudius. I will ensure you are in contact with the right people when we are ready. I am happy to have you on our team for this endeavor."

"The UTC and Sarters are working together, and a Genil with an Iungo on her arm is the Empress now." Laye was sick of the secrecy. *It's time for the truth.* Laye didn't regret one word as she betrayed her people and oath of secrecy with every syllable. "Mac has the location of the Vo-Pess home planet, Hyret in his ship logs. May I request that if there are any Vo-Pess defectors, they be given asylum?"

Destry was simply smitten at the efficiency of Laye's negotiations. "Of course. I suspect this arrangement will end up with highly favorable results. I will draw up the agreement and present it to both, you, and Mac, before you are sent home." Destry rose from her bench and led Laye to the door.

"You may join your family in the waiting room," Destry disappeared behind the wall, and Laye turned to find Zill standing in the hallway.

Zill seemed surprised as she approached him, and he put his hands on his hips, "I guess everything went well?"

Laye gave him a genuine smile. "Can you take me to the waiting room?"

He smiled back at her, and thrust her a damp cloth. "Please wipe your feet, there are little red flakes and soot everywhere. Destry is bad enough. I can't have another one of you dirt loving ladies leaving dust everywhere."

After a quick towel bath, Laye stepped into the waiting room, where Mac was seated in a chair with Fere next to him, appearing just as distraught. She headed for Mac, and he leaned up to reach for her hand before hauling her into him.

Mac whispered over her hair, "My father always had the money for the betterment of everything, including adequate medical care. He could have at the very least given us the means to try and save my brothers when they fell. Everyone but Yarle and I were disposable to him."

Laye wondered how much Mac knew when he asked, "Did your conversation with the queen go well? Will K'hurian be accepted?" *Mac knows everything.*

"Yes. K'hurian's agreement is being drafted."

He squeezed her to him as he whispered into her hair, "I am conflicted over this. We can talk about it later, but I am so thankful for you, my little butterfly," as he kissed her forehead, and Laye rested her head on his shoulder.

Laye reassuringly smiled, knowing exactly why he was conflicted, "I would have taken the deal without question once I heard my first assignment."

Mac smirked, "Excited for that one?" She couldn't help but laugh, "You have no idea."

THIRTY-FOUR

ARE YOU THERE, YARLE?

They waited for hours in silence, stewing over Yarle's life before one of the Sarter surgeons, Doctor Trather, finally came out to speak to them. "His body will recover, but we are not sure how long his brain went without oxygen. He died two more times as we were trying to repair the artery. We won't know anything until he wakes up which could be at any time. You can see him when you have bathed," Dr Trather explained as he eyed Laye and Fere with disgust, Laye read his name on his tag as she stood from Mac's lap.

Dr Trather sniffed the air and curled his lip at Laye and Fere. "I will have Zill escort you to a private room."

A few moments after the doctor disappeared through a door in the back, Zill came in the main door, "This way." He led them to a private hospital room with a full bathroom, "There is a particle replicator in the back of the room, please make yourself some clothing and if you need food, you can access it there as well."

Fere collapsed on the chair, still in a mental fog. Laye

knew that feeling of longing while avoiding hopelessness too well. Mac pulled Laye into the bathroom and turned the shower on. Laye shut the door and took her clothes off, tossing them into the trash. Mac took off his armor and had nothing under it. Laye smacked him on the rear, and he glared at her like she had committed a heinous crime.

She ignored him and stepped in the hot water, Mac followed her in and grabbed her. He held her to him, and wouldn't let go, even when Laye knew they should get out. Mac lifted Laye up, and she wrapped herself around him. He eventually turned the stream off, and they wrapped themselves in towels before figuring out how to work the particle replicator inside the wall in the back of the room.

Fere went in and showered, taking a while. Laye and Mac waited for her after they had dressed in some comfortable grey shirts and loose pants. Laye rested her head against Mac's shoulder, "Thank you for trusting us."

As he recalled the massacre in his canyon home, Mac scoffed, "Who am I to question you?"

"How do you feel about us going on this next mission?" Laye asked, apprehensive about the answer.

Quick to answer, Mac grumbled, "I fucking hate it. As soon as Destry said it, I had some serious destroy a world feelings, but I knew you wouldn't just say yes, I knew you would be excited about it. You miss your job, you just hated the control. I won't be the one to hold you back from what you want."

Laye could have cried, she looked up at him and he wrapped his arm around her. "You're saying I could have said no, and you wouldn't have been upset about losing the immediate voting inclusion?" Laye asked, she had to know.

Mac tugged her close, and answered, "We could have eventually earned it the hard way. I wouldn't have cared which path you chose."

"The big bad warlord has grown as a person?" Laye pursed her lips at him.

Mac scowled at her, and touched the center of her neck, "No, not entirely. Did you forget I have a tracker in you? You're mine, I'll always come for you."

Laye laughed under her breath as she leaned against Mac's chest. They waited quietly until Fere finally emerged from the steamy bathroom. Laye had already had clothes for Fere when she came out.

"Thank you." Fere returned into the bathroom to change. The waiting was destroying all of them, Fere sounded like a meek desert mouse. Her heart was in a vice, she had never been so afraid of anything.

When Fere was ready, they went back into the waiting area, and the doctor there speaking to Zill. Zill walked by them as they followed the doctor to the recovery room. Yarle had sensors all over him, and the wall was covered in different readings, one was a fully body hologram with real-time visuals of his organs. Fere took in his condition, "May I touch him?"

"Please, it helps the patient recover if they sense a loved one is near." The doctor moved on to another patient in a room across from theirs.

When the door shut, Fere slowly moved toward Yarle's head, "Do you think I should try and sense if his feelings are still there?"

"You might not be able to read anything if he's not awake." Laye wasn't sure it was a good idea, but Fere wasn't sure of what else to do, so she lay her hand on

Yarle's arm and whispered to him, "I need you to wake up. We all need you back. I need you back."

"I need to try it." Fere didn't turn around, but Laye understood. Laye slid a chair over next to his bed and Fere sat down before she leaned over to angle her face near Yarle's so one of her antennae could reach out and wrap around one of his horns.

Fere reached out for him, "His feelings are intact."

"His brain is responding, keep going," Laye held her eyes on the screen above Fere with Yarle's brain activity.

Fere pushed her feelings outward. She could feel Yarle trying to respond, and she rubbed her hand up and down his arm. He gave her strong feelings of relief mixed with anger. Unable to help it, Fere laughed under her breath, "He is relieved but angry beyond reason, I think he's going to be fine. We might just need to convince his mind to allow him to wake."

Laye could sense the release of tension in Mac beside her, he found a chair and dropped in it, "Thank you, Fere. He is furious with me, and he will get over it."

"He's going to be a lot more pissed when he finds out what we traded." Laye whispered to Mac.

Fere didn't respond but Laye knew she had been listening. She knew what would happen next. Without moving Fere whispered to Laye, "Fausta?"

Laye quietly confirmed, "Yes."

"I was hoping you would say that," Fere couldn't help a delighted grin, "and now, Yarle is enraged." Fere began laughing under her breath before slapping a hand to her mouth. Fere unraveled her antenna from Yarle's horn, and turned to Laye. "Yarle will be with us in a few moments, and we *will* need to restrain him. *Now.*"

Mac leaned his head back and groaned, this would not be pleasant.

Laye triggered the door as the doctor was leaving the room across the hall. "Hi, so we have a strong feeling Yarle will be waking any moment, and we also have a profound suspicion that he will be a monster when he does. We need the room soundproofed as well as containment fields erected. Now, is a great time."

The doctor stared at her blankly before narrowing his eyes, "How do you know exactly?"

Laye shot her antenna straight above her head. "You don't have clearance for that. Just do what I asked."

His eyes nearly fell out of his head as he took in her antennae, but the doctor flew into action, running for Yarle's bed and pressing a few options before turning to Laye, "He's held down in a forcefield we use for prisoners after medical care. It should hold but we've never had a K'hornibus in it. I'll put another field around the room until he calms down, including a sound barrier."

Laye nodded to the flustered physician, "If you have questions, consult your queen." He understood and tapped some options next to the door before disappearing down the hallway in a rush. The room was quiet for a few moments before something like a grumble, and then a rough whimper came from Yarle's lips.

"Here we go." Fere took a step back.

Laye shook her head as she backed up next to Mac. "K'hornibus hold the top seat for fury, I can almost feel him, Mac. He is not happy about us going after Fausta."

The moment she mentioned Fausta, Yarle released a gurgling hiss, "Anger has always served us well." Mac agreed as he watched his brothers closed eyelids flutter. *Laye and Fere are doing this on purpose, and I almost feel bad for you. Almost. This is what you deserve for lodging a rock up my nose as I slept when we were ten.* He still had nightmares about the nurse digging in his nose after the rock.

Yarle's head shook slightly as he opened his mouth and growled. A deep slow breath filled Yarle's lungs before his eyes flew open, and he roared in the small hospital room.

Fere slapped a hand over her mouth as Laye asked, "He's not going to bust an incision, is he?"

"No, he was bonded. He'll be fine." Mac stood up and put his arms around Laye.

Yarle's head thrashed as he screamed, "SAY'S WHO? Release me from this fucking invisible trap!"

"And let you loose to kick my ass, I don't think so." Mac scoffed as Laye rubbed Mac's arm in reassurance.

Yarle seemed to be fighting the force field and winning as he tipped his head up trying to eye Mac. "I'll fucking kill you! Fausta?! For WHAT TRADE?!"

Fere came up and lay her hand on Yarle's chest, "It's for immediate voting rights in the Sarter Kingdom council. It's worth it. It's just going to be a few missions."

"No! You can't go, I can't let you go! I just found you! Mac, fucking do something! I'll fucking kill you, Mac!" Yarle's words were spoken in an angry, yet devastatingly sorrowful tone.

Fere's heart broke, but she knew this was the right thing to do, "Eliminating Fausta is our life's work. We were raised and trained to kill her. This has nothing to do with Mac."

Yarle's head fell back, and his eyes squeezed shut, Fere pulled the sheet down that was covering his chest and began rubbing around his shoulders.

He could hardly take in a breath, gasping, "You can't

do this. Why do you have to be the one? Why does this rest on you? I can't accept this!"

Mac sat down as Laye approached Yarle on the opposite side of Fere, "I know you haven't truly been able to see Fere in action, but she's just as good as I am. Have faith in her, she is one of the best assassins in the galaxy. If anyone can take out Fausta, it's us. We will have the best tech, and there will be no room for error. The new Genil UTC empress is joining us in planning this mission, making this greater than anything the galactic center has experienced in hundreds of thousands of years. The standoff between the Sarter's and the UTC is over, and this last mission will ensure peace in the galaxy."

Yarle clenched his jaw, and hissed through his teeth, "I'll never accept this. If anything happens to Fere you will need to kill me, Mac, because if you don't? I'll kill you, and everyone involved."

Mac answered nonchalantly, and without looking up, "I know."

THIRTY-FIVE

THE CALL

Within the day, they were sent back down to K'hurian on a medical transport, and Fere and Yarle were resting in his bed. Yarle was wrapped around Fere, and she was beyond antsy, but knew better than to try and peel herself away from him.

"If you would have been able to watch us take over the Shrout main home." Fere began, but Yarle cut her off.

"I don't want to hear about it. I'm going camping by myself in the salt while you're gone." Yarle squeezed her closer, and she could hardly breathe.

Fere felt guilt overwhelm her. "Are you going to be different when I return?"

"Not unless you come back in pieces, or not at all," Yarle grumbled above her.

She felt a sliver of relief, she had never even had a nick when on a job. There was a knock at the door and Yarle snapped, "What?!"

Laye opened the door a crack and only showed her face. "Our equipment has been delivered. We start preparing tomorrow and we are scheduled to leave in two days. They gave us a new ship too. It has a cloak and Iungo transport tech."

Fere tried to sit up, but Yarle held her down, "Transport tech?! They're *giving* us the ship. Yarle, let me up!" Fighting Yarle's grip, Fere put her strength into pushing his arms off her, and his eyes popped open as she did just that.

"What the fuck?!" Yarle yelped as Fere slipped out of his grasp.

Fere stood next to a stunned Yarle, "I've been asking you to trust me. Are you going to make me fight you to prove myself?"

Laye laughed maniacally as she jumped toward Fere. Fere ducked and rolled as Laye landed on the other side of her. Laye spun yet Fere was ready, blocking each of her strikes. The two vaulted away from the bed and rolled across the floor in an impromptu sparing match. Yarle shot up from the bed as he snapped, "What the fuck is going on?!"

Fere and Laye were back on their feet, sending and dodging punches and kicks. Fere soared into the air and kicked toward Laye's head. At the same time, Laye leaned back to dodge the kick. The entire moment happened in less than a second, and Yarle grasped his pillow to his chest wondering if he needed to shout for Mac. Fere spun and slammed into Laye, knocking them both to the ground where they wrapped their limbs around one another but seemed to slip through each other's grasp repeatedly. They were silent as they tried hold after hold, attempting to pin one another.

Yarle was positively horrified. "Enough!" Fere and Laye both collapsed in a heap of laughter on the ground.

They used to have sparing drills where they were forced to run through every position they knew within a matter of minutes, which is what they just displayed for him. "I don't ever want to see that again," Yarle admitted with his arms crossed as he glared at Fere, still laughing on the ground.

Fere sat up and wiped her eyes, "I think I can handle myself. You don't have to worry about me."

Yarle began to say something, but was cut off when Mac barged in, "What is happening in here?"

Laye was still on the ground and Mac stood over her, "Yarle wouldn't let Fere up, and she asked if he wanted to spar. He obviously can't right now, so I obliged."

"Right here in his room?" Mac asked, his brow creased with concern.

Laye couldn't help but laugh all over again as she wiped sweat from her eyes, "Sorry, we haven't sparred in a while. I was a little excited."

Fere helped Laye off the ground as Yarle lay back against the pillows with his arms firmly crossed. Once on her feet, Laye explained, "Fere and I need to go through the equipment and familiarize ourselves. Yarle is, well, being Yarle."

Behind her, Yarle frowned, "No one thought to ask me anything. I don't agree with any of it, and I never will, no matter how this turns out. I'm fucking furious."

Fere and Laye left Yarle's room as Mac went inside to sit down in the chair next to the bed, Yarle was on bed rest for another day before he was cleared and he would try and climb out of bed if someone wasn't next to him at all times.

Laye led Fere into the living area where they spotted two large metal boxes with control panels on top. Laye went up to one and set her hand in the center of the top, and the box unsealed. The top opened on its own, and it revealed two types of body armor with instructions as well as a collection of weapons from all over the galactic center. A high-tech helmet sat on the weapons compartment, and Laye picked it up to examine it.

Fere opened her box, and began reading the instructions, "This is Iungo tech."

Laye turned and stared at Fere and struggled to find her words, "Is this their rail gun catching armor?!"

"Yes. Put your suit on we have to try these out!" Fere insisted.

"Where do you think you're going to test those suits in my city?" Mac was leaning on the wall behind them.

Laye bit her lips before quietly asking, "Can we use the transport? Wait, who is with Yarle?"

Mac grinned, "Yarle is having a post-op exam with Iker. Your ship from Destry is parked outside."

"What!" Fere and Laye each shimmied on the new armor as fast as they could before rushing outside.

They forgot rail guns to test with, and Mac took one out of each box before he followed them outside. Fere was sitting at the controls while Laye was in the back meddling with everything she could see. Mac handed them the rail guns and she scoffed at herself, "See? That's why we can't learn tech the same day we leave. It's too exciting."

"Please don't blow each other's heads off." Mac begged her as she flipped through the engine information.

Laye gasped with a hand to her chest, "Us? No, fucking, way!"

"What?" Fere asked from the front, too absorbed in the controls to have been listening. Laye looked over at Fere, "Read about the engine tech." Fere's hands flew to the controls, and she flipped through the same document as Laye. "You're kidding me. It's just magnified electromagnetic radiation blasted at a confined space?! The result is transporting. Shut your fucking sugar lips, this can't be right?"

"Oh, it's right. Look at this." Laye tossed Fere a small device, "It's a site-to-site wearable transporter. This says here that it works with our suits."

Fere scoffed, "Is this whole fucking ship Iungo technology? How did the Sarter Queen score that deal?"

"She must have become good friends with the Iungo. I don't know why else they would share so much tech unless maybe they know who we are going after," Fere explained as she put the transport tag on her armor in the center of her chest.

Laye did the same and saw a purple light emit as it connected "They had to know their target was Fausta. No one would just give away this kind of technology."

"This ship makes me think the Sarter Kingdom and UTC have been working on this for more than a few months. They must have been waiting for someone willing to do the job." Fere ran her finger over the console.

"I need to go back inside and make sure Yarle doesn't hurt himself. Don't have too much fun." Mac patted the side of the ship before he turned and went back inside.

Laye hopped in the front seat of the small ship, "Did you figure out how to turn on the cloak?"

"Not yet." Fere pushed a button, and the ship buzzed before a notice popped up, cloak enabled. Fere tipped her head to the side, "Well, I guess I found it."

"Let's try the transport engine," Laye offered as she peered over at Fere.

Fere bit her lip in excitement. "We are parked in Mac's courtyard. Do you think that's a good idea?"

"Why not?" Laye shrugged. Fere didn't have a good reason not to, so they started up the engine and plugged in the coordinates they wanted in the desert. In seconds, they were looking out onto the seemingly endless sand.

Fere whistled, "Now that is something."

"Let's try the site-to-site transporters," Laye offered. Tapping the options on her forearm, she selected the coordinates she wanted and pressed the option to jump.

In seconds she was standing outside of the cloaked ship. "That was fast."

"I have the guns. Let's try out these suits." Fere had appeared next to her after transporting.

They moved several yards apart and faced one another. Laye pulled her rail gun, and pointed at Fere, who was ready for the shot. Laye fired, and Fere caught the round with her suit. It spun around her body, and she slung it from her arm into the sand.

"My turn!" Fere cried out as she lifted her weapon from its place on her belt. Fere fired at Laye, and she spun into the round, the current of the suit mimicked the tech to shoot the bullet and twisted it around Laye. She felt like a goddess as the round twirled her body, she aimed with her arm and the projectile slammed into the sand.

"Blessed Relit, we could take out a whole room of commanders with this tech," Laye burst with excitement.

Fere wondered if that was the plan, she hadn't asked for details, "Are those our orders?"

"No, just Fausta. I'm just saying, maybe we should aim for more than just the head. Maybe we should cut off the whole top half of this problem we all seem to have in the galactic center. We know the First Humans don't have any real training." Laye offered as she met Fere's gaze.

Nodding, Fere agreed, "Understood. Let's have ourselves a good night of fun, and we get down to business tomorrow. The UTC is supposed to be sending us Fausta's location in the morning."

Laye grinned deviously, "I do like a good fuck before a battle."

Fere burst into laughter and admitted, "Me too."

THIRTY-SIX

BATTLE PREPARATIONS

When Laye went in Mac's bedroom, she found him sitting in his chair reading on his tablet. Laye left her armor in the box in the living room, and she was wearing her usual fitted underclothes. Without looking up from his tablet, Mac pointed to a camera he had set up and he demanded, "Take your clothes off."

Laye complied, and he peered over at her with a sour scowl, sniffing the air, "You are not getting in my bed smelling like that. Take your ass to the shower."

"Why don't you make me?" Laye taunted. Mac tossed away his tablet, and grabbed Laye, swinging her under his arm as he headed for the bathroom.

"Feeling naughty today?" Mac spanked her bare ass before he turned the shower on, not allowing her to escape from his grip.

He grabbed the soap to wash her lower half and rinsed her before reaching down and toying with her center. Mac heard her gasp and explained, "I found a way to make the desert sage oil more suitable for your pussy."

"Mac, if you put that on my pussy, you better gag me first, or someone will think I'm being murdered," Laye admitted from under his arm. She nearly started clawing at his leg at the thought.

Mac laughed, "I had all my rooms soundproofed."

"Oh fuck," Laye breathed as she felt Mac twirl his finger over her most sensitive place. *Sugar balls! He has the oil on his fucking finger!*

She began throbbing with need as she fought Mac, her legs failing around wildly. He slapped her ass again, and she jolted with pleasure, her core was thrumming with desire as he turned around with her under his arm. Her upper torso was now in the steam of water, and she could feel a breeze of air pass over her center. She was so sensitive she could feel every movement pulse in her core.

"Soap up so I can tie your ass down and have my way with you," Mac demanded as she became eye level with the soap. She wiggled in his grip as she reached for the soap, "Please just let me cum, I'm already there!"

"No, wash yourself well and hurry up," Mac demanded as he slapped her ass again. She almost came with that slap and moaned as her hands rubbed the soap over her breasts, her nipples were hard and desperate. She quickly rubbed soap over the rest of her skin. "I'm clean, fuck, please let me cum," Laye pleaded as she rinsed off.

Mac lifted her from under his arm and held her in the stream as he rinsed her once last time before he slung her over his shoulder. She grunted trying to rub her thighs together as he grabbed the oil. "If you don't hold still, I'm going to rub this oil all over you, and watch you flop around for an hour," Mac threatened as he spanked her ass again.

Laye furiously shook her head, begging, "Mac, don't you fucking dare!" She fought him further, and he slammed her wet body onto the impossibly soft bed. She was already shaking with need as he took her hands and tied them to the headboard before he tied just her left leg to the bottom of the bed. Laye tried to play a string and bow instrument with her leg to stimulate herself, but Mac pried it away.

"Fuck me! Just do something!" Laye would scream if he didn't let her cum. Shaking his head, he took the oil off the nightstand, and Laye wildly demanded, "No! No more of that!"

Mac smirked down at her deviously. "Shh, if you're too loud, I'll gag you."

Laye reared back trying to pull away from his oil covered fingers hovering her nipples, "No, no, no!"

Mac twirled his fingers over her nipples, and she squealed, "Fuck you!"

Mac gave her a deep laugh, "I told you not to fight me. Now you're going to pay."

Laye would find her revenge, she didn't know how, or when, but he was getting edged to death at some point. Her mind spun with pleasure as the oil began doing its job, causing her nerves to scream for contact.

Mac gently brushed his fingers over her nipples, and she trembled as she pleaded, "Please, Mac, I'll be good I promise."

"Too late." Mac reached down and pulled something from his drawer, Laye took one look at it and knew what it was. Laye blew out a long sigh, "You better not put that in me without making me cum first, you fucker!"

Mac smiled down at her while he slid a new vibrator inside of her and switched it on. He was delighted when she cried out and began whimpering for him.

"That's good, those are the sounds I wanted." Mac peered down at her shaking form and grinned.

Laye was nearly in tears as she begged, "I will do anything just let me cum!"

"What will you trade Laye?" Mac twisted and angled the vibrator inside of her.

Laye cried out again but this time her words meant something, "I'll always come back to you, I swear. I belong to you and only you." Mac paused a moment and admitted, "I didn't know there was a right answer, but I think that's it."

Taking a cloth, Mac cleaned the oil off Laye's nipples and pull the vibrator out of her, but didn't untie her. She leaned her head back and unapologetically moaned as the cloth slid over her breasts. Mac reached down between her thighs and gently wiped away the oil there, and she surged from the contact.

"Do you know what I like the best about this new formulation?" Mac asked as Laye tipped her head up to stare at him.

He had a devious stare as he admitted, "The affects continue after the oil is wiped away."

Laye screamed as he descended his mouth onto her, dragging his tongue up her center. All her muscles were tense, and she was squeezing her legs around Mac's head as she felt his hand slide up her skin and pinch her nipple. The moment he touched her desperate flesh, she exploded. Her orgasm slammed into her, and she flailed around, fighting to take a breath. Her mind felt like it went blank as the pleasure crested and she shattered for him.

Mac didn't rush as he untied her and crawled over her spent form, "This is how I always want you, spent from pleasure so great you scream. This is what you deserve."

He slid inside of her, and she groaned with how filled she was. He thrust, and she could feel herself coming undone all over again. Mac pushed himself into her and Laye was already so close when she felt him separate inside. She ground against his split and rolling length. Mac grabbed her hips and pressed her into him as he leaned over her. His length angled up at the ends and fluttered.

Mac roared as he tipped over into her, she felt his cum jet out of the center of his split length. "Fuck. Why do you always make me so hungry? I always want to eat fresh snake meat after I cum in you." Mac had his hands on his hips staring at Laye under him.

As he untied her, she laughed, "Do you want me to fetch you something out of the kitchen? Do you need a little plate service after you get off?"

Mac lie on the bed next to her, "If you're offering, I'm taking it."

"I'm surprised you want food in your room." Laye admitted as she rose up.

Mac questioned, "My room? Do I look like I occupy this room by myself anymore?"

"Oh, I just assumed." Laye stopped reaching for her robe and turned to Mac.

Mac was leaned against his headboard with his hands behind his head, "Did you assume because I say I own you? Because that is far from the truth. That's a fucking game. This is just as much your home now, like it is mine, Yarle's, and Fere's."

Laye hadn't genuinely thought about it and was happy just belonging to him. She hadn't considered she was anywhere close to his equal when it came to the rest of his life.

"You have children, and they would come first," Laye understood K'hornibus would often choose a child over a significant other.

Mac rose up and approached her, tipping her head to look at him. "No one I love is going to ever go without anything as long as I'm alive, or after I die. That includes you. Now, I believe you promised me a plate of food. That's a big deal here, it's kind of like offering a glass of water."

"I'll go fetch your plate," Laye whispers as she smiled at him. Laye dressed in a robe before she made her way out of his room and to the kitchen. When she arrived, she found Fere was leaned against the counter with her thumbnail between her teeth.

"What is wrong?" Laye asked as she pulled a plate of meat out of cold storage and put it on the counter. She resisted the urge to rub her chest again, the oil was still making her nipples tingle, and her robe continued teasing them as she moved. Laye began preheating the heating box. "Fere? What is wrong?" Fere paused a moment, but finally answered, "Yarle is so angry he will hardly speak to me. I think being shot, and almost dying scared him more than he wants to admit."

Laye thought briefly before she suggested, "Mac told me bringing them food is like bringing them water. I'm making Mac a plate, you should make Yarle one. Maybe it will snap him out of it."

Fere's eyebrows slowly raised, and she tipped her head, "That's a great idea. I'll try anything at this point."

Fere took another portioned plate of meat, and set it

next to the one Laye pulled out before asking, "How did you and Mac meet anyway?"

What began as a giggle turned into a full-on belly laugh as Laye tried to figure out how to explain it. Fere, contagiously giggling, tapped the counter, "That bad huh?"

Laye nodded, nearly in tears, "He caught me, and I didn't want to die, so I got naked in the creek and felt myself up."

"You fucking did not!" Fere was now laughing along with Laye as she continued. Laye grabbed Fere's arm as she peered around the corner to make sure no one was listening before she rapidly rambled, "He tied me to a table and gave me an orgasm with an electric bone saw handle. I thought he wanted to cut me up. I guess I looked depressed or something, and he felt bad for me."

When she turned back, Fere's mouth was dropped open. "Are you fucking kidding?"

Laye shook her head no and started laughing all over again, "Not at all. That was my first orgasm!"

Fere's eyes flared, "Yarle was my first!"

Laye slapped a hand over her mouth. "None of those elite Vo-Pess men knew a damn thing about women. I wouldn't be surprised if we find more defectors the way Mac came for me."

"I've almost convinced myself I would have run after them and made them take me if they hadn't. You're right about defectors. I know we will eventually see more of our intelligence people, which is a fact. They can't erase that we made it away and they know damn well they can't ever kill us. Mac and Yarle would burn the planet," Fere admitted, those two steps toward Yarle had been the easiest steps of her life.

THIRTY-SEVEN
THE PLATE

Fere played a balancing act with the plate of food and glass of water at Yarle's door. The plate was carefully tucked under her arm while she balanced the glass of water in her hand. She opened the door, and took the plate wedged under her arm back into her hand. When Yarle noticed she was holding a plate of food and a glass of water for him, his anger fade away with every step she took toward his bed.

Taking the plate from her first, he reached for the glass, "Do you know what it means to serve me food and water?"

Fere shrugged, "It means enough for you to talk to me. I can't leave with you upset, I'll do anything for you to feel better before I go."

"It means forever," Yarle explained as he bit into the snake on his plate.

Not taking her eyes from him, Fere didn't waver, "That's about right."

He set his plate down and pulled her over to him

before picking it back up and eating as fast as he could. Yarle chugged the water then set his plate on his side table before he turned around to face Fere.

"I don't like that you're going on any kind of mission without me. When I was dying, all I could think about was how you would be alone. I know you can take care of yourself, it's not about that. I was shot in the first five minutes of the mission, and that could have been you. I thought about how I would feel if I had been the one left alone. It was too much, and I snapped. The moments before I blacked out, Mac was yelling at me to hang on, that we had a chance to change everything with you and Laye. He told me I couldn't die, I had to be supportive in your future missions. He had spoken to the queen about Laye when she questioned him about my injury. I've never been so furious as I listened to him freely offer you and Laye for our planet, but I was already too sedated to say a damn thing about it. I couldn't comprehend ever putting any of us in danger again, and for him to offer such a thing when I was actively dying. When I could hear your voices in the hospital discussing going after Fausta, I have never wanted to destroy everything in my path more in my life," Yarle admitted, his arm was around Fere and squeezing her to him.

Fere felt guilty, but she knew Yarle wouldn't have come out of that state easily. "We knew you would fight harder to wake up if you knew the truth. They bonded your insides, so you were in no danger, I'm sorry it was so traumatic. I wouldn't have done that if I had known."

"It's not that at all, I would have been furious when I woke up either way. I'm a selfish man and the idea of my woman going on another mission for Mac is out of the question. But to hear Fausta's name? I was enraged. I hate all of it and the last thing I want to do is support something putting you in danger. When you walked in with a plate for me though, I realized forever is not all about me. This is about what you want too and if you want forever with me? I know I will have to make fucking compromises I don't like." Yarle rubbed his hand up her arm, and she rest her head on his chest.

Fere still felt a pang of guilt. "I'm sorry you have to change so much for me. That's not what I wanted."

"Learning how to not be so damn selfish is probably not a bad thing." Yarle whispered over her hair, his lips brushing her antenna. She felt his strong feelings for her briefly. "When you were still out, I felt for you through my antenna. I felt great anger and relief."

"I remember waking up to you inside my head. I was angry, but I was so relieved to feel you that nothing else really mattered until I heard Fausta's name." Yarle admitted, the memory still fresh and boiling inside of him.

Fere sighed, she had felt alive when she realized they were going after the ultimate enemy of the galactic center, "I need this, it calls to me."

Yarle sunk his head as he relented, "I know. I know there's nothing I can do, and I don't want to change anything about you. You're perfect the way you are and if that means I have to deal with you being an assassin for Mac or the Sarter Queen then so be it."

Fere crawled over Yarle to straddle his lap, and he leaned back as she lay over him, resting her head on his chest. "Thank you. I can't just forget what I trained for my entire life, this is my chance to end it, and I want nothing more. I can just be me once it's over, I can let it all go."

Yarle understood and he kissed her forehead, "Will you

be able to let it go, or will you be left with a desire for more?"

Fere smiled against his chest, "You're all I need and want. I just want a peaceful life with you, the idea of helping you, Laye, and Mac heal your planet is thrilling. I can't wait to see it rain, and watch the plants grow."

"It sounds like you love K'hurian as much as Mac and I." Yarle set his hand over her head and brushed her hair from her face.

Fere bit her lip before she answered, "No, I think I just love you, and our future."

Yarle's heart leapt, K'hornibus didn't say things like I love you, but hearing it made him think twice. He lifted her so she was sitting on his stomach, and he guided her face to his so he could kiss her. He couldn't live without this woman, and he couldn't pull her close enough, he fought the urge to squeeze her to him.

He kissed her like he would never see her again, her heart broke with his soft touch and the way he held onto her. Yarle lifted her up by her hips, her light frame allowing him to move her easily. He bit the hem of her undershirt to lift it up and she pulled it off, exposing her breasts to him. He lifted his face and put his mouth around her nipple, and he licked and sucked on each of her sensitive nipples before he kissed down her skin.

Fere grabbed the headboard as Yarle lifted her up and sat her center on his face, he growled as he dipped his tongue inside of her. Her heart skipped as she felt him nip and suck at her nerves, the sensation making her shiver. His fingers stroked the edge of her wings while he held her up by her hips and licked her thoroughly. Fere sucked in her breath. Yarle was devouring her, and she felt herself prepare to shake, her muscles tensed trying to stop it. Yarle sensed her body shift and gripped her hips in a bruising hold as he flicked her along her row of nerves, Fere couldn't resist it anymore. When she let loose and violently shivered, Yarle held her center to his mouth and lay his tongue against her. It caused a vibrating sensation, and she yelped as she cracked open. Fere's shaking became more intense by the second as her orgasm slammed into her, she could hear Yarle laughing under her as she cried out. He didn't pull away but kept going as her shiver dragged on, the combination of her shaking and his rough tongue was giving her the longest stretch of pleasure yet.

When she finally slumped over, Yarle couldn't help but roar with laughter, "That was the craziest fucking thing I have ever done."

"I fucking love it when you touch my wings," Fere admitted, she knew he would have his way with her by the way he looked up at her. His eyes were full of wonder and joy. Fere's eyes went wide as she reeled over the possibilities, "Don't come up with any fucking ideas."

"Oh, I have some ideas. You'll just have to make sure and come back home so we can try the rest of them." Yarle stroked his hand down her wing, and she came unglued.

Fere yelped as delightful sensations overwhelmed her, "Oh, fuck. It feels too good." He grinned as he moved her over him and lay her next to him face down, his hands unable to help moving over her wings. She quivered under his light touch, and she squealed, holding back another shiver.

"This is too much fun," Yarle admitted as he released his length. He lifted Fere up where her back was facing him as he slid her onto his length, his hands gently drifted over her back to caress where her wings were stored away. She let herself go as she moaned and wiggled and ground onto Yarle's length. She felt him split as he traced the edges of her wings before moving his finger along the veins, Fere felt another intense shiver building. Fere couldn't hold back as her body took over, and Yarle grabbed her hips to keep her from lifting off. She froze in a state of vibration as her second orgasm rocked her, sending her mind into orbit. With his length split and rolling mixed with the vibrations, he tipped over and felt a detonation of pleasure. Yarle burst into her and groaned as his length pulsated. Fere released a high-pitched sigh as she lay back against him, her skin slick with sweat.

"You have to come back to me. You cannot be caught, do you understand?" Yarle grabbed her shoulders, he had not even pulled his length out of her yet.

She nodded in agreement, "I will. I swear to you. I will come back to you. I will come home in one piece, and we will have our life together."

Yarle closed his eyes and begged the sands that she was speaking the truth, that this perfect woman he found wouldn't be harmed. He was already full of dread and had no idea how sleep would happen.

THIRTY-EIGHT

FAUSTA URSUS III OF THE HOUSE OF VENUS

Laye and Fere stood in Mac's entryway as Mac and Yarle said their goodbyes. Mac was a picture of pride in Laye, but Yarle was haunted and cold. Fere knew he hadn't slept and still felt apprehensive about her leaving.

Hooking his hands under her arms, Mac raised Laye up and kissed her. "Go kill her and come home, we have a celebration to plan. Destry is so confident in you two that she is already preparing an award dinner."

Laye laughed, "I have always wanted to fly with their Alis. I think it would be exhilarating." *They would probably try and eat me, but it would be worth it.*

Yarle held Fere to his tense body, and she could almost feel his agony radiating. "I'll be back soon, a few days at the most." Fere's heart sank in her chest at his hand squeezed her shoulder, he was holding back, and she knew it.

Laye opened the door behind Fere, and she pulled away. Yarle cringed as he let her go. Fere hated that his eyes being full of worry was the last thing she saw of him before she left home and boarded their transport.

Laye saw it all unfold and when they sat down and buckled their harnesses, she reached over and took Fere's hand, "He will be alright because we are coming home."

"I know. I just wish he had more faith in me like Mac has in you," Fere explained as she held Laye's hand.

Laye smiled at her, "Yarle hasn't really seen what you can do like Mac has seen me. Even if he did, Yarle is a vastly different person that Mac, maybe he sees more than just a warrior in you and doesn't know how to express that. Maybe he sees a partner and your gentle side, he might be scared of the other part of you and that's alright. This is new and he will grow. Mac has become the man of my dreams, and I think Yarle is doing the same for you. You just haven't had as much time as we have. Now that I say that, we haven't had much time either, this has all happened so fast. When we come back and become settled, life will be perfect. I promise."

"You're right. Let's kill this bitch so we can come home and back to our men." Fere slid her helmet on and the controls inside lit up. Laye did the same and the transport linked with the helmets before they mounted the site-to-site transporters to their armor in the center of their chests. The transporter engine was ready in moments, and Fere plugged in the coordinates while Laye prepped the ship for transport.

Laye nodded to Fere and pressed the option to engage the engine, snapping them out of existence. They appeared above an unnamed planet, just a line of numbers and the greater system it's located in. *I am not reading all those numbers out, they should have stopped at three if they wanted people to pay attention.* Reading further she discovered there was thin atmosphere, and it was uninhabitable other than the hidden First Human backup command base. Only a few ships were docked, and no satellites were in orbit.

Laye read there were only a few detectable life forms, "These readings cannot be correct. This only shows five people in that base. There must be over thirty humans down there."

"Where should we start?" Fere asked, flexing her hands in anticipation.

Laye pulled up the map to the view screen. "We need to find a place we can transport in that looks like it's hidden away. Maybe we can move through most of the building without tripping the alarm."

Nodding, Fere suggested a place on their transport selection map, "Right here would have almost no obvious foot traffic."

"Alright, give it a few more minutes. Let's watch the foot traffic patterns a little longer." Laye suggested as she reviewed the evolving image. They sat for a moment watching before Laye agreed, "We move here, then here and see if we can take out whoever is in this larger room here?"

Fere nodded, "That's perfect. Let's go."

They entered in the coordinates, and both engaged their transporter at the same time, they appeared inside the base, down a dark hallway. Everything seemed fine until they took a step.

Alarm bells rang out, and the two ran down the hallway for their first target. They slammed into a force-field as a commander hit a panic button on the wall outside of his office. "I caught the intruders."

Laye and Fere felt an electric current pass through them as their equipment fried. They each tossed away their sparking helmets as commanders rushed them. The force-field must have held onto electronic devices because they were freed the moment the current ended, but it was too late. Human commanders surrounded and overtook them, Laye and Fere both hit the ground under the heavy weight of the humans. *Sugar balls! We were caught within the first minute!*

They felt restraints slide on their wrists and ankles before they were jerked up. Two commanders with knives cut away their armor, nicking their skin as the knives slid down their bodies.

"Did you think you could just strap yourselves with Iungo tech and rush us? As though we wouldn't be prepared for you? You will wish you never came here. Take them to our interrogation room." Fausta Ursus III stood before them as their armor was pulled away and they were disarmed.

Laye's skin pebbled in the cool air, *how did we end up doing this half naked again? We really need to wear more clothes under our armor next time.*

In nothing but underclothes, Laye and Fere were fearless in the midst of their enemy as they were led away. After a short trip down a hallway, they were being shoved into metal chairs and Fausta was close behind. After being restrained, Fausta narrowed her eyes around to her commanders, "Get out. I have questions for these two."

Once the door closed, Fausta reached for a knife and approached Laye, placing the knife under her chin and forcing her face up, "Do you think I'm not aware of your little boyfriend, the K'hornibus. I know all about how he found Hyret, and he let us know where to find it when he did. We have trackers on every ship made on Melior, when you employ only rich people, they're quite loyal." Laye stared at Fausta, feeling her slip the knife into her skin. "Where should we start?"

Fausta dragged the knife across Laye's chest and Laye didn't flinch, if Fausta thought she would try to pry something out of Laye? She was dead wrong, because next to her, inconspicuously, Fere was busy dislocating her thumb and slowly working the restraints off her hand. Laye was fully aware of her ability and kept Fausta busy.

"What do you want from me, Fausta? Just cries of pain. Do you want me to sob for you because we were caught?" Laye taunted her, causing Fausta to slash the knife down her arm.

Clear blood poured from her as Fausta reached over and slashed at Fere, opening the skin below her breast. Neither made a sound nor moved as Fausta cut them, this time on their legs. Fere felt her clear blood slide down her belly as she finally freed her thumb and felt the cuff slip from her hand.

Fere made a slight whistle with her lips, and Laye slammed her legs against the sides of her chair, engaging Fausta's attention. Fausta jammed the knife into Laye's leg as Fere leaned away preparing to attack. Just as Fausta moved to stab Fere, she swung the metal cuffs around and slammed them into the side of Fausta's face.

Like a sandbag, Fausta hit the floor with a thud, and Fere worked to free herself. She exhaled a trained breath before dislocating her other thumb and squeezing her hand out before she set both of her thumbs back into place. Laye was already moving her chair across the room toward Fere when Fere stood up and waddled with her chair right over to Fausta's face down, knocked out body to grab the removal control device from her back pocket.

Assessing their wounds were mostly superficial first,

they worked quickly on the cuffs and had them removed in a matter of seconds. Just as the cuffs from Laye's ankles fell away, there was a shout behind the door, "They're out! Sound the alarm, the Empress is down!"

"The empress?" Laye kicked Fausta's leg and laughed as she took two small knives from Fausta's hips, "Not anymore!" Fere and Laye were ready on either side of the door when it swung open, revealing a crowd of commanders vying to slaughter them. They each had one small knife, and the determination of a lifetime of preparation as they attacked. Slicing across the first commander's throat, Laye yanked him down as she cut across the face of the next. Fere next to her jumped over the first two kills to jab her knife into the temple of the third as she grabbed his long knife from his belt.

Laye took a rail gun from one of the downed commanders and covered Fere as she cut down commander after commander. Laye aimed and fired, taking out six commanders as Fere ran over to another, and gutting him where he stood. They moved into the main room, and found a few commanders hiding behind their desks, Laye aimed and shot them each through the thin metal desks.

"Is everyone dead except for Fausta?" A man ran for the ship docking bay, and Laye raised her gun and shot him down.

Fere nodded, "I think that may have been the last one. None of the ships are gone. Oh, look! It's our armor, and site to site transporters so we can transport back on the ship." Gathering their things, she tapped on the armor sleeve and the screen lit up, "It works, we can go home without calling for help."

Laye grinned as she heard Fausta groan behind her, "Let's have some fun before we go home. I bet we will have some time off after this, considering we took out all the commanders too."

"We killed thirty-seven. Let's make it thirty-eight." Fere always counted the bodies, and she was staring at Fausta like she was the ultimate hunting prize. They made their way over to Fausta and lifted her into a chair before tying her to it. Laye backhanded her across the face. "Wake up. It's time to pay." Fausta raised her eyes to Laye and Fere. Fausta frantically searched the area as she slowly realized she was bound to the chair in which she had Laye just moments before.

"Surprise. It looks like you're the one in the hot seat now," Laye purred as Fere handed her a knife.

Laye started by slicing Fausta across the top of her right knee, severing the thick tendon there. Fausta screamed as Fere pointed to the left knee, "Let's be sure she can't run away."

Laye slashed her across the top of the second knee and they reveled in Fausta's cries. Fere motioned for Laye to hand her the knife, and she took it only to slice down Fausta's side, spilling her blood all over the floor. Fere kept going, cutting Fausta across the chest, deep enough to sever all he muscles as she dragged the knife across. Fausta gurgled and cried as Fere playfully asked Laye, "Should I end it or keep going?"

"Let's go home, Fere. I want to deliver this woman's dead body to Destry's feet. I know she wanted her alive, but I just don't think we can manage that. She and her faction have been a leech in the galaxy for far too long. They caused our world to become an authoritarian nightmare and millions of our people have suffered for it." Laye gave Fere the signal to take her life, and Fere was delighted to.

Fere leaned over in Fausta's face as she sat stunned, and now too low on blood to speak. "It has been my ultimate pleasure making you scream. I hope you have fun being tortured for eternity in the flames of your hell." Fere dragged the knife across Fausta's neck and hovered over her as the light left her terrified eyes. Fere and Laye both stood in silence, surrounded by the spilled crimson blood of the disgraced former empress.

With their deadly skills, they had done the galactic center a great justice. This was the end of a reign of terror which had seen the elimination of many entire species, some before they had the chance to even evolve. This woman and her people had been behind it all, and had believed in their human domination, when humans weren't even supposed to exist at all. They had been created long ago and had caused nothing but havoc ever since.

Fere handed Laye her transporter, and they each held onto one of Faust's limp hands as they transported back to their ship.

THIRTY-NINE
AFTERMATH

When Fausta's dead body hit the floor of their transport, they haphazardly shoved her into the storage cabinet and slammed the door. It wouldn't shut and they kept trying before they realized Fausta's arm was nearly cut off in the door, Fere laughed under her breath as she kicked the arm inside and the cabinet finally shut. Laye reached for the dermal bonders, and they each attended one another's wounds before sitting down in the front seats.

They sat in silence, looking down on the desolate rocky world below them and decompressing a bit before Laye plugged in the coordinates of Destry's private landing pad at the Sarter Palace. The ship materialized, and they opened the door as they watched two Sarter guards run for the communication hubs on the side of the door.

Within moments, Destry was running outside and toward them with her brother Oran in tow. "You, did it?" Laye popped open the storage cabinet, and she and Fere each grabbed a leg and dragged Fausta's mangled body out in front of Destry.

"I knew it. I knew it when I met you." Destry leaned over Fausta and shook her head with disgust.

Fere smiled at Oran, "We killed all the commanders too. You might want to have a crew clean it all up and gather their intel. They left several ships behind."

Destry grabbed her brother's arm and shook him, "I told you they would do it!"

He scowled, "Fine. I hate that you're on a winning streak, but I'm glad you won this one."

"You're glad I won this one?!" Destry smacked her brother's arm, and he laughed, "What?" Laye rubbed her sore neck. "Is there anything else you need from us?"

"No, and if you two carried out what I think, you may have eliminated all the targets Empress Claudius and I would have had lined up for you. We will evaluate your kills, and let you know, but you may have already fulfilled your end of our entire deal all at once," Destry explained as she hooked her arm in Oran's, and they turned to return to the Sarter palace. Two guards at the door lifted Fausta 's body and followed them inside.

Laye and Fere turned and climbed in their transport and closed the door before Laye asked, "If we took out all our targets in one mission, what the hell are we going to do the rest of our lives?"

"I don't know, but I want to start on the rest of our lives tomorrow. I'm fucking tired, and I want to sit on Yarle's hard dick within the hour, so step on it," Fere demanded and Laye screamed with laughter as she punched in the coordinates. In seconds, they were parked in Mac's court-yard, Yarle was still sitting on the steps in front of Mac's door with his camping gear piled next to him.

He hasn't even left to go camping yet! Fere moved from her seat, and the door hardly had time to slide open when Fere burst from it and flew onto Yarle.

"You're back already?!" he cried out as he wrapped his arms around her, and he yanked off his mask to bury his face in her neck.

Mac opened the door and stood in the doorway, meeting Laye's eyes, "We tortured and killed her. I think we might have killed all our future targets too. It's over." Mac's face became stone, "You took out the former fucking empress and maybe all your future targets too? You were gone for three hours!"

Laye nodded as she closed the gap between her and Mac, he wrapped his arms around her. Fausta was dead, and they could move on. Mac was overjoyed and he pulled his mask off and tossed it behind him before he lifted Laye up. She entangled herself with Mac while Yarle lifted Fere to her feet.

"Call Cicilo and tell her to have food delivered. Drag your mattress into the living room like we used to do when father would leave." Yarle suggested as Mac set Laye down.

Mac laughed, "That's a great idea. I bet they've never seen the Pirate Chronicles."

"Oh, we have to show them, I binged it two days before we found Laye, and I forgot all about it. I still need to see season two," Mac admitted.

Yarle scoffed, "There are four seasons Mac!"

"Oh, I am behind." Mac laughed as they headed for their rooms. In minutes, Mac and Yarle had their mattresses in the living room, and blankets and pillows spread out. Fere and Laye crawled in the middle, wiggling in the covers and finding comfortable spots as Cicilo came in with bags of food in her hands.

"The Sarter Kingdom just announced the death of Fausta Urusus III. Did you hear?" Cicilo raved as she handed over the bags to Mac.

Smirking at her, Cicilo's face fell, and she focused on Laye and Fere. Both were still disheveled and had bits of blood still stained on their faces. "Yes, we are aware of Fausta's death." Mac admitted quietly as Cicilo raised her eyebrows at Laye and Fere. Cicilo coughed into her arm, "I see. The timing of Fere and Laye's return is notable."

"It is, isn't it," Mac agreed as he beamed over Laye.

Fere laughed, "Cicilo, you should buy a nice dress. There will be a dinner soon, you can tag along and see the Sarter palace if you would like."

Cicilo beamed as she whispered, "I would love that."

She backed out of the room, and Mac watched her run for her transport and likely off to find a dress. Behind him Laye couldn't help laughing, "Well, now she wants to fuck me and Fere too." Mac and Yarle roared with laughter before they both crawled over the couch and onto the beds next to Laye and Fere.

"I just bought a lot of alcohol, and I don't even know if you can drink it or not? I think my brain shorted out when you were gone," Mac admitted as his brow creased. Laye and Fere nodded and reached their hands out with big smiles as they both giggled. Mac handed out glasses filled with a specialty liquor that seemed as though there were swirling stars in their cups. Laye took a sip and guzzled it down before handing Mac her glass for more.

"That's liquor, you might want to slow down." Mac explained as he filled her glass anyway.

Laye shrugged and batted her lashes at Mac, "You're a big guy, you can handle me drunk."

Mac awkwardly laughed, in a bit of disbelief about his next words. "The fuck I can! Don't you dare drink too much. This is your last cup for the next hour."

"Fine. You're probably right." Laye admitted as Fere stuck her glass out for more. Mac sighed as he filled her glass, "We haven't even started the show yet."

A tablet made a sound behind them and Mac reached over to grab it, "It's from Destry. It looks like Laye and Fere managed to take out every target on Destry and Empress Claudius' hit list. You're both instructed to rest up and prepare to be awarded by the UTC and Sarter Kingdom for eliminating their entire most wanted fugitives list. Your obligation is satisfied, and K'hurian is awaiting the nominations for our representatives to join the Sarter Kingdom Ruling Council. Destry only asks if you would like to be revealed, or if you would like the ceremony to be private."

Laye and Fere faced one another simultaneously whispering, "Private," before Laye turned to Mac and he nodded before he responded. Fere turned to Yarle who looked as though he saw a ghost, "You two really killed them all?"

"We were discovered when we transported in. The tech we were given was familiar to them, and they easily captured us."

Fere admitted and Yarle's eyes flared, *oh shit, I said the wrong thing.* Yarle shot up from his relaxed position, "You what?! You were captured?!"

Fere and Laye laughed nervously as Fere raised her thumbs and wiggled them at him. "I can dislocate my thumbs, and we used to get caught all the time on purpose. It was kind of our thing."

"I'm glad this is over, I don't know if I can listen to anymore." Yarle admitted, his heart was raging so fiercely he thought he might have to go for some air outside. Fere wrapped herself around him, "We don't have to talk about it."

"I want to hear all about it, but Laye can just tell me later." Mac admitted as he shrugged, and Yarle was glaring at him.

Yarle grabbed the controls for the visual media and turned on the program, The Pirate Chronicles, before lying back. Mac passed food around, meat for he and Yarle and honey for Laye and Fere. They ate as they watched the introduction for the show.

"It's about a pirate ship which travels the center. It's not accurate at all, but it's a good show and the actors are great." Mac explained as Laye handed him her empty jar of honey.

They found comfortable places and watched for a little while. The episode was about the captain finding a woman who needed rescuing from being stolen away by a hoard of evil men. Laye could hear heavy breathing next her, and she peered over at Fere.

Laye slid her hand over her smile as Yarle noticed, "What?" Laye pointed over to Fere, who was asleep with her mouth dropped open, "She has never fallen asleep that fast."

Yarle smirked, bursting with pride. "I guess I'm just that good."

Fere twitched and Laye held in a laugh as Mac tugged Laye close to him. Her friend had never appeared more peaceful. Laye and Mac tried to focus on the show and before long, Laye noticed Yarle had fallen asleep too.

"Thank you for taking her away from Hyret when you came for me. She deserves this." Laye rubbed Mac's arm as she looked on her friend with love.

Mac tipped her face toward him, and he kissed her. "I saw how much she cared about you. She gave herself over, we didn't have to take her."

The way her life had worked out in the end was overwhelming her, and she felt curious emotions welling inside. Emotions she didn't understand. Mac whispered into her hair, "It's alright to let yourself be happy."

How did he always know? She wiggled around and wrapped herself around Mac.

"Do you want another drink?" Mac asked as she buried her face in his big chest. In a muffled tone, Laye answered, "Yes. More alcohol."

"Here," Mac had a glass hovering above her head, and she took it. He held his filled cup up to the light of the display watching the swirls, "I think this might be the best day of my life."

"It's the first of many. What are we going to do with all our time?" Laye asked as she tried dreaming of the possibilities.

Mac scoffed as he reached around her, and grabbed her breast, "What the fuck do you think we're going to do?" Laye's eyes widened as Mac laughed, and held her to him, "Why are you so surprised?"

FORTY
DECORATION

Laye and Fere stood in Mac's closet trying to figure out what they would wear as Yarle and Mac sat on Mac's bed, waiting. They had been ready for over an hour in custom black suits ordered from Melior. Without the threat of the Shrout, this would be the first time they would be making a public appearance without needing masks to hide their identities. Laye and Fere had options spread out everywhere. Laye finally had enough. "Can we call Cicilo? We need help!"

Mac smiled and grabbed his tablet to call for Cicilo to come and help them find something to wear. A few moments later Cicilo knocked before she opened Mac's door, "May I come in?"

Mac pointed to the open closet door, and Laye stuck her head out, "Please help us, we have no idea what we are doing." Cicilo smiled but when she stepped into the closet, she stood stunned. Laye and Fere were standing completely nude before her. They would need to find Cicilo a partner, Laye was receiving some intense sexual desire from her. Laye cleared her throat, "We need dresses."

"Oh yes, I can help." Cicilo brushed by the two before pulling a black floor length, cross strapped dress out for Laye and a sleek black sparkling high neck gown for Fere.

Cicilo bolted from the closet, "I'm off to dress myself."

"Thank you," Laye started as Cicilo burst out of the room and shut the door behind her.

"Is Inex single? I think Cicilo needs to get laid." Mac and Yarle chuckled to one another as Fere and Laye slid their dresses on, each one more than satisfied with Cicilo's choices. The dresses were beautiful and fit them perfectly.

Yarle and Mac stood up and escorted their women to the door, Cicilo stood with their masks. She was wearing a fitted dress to her mid-thigh, her ample chest filled out the low-cut top.

"We don't need to hide anymore, we just need them for riding now." Mac explained as he took the masks and set them down on a nearby table.

Cicilo nodded at him as they passed her to climb into the back of Mac's transport, Cicilo found her place up front. The door shut and they were taken to where Mac's ship was parked. They boarded his ship and found their seats, Inex was sitting at the helm ready to take them to Vistalia.

They were in orbit, and opening a wormhole in minutes, the green and blue Sarter home planet appeared under them in seconds. The world sparkled among the cluster of stars all around, its own system star was bright behind them.

They received a message from the surface in a soft feminine voice, "Welcome to Vistalia, honored guests. Please proceed to the landing coordinates."

Inex brought the ship down on the queens private landing pad and waiting to greet them at the doors were Queen Destry and Empress Livia Claudius. Thunder clapped above them as they filed out of the ship toward the doors.

When they were standing in front of Livia and Destry, they bowed and Destry introduced them, "Livia, this is Laye and Fere."

Livia, a beautiful bald, brown skinned woman, grinned, "It's a pleasure to meet both of you. If you will follow us," Livia opened the door, and they trailed behind her as she led them into an open atrium.

There was a table in the center with two system star award pendants, the galactic center's highest honor. They represent the stars in each system and their life-giving light. Laye and Fere had not been expecting such a grand gesture, and they both stood frozen as their eyes fell on the shining pendants. Mac gently touched Laye's back as he whispered, "You earned this."

"I see you are aware of this particular honor?" Livia asked as she picked up the first pendant and went to pin it onto Fere's dress.

When the pendants were pinned on, Destry stood before them, "You have made our galaxy a safer place for everyone. We thank you with these system star awards, but we will forever be in your debt. Oran and I have decided to generously share in the cost of your terraforming project for K'hurian as a gesture of thanks."

Destry handed Mac a tablet with a hologram of K'hurian turning above it, "This is your official acceptance into the Sarter Kingdom, and Livia has extended honorary citizenship into the UTC for all of you."

"To express my gratitude, I am happy to offer my

assistance in your terraforming project. I know water is your most sought-after resource, so I have an ice planetoid being moved to orbit K'hurian, giving you the rest of the water you need to heal your planet. It is the least we can do for you. You may call on Destry, or myself, if you ever have a need," Livia instructed as Mac bowed to her in thanks.

Destry hooked her finger at a nearby guard. "You requested a private celebration, so we have a dinner for you four in my personal gardens."

Laye was star struck, and Fere behind her was nearly hopping with each step. The queen's garden overflowed with tropical foliage, and there was a glass table in the center with place settings for four.

Destry led them to the table, "Enjoy your dinner, someone will come and escort you back to your ship when you're finished. It was truly a pleasure to meet each of you."

Destry tipped her head to them and glided off when a Sarter man approached the table to take their order.

"I wonder what Inex and Cicilo are talking about." Laye blurted out as everyone decided on what they wanted to eat. *I wonder why she didn't join us, she must have a reason.*

Mac eyed Laye before answering, "None of our business, why do you care?"

"Inex looks lonely, and Cicilo feels like a sexual ticking time bomb," Laye pointed to the menu, "They have a whole natural syrup and nectar selection!"

Mac rolled his eyes, "Inex is not talkative, I doubt anything will happen."

"You and I both know you don't need words to have sex." Laye retorted, giving Mac a sly grin when he narrowed his eyes at her. Fere coughed as she sipped her drink and Yarle pretended like he hadn't heard. They all fell silent when they realized the waiter was standing and waiting for their order, he either hadn't been listening or didn't care.

Mac ordered first, "I want the Sarter bird, Yarle I think it's for a table."

"Good with me," Yarle agreed as he kept reading the menu.

Fere went next, "I want elec fruit nectar."

"That variety has an intoxicative effect similar to a drug called rush." The waiter explained without looking up from his tablet. "That works, I'm always down for a good time." Fere admitted and Yarle next to her chuckled under his breath.

Laye perked up at that, "I want that one too."

Within a few moments their food was being brought out and spread over the table. The bird was Laye's size, and she scowled at Mac, "That could have been me!"

Mac and Yarle laughed as Fere asked, "Can we just eat please? If you keep making me laugh something is going to come out of my nose."

Laye patted Fere's knee as she dipped her tongue in the jar of thin nectar, "This is interesting."

"It tastes like we are going to need babysitters." Fere admitted as she bashfully eyed Yarle.

Yarle shook his head, "I do not think so. I would need a sedative dart gun to agree to that."

"I bet we could ask Destry!" Laye offered, and Mac sighed.

Mac rested his hand on her leg, "We are absolutely not doing that. If you want to be that twisted, I'm putting you in a padded room you can't break out of."

Laye creased her brow, "You're no fun."

Fere and Laye slurped down their nectar and to Yarle and Mac's opposition, and they each received a second serving. Mac and Yarle devoured the giant roasted bird as Fere and Laye chatted about how Gerne always seemed to have something up his ass. When the meal was finally over, Fere and Laye giggled the entire way back to the ship.

The doors of the palace opened to the Queen's private landing pad and Laye saw the unmistakable ducking of Cicilo's head as she climbed off Inex lap and moved back into her seat. They had forgotten to shade the ships front window.

Laye patted Mac on the arm and he groaned, "Alright, I admit, you did see that coming."

Laye smiled to herself as she skipped back to the ship, the landing pad was covered in fresh rain. She missed wet days after a rain, it was the only thing she missed at all from her former life. *I can't wait to see it rain on K'hurian.*

They climbed aboard the ship and Inex and Cicilo did everything except look at one another, but the residual warmth on the ship's bridge was answer enough.

"Is everything prepared at home Cicilo?" Mac asked as they found their seats. Clearing her throat, Cicilo answered, "Yes Sir. They wrapped up about thirty minutes ago."

"What is going on?" Laye demanded as Mac bit his lips together. Laye turned to Yarle and Fere was already staring at him. "I am not saying a word, don't ask."

"You two are hopeless." Mac teased as Inex took them into orbit and opened a wormhole to take them home.

They arrived back at K'hurian but when they descended, they didn't go to Mac's courtyard. They landed at several enormous, metal and glass homes. The perfectly placed glass bent the light, and the glow made the homes look ethereal.

"Mac, what is this?" Laye asked as she stared out of the front window.

The doors opened, and Mac rose from his seat, "Come see our new homes. Inex, you and Cicilo can have the night off."

Laye was so thrilled she nearly shivered, her hand reached out for Mac's as he led her out of the ship. Yarle and Fere followed behind them.

They entered a courtyard of desert plants, and from there was a path leading to several homes. With the major improvements to the city completed, it had been time for their homes to be built. "This is ours, and that one belongs to Yarle and Fere," Mac explained. Laye ran for their home and didn't wait for him.

She burst through the doors and found their living room so large she could fly from one end to the other. He came up behind her and put his arms around her. "You should be able to fly anytime you want."

FORTY-ONE
SUPRISE GUESTS

The next day, Laye was busy exploring her new home when she heard a knock at the door, she heard Mac's steps, and she went to see who it was. Laye saw Mac open the door, and it was Cicilo, "You and Laye are going to want to see this. I need to grab Yarle and Fere. Inex is ready in the transport."

Mac waved to Laye, and they headed to the transport and waited for Cicilo, Yarle, and Fere. Inex smiled at Mac when he climbed in, which was nothing like him.

He just hoped Laye didn't notice, but she clearly did when she was jabbing him in the ribs after he sat down. Fere and Yarle climbed in and sat down as Cicilo climbed in the front.

"Do you know what this is about?" Yarle asked Mac as he put his arm around Fere.

Mac shook his head, "Cicilo, spill it."

She shook her head, "You wouldn't believe me." Mac sighed, she was probably right.

Mac sat back and they took off for what seemed to be

the middle of the desert. They landed and their transport door slipped open, revealing a small space vessel sitting in the middle of the sand.

Laye and Fere spoke at the same time as instant recognition fell over them, "That's Vo-Pess." Laye stuck her antenna up, and she gasped as they scrambled out of the transport, "There are three empathic Vo-Pess in that ship."

Fere and Laye began running in the sand, they could hear Mac and Yarle behind them. When they arrived at the ship, the loading bay opened to reveal two adult Vo-Pess. A lavender man and a peach woman, both with black hair, stood in their Vo-Pess nano tech armor, each of them wary of Laye and Fere.

"Are you Laye and Fere? I am Rane and this is Vers. We desperately need asylum for us and our passengers," The woman asked, her hand intertwining with the man's.

Laye and Fere nodded and said, "Yes," simultaneously and without thought as the two people parted to show their passengers. Fere sucked in a harsh breath and grasped her chest, it was three freshly emerged Angle Wing's with maroon skin. Their black hair was still stuck to their skin from being inside the cocoon.

"They're all empathic." Laye whispered as she held her eyes on the three girls who looked identical to her best friend.

Vers held his hand out for the girls, "This is Tero, Yeri, and Heny. Rane sensed they would be empathic when she visited the spawning forest. We were in the courtroom when the K'hornibus came for you, and we knew this was the only safe place for them. We couldn't allow the Vo-Pess to put them through what we all went through."

"What about you and Rane? What do you need? Are you bonded?" Laye asked, but she wished she hadn't.

They both froze and Vers finally admitted, "She was bonded, and we defected and ran away together. We don't expect anything. We only ask for assistance finding us work, something the Vo-Pess wouldn't be concerned with."

Mac slowly approached behind Laye and set his hand on her shoulder, "I have just the place for you and Rane."

Fere turned around to Yarle, and he mouthed, "What?" Pulling him down and forcing him to bend over, Fere asked, "Can they stay with us? I think I am their sire." Fere knew the eggs she lay long ago, her spawn, would be emerging soon. *I know these are my daughters.*

Yarle looked up at the girls, and down at Fere, there were all identical to her. Yarle felt his fatherly instinct claw at him and could have it no other way. "They are more than welcome to stay with us, you never need to ask about something like this. The answer will always be yes." Yarle offered as Fere spun on her heals to see what the girls would think. They each nodded as Rane agreed, "They haven't sorted out many words yet, you'll need to start from the beginning."

Fere grinned from ear to ear, she had never been so excited about anything in her life, "We can take care of everything." The girls saw Fere smiling and all their eyes flared with excitement, behind them Yarle was nearly as excited as Fere was. He had hardly been able to see his adult children when they were kids, he felt like this was his chance to be the father he wanted to be.

Laye pulled Rane aside, "They were not claimed, correct?"

Rane nodded solemnly, "They were not. We hid and waited for them to show signs of emergence, and we cut them out right before. We couldn't risk one of the elder's sons showing up early."

"You made the right choice, they are safe here. You and Vers can stay in our home until we find somewhere that fits your needs." Laye offered as Mac slid his hand over her shoulder.

Rane looked over at Vers, "We need to remove our trackers."

"I dare the Vo-Pess to come near my planet. I'll have the Sarter's send a doctor." Mac growled over Laye's head.

Rane smiled at Mac, "That won't be necessary, we just need a knife."

Vers and Rane tapped their amor tabs before Rane took a knife and sliced into Vers arm to dig out his tracker. She stomped on it before handing the knife to Vers for him to the same for her. When they finished, Vers moved to the front of the transport, "I'm setting it to self-destruct in ten minutes."

Everyone moved toward Mac's transport, and after they had begun their trip back, the heard the transport explode behind them. The three girls huddled around Fere, and they seemed to feel safe with her. Laye wondered if their people's spawn were once raised by their sires, the idea of that sounded too good to be true. She was just thankful these Vo-Pess girls would have a better early life than she and Fere.

They landed back at home, and when the girls saw the open doors of the house Fere was walking towards, they grabbed one another's arms. Laye and Mac stood with Vers and Rane watching the girls act full of glee as they went inside with Fere and Yarle.

"I can't believe we pulled this off. They weren't on the tag list yet, it will be weeks before the Vo-Pess know they're missing, and even then, they might attribute them to a failed emergence. The elders are soon to begin a civil war, and much of our former society has crumbled. I honestly don't think anyone will be coming, at least not any time soon." Vers admitted as he reached for Rane's hand.

Mac growled, "They won't be coming at all, or I'll go back and blow the planet out of existence."

Laye rubbed Mac's arm, and he led everyone inside offering, "Please make yourself comfortable, I'll show you to your room after we find you something to eat." Following Mac to the kitchen he and Laye pulled a tray out and filled it with water and a selection of honey for them to choose from. Laye carried the tray in and set it on the table in front of the couches.

Rane and Vers ate some honey before each drinking down the tall glasses of water. They seemed like they had been through something similar to Laye and Fere.

"I contacted my friend Benitian Venclair, he runs Sinex station. His business is not always legal, but it fits what you are asking for." Mac offered as he wrapped his arm around Laye.

They each nodded and Vers answered, "That sounds great. We can start right away, we are happy to work for our stay here as well."

"You are our guests, and we expect nothing from you. Let me show you to your room." Mac rose up and helped Laye to her feet as Rane and Vers followed. Mac went down a hallway that led off from the living area and opened the door to a room with an attached bathroom, "You'll find fresh sleeping clothes in the closet, we can have some additional clothing delivered for you tomorrow."

They nodded as Mac shut the door behind them and he and Laye headed to their bedroom. The moment the door shut, Mac switched on the sound blocker.

Laye waited until she heard the buzz of the sound block before she purred, "The fact a transport full of Vo-Pess showed up wanting you to save them like you saved me? Something about that makes me hot."

Mac narrowed his eyes at her, "You can't say that without taking your clothes off." Laye had her clothes off in a flash, and Mac laughed, "I can see that I have met my match in every way."

"Why the hell do you still have clothes on?" Laye stood nude in front of him with her hands on her hips. Mac stripped down, and Laye jumped onto him, she couldn't wait any longer. They were a flurry of roaming hands as she and Mac landed on their bed. He hovered over her and kissed her, sliding his hand under her head.

He kissed her down her chest to her nipples and licked each of them before he knelt between her legs. Lifting her legs, he set them on his shoulders and dove between her thighs. He wasted no time and found her needy row of nerves, running his rough tongue along them and making her squirm. Laye's hips shook as he gave her everything she wanted, and he wrapped his hands around her thighs to hold her to his shoulders. He growled as he ate her out and the sensation added to her pleasure. Mac let go of one side of her thigh to rub his fingers over her wing, she gave him a pleading whimper as the tingling sensation spread through her body. Laye couldn't hold back any longer as she tipped over and cracked open, her pleasure spilling out as Mac continued to lick her until she was clean.

She felt him grasp her hips and he flipped her over, her legs were hanging over the edge of the bed as Mac lined himself up. He thrust into her from behind as he stroked his fingers down her wings along her back. Laye felt herself reach a place of ecstasy as Mac's length split inside of her and began rolling. He continued stroking her wings and she felt a shiver building. "Mac!" Was all she could shout before he grabbed her hips, and she violently shook. Her second orgasm hit like a rocket and Mac came along with her, his pleasure spilling inside of her. Mac grumbled something about his queen as she finally slowed and slumped against the bed.

He ran his fingers over her wings, and she groaned under him, "You were made for me."

FORTY-TWO
EPILOGUE ONE

Tero, Yeri, and Heny played in the sand on the beach as Yarle and Fere watched them. They were on a family vacation on Keru's floating city at one of the most beautiful resorts in the galaxy. Yarle had surprised them with the vacation just days before.

In just a few months the girls had begun speaking and were already doing well with their studies. Vo-Pess were nearly full sized at emergence and had fully developed minds which simply needed to be imprinted with information. Fere had never felt so fulfilled as she did when she assisted with their studies, it had developed into an idea that she could begin a free public school in K'rin.

Her and Yarle were spread out in sunning chairs with drinks as they relaxed on the beach. In the distance, whales the size of spaceships lunged from the endless sea just to slap their giant bodies against the water.

A plana waiter approached with their lunch order, and the girls gathered around. Fere handed out honey as Yarle tore into his giant bird leg.

"Yar! That leg is as big as mine!" Laughing, Yeri yelped as Yarle waved the steaming leg at her.

Within a week, Yarle and the three girls had bonded as Yarle taught them K'hornibus wrestling three times a week.

Fere decided that they could learn skill from her when they were older, she didn't want to do training before they were ready. She wanted them to experience a childhood, something she never had.

Yarle finished his bird leg, and set it down on the tray, "I have a surprise for you."

"Another one?" Fere perked up as she reached for a glass of water. Yarle grinned and waved at someone behind them, Fere turned to find Mac's oldest daughter Mere was heading toward them with a bright smile.

Fere was overjoyed, "Mere! Don't you have class?"

"It's summer break. I have four weeks off! Uncle Yar called and asked if I would watch the girls so you two can go on a real date. I'm taking them back to my apartment for painting and crafts, and my sisters are impatiently waiting for us." Mere had her arms out as the three girls rushed her, all squealing.

Heny was leaping up and down, "Can we go now?"

They knew they would have several more days at the beach, so cousin time took precedence. "Of course. Have fun!" Fere waved to them as they happily drudged through the thick sand with Mere.

Fere turned to find Yarle standing with his hand out for her, "We have dinner plans, and we need to dress." Taking his hand, Fere wondered if he was taking her to the tower restaurant. She had looked it up on her tablet, but she had not said a word to him about it.

They returned to their room, right off the beach, and

Yarle had a dress laid out for her on the bed. It was a sleeveless iridescent lavender with a dipping V cut. She ran her fingers over it and smiled.

She and Yarle dressed, and he wore a black suit. "Where are you taking me?" Fere had to ask, the mystery was sending her into a whirlwind. Yarle grinned at her, "You'll see when we pull up." He led her into the hallway of the hotel before guiding her to the front where a floating transport was waiting for them with its doors open. They climbed inside and sped away toward the center of the city.

They stopped in front of the tallest building in the City, and Fere could hardly contain herself, "How did you know?!"

"The girls saw you looking it up. They told me I needed to take you here." Yarle admitted as he slid his arm around her. Fere refrained from screaming with delight as they went inside the building and found the lifts. She and Yarle walking through the building's main floor, had garnered the attention of nearly everyone. News of the K'hornibus planet's shift in power and the recent development, they had made in their society had their names smeared on every headline. The Shardlow's were now well known in the galactic center, and they had not gauged the scale of it all until that moment.

"It looks like we might be using the back door out of here." Yarle admitted as he pulled a small communicator from his pocket. Yarle slid his device back in his pocket, "We will have escorts to take us back to the hotel, there are already people gathering downstairs."

The lift stopped and opened to the restaurant. The space had windows floor to ceiling, the foliage in the room was vibrant and made her feel alive.

Fere moved to the windows and looked down over the cityscape and out into the Keru ocean. Yarle wrapped his arms around her as she admired the immense beauty of the vast stretching water. The floating city was in the process of moving from its summer position to its winter position, the move was to protect the city from cyclones that frequented the upper hemisphere.

A storm in the distance lit up the evening sky as it rolled in, lightning was striking on all sides of the clouds and illuminating the water. Boats began heading in from all over as the wait staff led them to their table. They were taken to a table on the covered balcony and Fere asked, "Won't we get wet out here?"

"No, we have a forcefield around the tower to protect it from the elements. You will be quite comfortable," The waiter answered as they stood at the end of their table, ready for their drink order as they poured two glasses of water.

Brining attention to their Sarter waiter, she asked, "I want something fruity tasting, made with Vistalia liquor?"

"I want a glass of Sarter Three." Yarle waited until the waiter left and put his hand on Fere's. Fere met Yarle's eyes, and he pointed to the sky, "There is one more thing." Fere watched the sky where he was pointing. As the system star fell on the horizon, a lime-colored meteor shower began over their heads. She leaned back in her seat as thousands of bright green streaks crossed the sky and lit up the shadows of the city like daylight. It was the most beautiful thing she had ever seen, the waiter set their drinks down, and she grabbed for hers.

Fere didn't take her eyes from the sky as she sucked down her drink. It was outrageously delicious, and she didn't notice how strong it was until she had finished it.

She set the glass down with her eyes wide, and Yarle laughed, "That was probably enough alcohol to last you all night."

Fere grabbed her water and drank it down as Yarle sipped his liquor as the two were lit up in soft light from the meteors above. Thunder clapped all throughout the clouds rolling in and Fere breathed in the crisp, salty air. This was the perfect night.

"How long will the meteors last?" Fere asked as the server brought Yarle a steak, and Fere a bowl of warm nectar. Yarle cut into his steak and peered up at Fere, "All night."

"Is that why you booked us the room at the hotel with the glass ceiling?" Fere asked as she tasted the nectar. He nodded and she was left wanting to crawl under the table, right between his legs. Maybe she would do that when they arrived back at their room. Yarle nearly inhaled his food and gulped down his liquor. "I am ready when you are."

"Why did you eat so fast?" She asked as she set down her empty bowl.

Yarle sniffed the air as he grinned, "You think I can't smell when you're wet?" Fere cleared her throat, "Oh. Well, let's go then."

Yarle nodded to someone in the restaurant, and he rose up with his hand out for her. He led her to a door by the kitchen, "We are being picked up in the back, we have a growing crowd downstairs. Now the headlines are curious about you and Laye."

"Ha! The Vo-Pess are going to lose their shit over this! This is the best night of my life!" Fere had a hop to her step as they plugged the floor they needed into the lift.

Downstairs their driver met them by the back door,

they were alone, and no one followed. Fere relaxed against the seat while Yarle slid his hand between her thighs and up the center.

She couldn't keep her hands to herself either as she reached into his shirt, and he pulled her into him for a kiss. As they pulled to a stop, she crawled onto his lap, "This time you're going first. This suit better come off as soon as we make it inside the room."

He growled and kissed her as their door was opened by the driver, who quickly looked away. They couldn't keep their hands from another as they found their room, and they fell on the ground inside of the door when it opened. The door clicked shut behind them as Fere crawled up Yarle, unbuckling his pants and pulling them down. He was hard and ready for her.

Fere descended on him, and he groaned as she took him as far as she could. She stroked him with both hands as he took in fast breaths, Yarle's length was starting to split and roll inside of her mouth. She loved when his length split, she felt it moving in her mouth and it gave her a sharp thrill down her spine. The way he was grabbing her head, and twirled his thumbs over her antennae made her insides burn like wildfire. Yarle curled up and came with a groan, the thick cum shot into her mouth and she swallowed it down. He panted as he sat up and took his jacket and shirt off before he reached for her and lifted off her dress to toss it away. She straddled his lap, and he leaned down to kiss her lips and down to her neck. He rubbed his thumbs over her nipples as she ground her center on his thigh, the sensation leaving her wanting so much more. Yarle lifted her up and carried her to the center of the room before setting her down on an armchair.

He spread her legs, each one going over the arms of the armchair as he fell to his knees.

Fere watched through the glass ceiling as lightning filled half of sky and bright meteors lit up the other. Between her legs, Yarle licked her up her center as his hand wrapped around her throat, holding her to the chair. Her hips rolled around as she felt his rough tongue rub against her nerves just the way she liked. Fere could feel herself growing close, the immense heat inside of her was overflowing and she sensed the impending explosion of pleasure.

When she tipped over the edge, she tensed and Yarle growled, giving her a bit of extra friction. She shook and cried out as her orgasm overtook her. Yarle licked up her pleasure before he leaned over her, "Forever with you doesn't seem long enough."

FORTY-THREE
EPILOGUE TWO

Soaring through the desert as she headed toward the salt, Laye spotted where she wanted to make camp for the night. She landed in the flat spot and dropped her gear from the pack she had secured to the front of her body.

She made herself busy preparing for later, it was only a matter of time before he tracked her down. Laye pulled her bed mat out and took her flying clothes off to store them away. After guzzling some water and cooling off, she watched the glittering salt under the afternoon system star, this was her favorite place to be on K'hurian. She loved her home in K'rin, and she even enjoyed visiting the new Thine City being built where the former Shrout compound and surrounding outdoor camps had been, but nothing compared to flying over the mountains and seeing the sprawling sandy colored glitter of the salt.

The center of the salt the deepest places had begun to grow deep pools of standing water. It was the first time in thousands of years the planet had enough water that even the salt was becoming wet again. Laye's heart swelled as she imagined how it would look in the coming years with the Sarter technology and the gift from Livia. They would see ancient weather patterns begin again instead of the previous one rain a year. *I can't wait to see water crash over these shores, and honor the wind spirits by flying over the waves.*

They had been working with Destry to repopulate necessary creatures back into their ecosystems when the time came, and many of the creatures were already in habitats being developed in a ship that remained in orbit for the duration of the project.

Laye loved her life but after a few months with Mac, something seemed missing. It didn't take long for them to figure out what she needed, and he had been more than understanding.

"Shit!" Laye saw the time on her wrist communicator and hopped to her feet. *Did I really sit down and get distracted? What was I thinking? I need to hide,* it was already dark. *Fuck!*

Laye turned her lantern on and opened the top, so it shined into the sky before she set it down and took off down the hill. She could hear the purr of the bike in the distance, and she picked up her speed, her legs moved as quickly as she could make them.

She heard the bike shut off, and she ran straight into the hills, her heart was a raging engine in her chest. The sky grew dark aside from the distant stars that made up the galactic center, and she hurried up one hill and down another. She stepped as light as she could, trying not to make a sound as she moved around the enormous rocks with an occasional bush or scraggly tree growing out from underneath it.

She could hear crunching behind her, and she hid,

preparing to run. The moment she could see his spiked head over the previous hill, Laye bolted and took off up the next mound. The sounds of boots hitting the ground behind her made her run faster and she spread her wings as fast as she could. Laye hadn't even lifted off the ground when she felt a hand wrap around her throat.

How the fuck did he catch me so fast? Laye tried to fill her lungs with air as she tried to retract her wings while he held her to the ground. The air was cool and it chilled Laye's skin, her thin underclothes provided no warmth. She felt hot breath on her neck, "Where the fuck do you think you're going?"

Her core was already heated, "Did you think you could outrun me?"

Laye was putty in this man's grip, she was so wet her thighs were slipping. She wasn't saying a fucking word. "Doing this the hard way all the way out here was not wise." Mac, wearing his old mask for her, turned her around once her wings were up against her skin. She hadn't thought about that, and her eyes searched the darkness, she may have really fucked up this time. Did she even have water back at her camp? *Oh, shit.*

Mac tore her shirt down the center, and followed with her pants, ripping them off her. Laye was speechless trying to decide if this was the best or worst idea she had ever had as he tied her hands behind her back and forced her on her knees. He tipped her chin up as he pulled the desert sage oil out of his pocket, "You didn't pack enough water, did you?" Laye shook her head as he reached down and slathered her nipples in the oil, "This is going to be a fun night, I forgot all of mine."

"What?!" Laye reared back from his oil covered fingers.

Mac laughed as she tried to shift away from him, the tingle just beginning in her nipples.

He grabbed her hips and laughed maniacally, "Just where I want you."

"Mac, oh fuck! No!" Laye cried out as he wrapped his arms around her and rubbed the oil around her back entrance. He dragged her back and set her in front of him, her form shaking as she whimpered to him.

"I want to see how long the effects last. You're the perfect test subject." Mac explained as her muscles clenched.

Laye whispered through chattering teeth, "I'm going to get you back for this so hard."

Mac laughed over her, "Not today little butterfly, today I will have my way." Laye was dripping, and she knew he would hold her there until she was screaming for him to let her cum. It had all been her idea, but she was sure Mac had been more thrilled than she was. They could relive the moments he found her, the moment his life changed, for as long as they wanted.

He held her down by her shoulders, her knees were spread so her thighs didn't touch, and he didn't go near her breasts. Laye was going out of her mind as the oil did its job and made her nerves so sensitive a breeze could have made her cum. "Please, Mac. You have to touch me, please!" Laye could not comprehend anything but her aching need as he shook his head no.

Laye was desperate, "I'll do anything."

"I want another bowfruit pie." Mac admitted with a shrug. Laye laughed before she whimpered, "That's what you want? I'll make you ten! Just let me cum!"

Tossing away his mask, Mac grinned to himself as he lay a mat down and her on top of it. He knelt between her legs and spread them wide before he bent down and kissed her row of nerves. She would scream if he didn't hurry up. He reached up and wiped away the oil from her nipples, making her moan into the night. She panted as he twirled his fingers over her nipples and lingered there before he moved down and held her hips up to his face.

Mac licked his lips, teasing her and making her so desperate she felt her heart may burst. Laye cried out when he finally put his mouth on her center and licked her row of nerves. The oil on her back entrance was making every move seem like he was toying with her there too. Laye was overwhelmed with sensations as he nipped at her, and she finally fell over the edge.

Laye silently screamed as she broke apart, her core sending shivers down her nerves as Mac licked her through it. She felt him line her up with his hard length and she angled her hips to take him, he kneaded her hips as he thrust inside.

He lifted her up, so she was sitting on his length, and he stroked his fingers up and down her wings. She was sure this was her favorite part, Laye couldn't get enough of having her wings touched so gently and lovingly. It sent lightning through her as his length split inside of her. He began rolling his dual length as she tipped her head back and her eyes focused on the open sky, full of stars above them. He groaned and his length fluttered at the ends, Laye felt herself fall again. When she did, her inner walls clenched around his length, and he spilled inside of her with a growl.

His hands around her hips felt like home, and his warmth felt like forever. Laye was happier than she had ever been in her life, each day seemed to be better than the last. He pulled her off him and he cleaned her up with a cloth from his pack after he untied her.

"I may have cheated." Mac admitted as she put on some clothes he brought her.

Laye stared at him, "What does that mean?" She rubbed her own nipples, still feeling the oil and she wondered if Mac was ready to have sex all night. If there was no water to wash her off, he better have planned to take care of her.

Mac watched her rubbing her nipples and admitted, "I used the site-to-site transporters from your ship. I talked Fere into letting me borrow them." Laye gasped as she kept gently touching herself, "You did cheat!"

"If you keep rubbing your nipples like that, I will make you finish yourself off for me." Mac threatened as he kept his eyes on her.

Shrugging, Laye admitted, "I've never done that before, but this feels so good. I want you to help me."

Mac bit his lip as he sat on his mat and pulled her into his lap, "Fuck, come here." After he yanked her pants off, he pulled her shirt up over her breasts and guided her to lie back against him. He moved one of her hands to her breast and the other to her center, taking her finger and stroking it down the middle.

Laye inhaled in a harsh breath as he whispered, "I'll take care of your breasts, you feel yourself and learn what you like."

Laye slid her fingers between her thighs as Mac gave her nipples the attention she wanted. She was so wet already, and her finger slipped against her nerves, her insides seamed to dance with the delicious sensations. Mac kissed her neck and squeezed the tips of her breasts. Her fingers found the right rhythm, and she came undone with a squeak as Mac growled over her shoulder, "That's it my little butterfly."

They cleaned up and dressed before she located her camp, and they lay out under the stars. They remained silent for some time when something occurred to Laye.

"Did you really bring up pies in the middle of sex?" Laye giggled as she turned to Mac.

He looked over at her longingly, "What? Your bowfruit pies are delicious."

ABOUT THE AUTHOR

Lauren Logan is a neurodivergent, disabled science fiction romance author from North Texas. After high school and junior college, she attended the University of North Texas and studied Psychology and History. She met her husband in 2008, married in 2010, and they now have two little boys. They all enjoy watching science programs about astronomy as well as staying caught up on the latest Star Trek episodes.

In 2015 Lauren developed a passion for hair and began a journey that would lead her to hair school in her thirties. She specialized in vivid color and within a year and a half she had been nominated as a top 100 pastel colorist in the

Behind The Chair global hair awards. Unfortunately, the ultimate hair honor had come too late. A few months before her nomination was announced, Lauren had been forced to quit her dream career as a vivid hair colorist. The loss was devastating and she fell into a dark place.

November of 2020, Lauren was formally diagnosed with an autoimmune disease, Rheumatoid Arthritis. The disease course is aggressive and effects nearly all of her major joints, as well as both hands and feet. She has developed deformities in her fingers, making any chance of regaining her former hair career impossible. On rainy days you can often see her walking with a cane because the changing weather can bring on a flare. Since her diagnosis, she spends much of her time unable to leave her bed due to the constant pain and fatigue. The medication she is prescribed leaves her immunocompromised as well as having many difficult side effects.

Refusing to let her disability steal her ambition and kill her determination, Lauren began writing at the beginning of April, 2022. Over the course of one year, she completed two full length Sci-fi novels. Since the completion of the Reticere Series, she is now working on several stand alone novels in the same universe. Writing gives her hope and being an author gives her a future. She pours everything she is into her stories and she hopes you love them as much as she does.

For more information visit:
www.AuthorLaurenLogan.com

facebook.com/authorlaurenlogan

instagram.com/LaurenLoganArt

tiktok.com/@lauren.logan

www.ingramcontent.com/pod-product-compliance
Lightning Source LLC
Chambersburg PA
CBHW020226010826
48973CB00006B/1386